HIGHER GROUND

BY DEVON MAY

Cover Design by Acacia @ Ever After Cover Design.

Photography by Lindee Robinson

Models Shannon Lorraine and Tyler

Edited by Laura @ Hummingbird Editing.

BOOKS BY DEVON MAY

BECAUSE OF LOVE SERIES

Because of Us (novella)

Because of Her

Because of Them

Because of Me

STANDALONE

Higher Ground

AUTHOR'S NOTE

Higher Ground is a spicy small town romance set in rural Australia. To stay true to the characters and the author, it is written in Australian English. There may be times you spot a *u* where you weren't expecting one, or an *s* instead of a *z*. It is my hope that you are so invested in Byron and Emory's story that you don't notice them.

Trigger Warning: *Higher Ground* is a story of forbidden, all-consuming love, chasing dreams, and making hard decisions. It involves sexual content between two consenting adults. If any of the below is potentially triggering for you, please read on with care.

- Age gap relationships
- Use of emergency contraception
- Messy family situations, including both parental abandonment and children who go no contact with their parents

For those still waiting to chase their dreams.
It's never too late.

CHAPTER 1

EMORY

Dark storm clouds rolled in from the horizon, matching the heavy feeling of defeat that lingered in Emory's bones. The bright red stamped letter hung loose in her hand, and she so desperately wanted to just let it free. Maybe the wind would catch it and carry it away. Maybe it would get caught in the rain and washed down the gutter. Maybe she could pretend she never saw it. Maybe they could stay a little longer.

It would never work, though. They'd sent an email too and left a voicemail after she dodged the property manager's call. And even if by some slim chance it did, she'd only be delaying the inevitable.

In hindsight, Emory should have known they wouldn't be able to stay here forever. The warning signs should have started flashing six months ago when her baby daddy turned landlord switched the lease to a month-to-month contract. It was only a matter of time before he decided to kick her out.

So, okay, it wasn't a surprise when the email hit her

inbox a few weeks ago, but she wasn't ready then, and she definitely wasn't ready now.

"Clayton, buddy, let's go, time to go inside."

Emory's three-year-old son did his best to ignore her, running instead towards the back gate. Most days, she'd let him. He would play outside on the second-hand plastic slide she'd found at an op shop, and she'd watch from the kitchen window while cooking dinner. Some quick, mid-week, kid-friendly meal she'd found on the internet whilst doing her meal prep over the weekend. Or they'd play together until their stomachs growled, and she'd carry him inside for a dinner of toasted sandwiches and frozen vegetables. She might not have been a perfect mother, but she did her best.

But today was not like most days. Today, the rain was coming. She needed to cook a quick dinner and start making sure the house was safe from flooding, just in case. The water levels had never risen so high that this part of town went under, but in Gardner Creek, with a storm as big as this one? You could never be too sure.

The checklist had been running through Emory's thoughts all day. All the little things the State Emergency Service warned residents to be aware of. Make sure anything personal, valuable, or irreplaceable is placed on high, secure shelves. In the attic space or the cabinets above the kitchen bench. Pack emergency go bags, one for each family member. Download the Emergency Response app and set up the notifications. Be ready to watch the water rising and know when, not if, it's time to leave. It all pounded against the inside of Emory's temples, building into a headache she knew would stick around for days.

"Play, Mumma," Clayton called. He hung on the rickety old gate, adding just enough weight to its wooden frame to pull down on the handle. It swung open with a screech, taking the little boy with it. He cheered as he kicked his legs in delight.

Emory huffed under her breath, her deep brown eyes narrowing as she turned away from her son to hide her annoyance. If she had a free hand, she probably would have pinched the bridge of her nose. She definitely would have tied her long mane of mousey brown hair into a ponytail to stop the wind whipping it against her cheeks. Everything was beginning to hurt, exhaustion finally weighing her down after her long day. The bags hanging from her arms started to slip. Groceries, her work bag, her laptop bag, Clayton's backpack, and the tote full of academic texts she picked up from the small community library all threatened to empty onto the dusty gravel path that led to the front porch.

"Not today, Clayton, the rain is coming." She turned back to him with a smile, hoisting the bags back into the crook of her elbow and doing her best to keep her voice chirpy. It wasn't Clayton's fault she was in such a sour mood.

He whined, though, stamping a foot and attempting to hold his ground. Which was just about all Emory could take.

"Three." This time, Emory's tone was sharp and authoritative, but with an edge of the exhaustion that had washed over her. "Two ..." she dragged out the word until Clayton finally responded.

He plodded over to her, shuffling his feet through the dry, ankle-high grass. Emory had been meaning to mow it, truly, but between her shifts at the local café and looking after Clayton on her own and the three final assignments she had due, she just hadn't found the time. Then the weekly forecast had been announced.

Rain.

Everywhere.

A lot of it, for a long time.

What was the point in mowing the grass if it was just going to get covered with floodwater anyway? Emory had reasoned with herself, as though the imminent flood was the only reason she wasn't out mowing the grass over the weekend.

Shifting the weight of all the bags onto one arm, Emory pushed open the big wooden door to her tiny weatherboard cottage. The hinges creaked their disagreement. Clayton, finally having picked up a little speed, pushed through her legs to get inside.

"Shoes!"

He ignored her.

"Clayton, shoes!" she called, a little louder this time.

Loud, stomping footsteps echoed through the house as the little boy made his way back. Emory cringed at the thought of his dusty footsteps scattered through the house. She would have to mop. But then again, maybe the house would flood along with the yard, and it all would have been for nothing. Maybe mopping wasn't worth it right now.

"Bluey?"

If she'd been looking down into Clayton's deep blue puppy dog eyes, Emory would have said yes to any question he asked. But she wasn't looking at him. She was too busy dragging the bags into the small kitchen space.

"How much TV did you watch at Papa's?" she called over her shoulder.

Clayton, now with bare feet—although where on Earth had his socks disappeared to? Emory would have to find them later—came skipping into Emory's space with a wide grin.

"We watched O-naughts and Play School and Spider

—" With wide eyes, Clayton slammed both his hands in front of his mouth, gasping.

"Did Papa put Spider-Man on for you?"

Clayton nodded but kept his hands over his mouth. "It's a secret," he whispered through his fingers.

"We don't have secrets, remember?"

Bloody Byron and his obsession with Spider-Man. He was determined to make Clayton fall in love with his favourite superhero after he failed to do so with his own boys. It wasn't a bad thing, it was just persistent, and Emory wished he'd give Clayton a little more agency in the shows he watched. Even if he was only three years old. A little less screen time would have been good, too, but Emory could forgive that. Byron was doing her a huge favour watching Clayton, she didn't have the luxury to whinge over how much TV they watched together.

Clayton nodded again, this time pulling his hands down and clasping them together in front of his belly. "Sorry."

Emory couldn't resist. She dropped to her knees and spread her now free arms out for a hug. Clayton fell into them, and she clasped him tight, appreciating the closeness for a moment.

"Don't be sorry," she said, squeezing him and tickling under his arms. "Thank you for telling me. Let's put Bluey on while I cook dinner."

And brainstorm where the hell we are going to live. She knew more screen time was less than ideal for a three-year-old, but one evening of cartoons wasn't going to hinder him. And she really did need the space to figure everything out.

It was a mission to find the remote in its hiding place under the mountain of cushions Clayton kept referring to as his cubby, but once Bluey's family was playing musical statues and Clayton was happily dancing along, Emory was finally able to take a second to breathe.

She inhaled deeply, feeling the air fill her lungs for what felt like the first time all day. Every day felt like that. The same monotonous rush from the minute she woke up. Getting both her and Clayton fed and dressed and out the door, dropping him at his Papa's house whilst trying not to swoon over the one man in town she absolutely should *not* be swooning over, racing back into town to start her shift at the café. Every afternoon, she repeated the whole thing in reverse, usually with an added stop at the library to sneak in an hour of uninterrupted study. Today, she'd only meant to pick up the academic texts that had been shipped over from Sydney's immense collection of books, but spent longer there than she'd intended, getting lost in the aisles. For a moment, she managed to forget that she was stuck in a town where everyone knew her name, but no one ever said hello. It wasn't until Mya, the librarian and her best friend, kicked her out that she realised just how long she'd been in her own little world.

For a small town, Gardner Creek had a beautiful library. The refurbished old farmhouse became Emory's favourite place when she first moved here, and her safe haven when the life she thought she had built here started to crumble. Now, it was the means to her escape. She only had one month left of her marketing degree, plus a few exams. Then she could move back to the city and get a job and—if she was lucky—find her place in the world.

Until then, though, all she could do was make ends meet here. Juggle everything all on her own. Not that she wouldn't be doing it all herself in the city, because she would be. But at least in the city, she wouldn't be trapped in this place that always reeked of broken promises and pity invites. She didn't fit in in Gardner Creek, that much was clear when she first moved here, hanging off Jaxon's arm when he returned from his brief stint at city living. And it was somehow even clearer now that she was alone.

Because she was. Alone, that is. Even when the café was crowded and she made small talk all day. Even when she sat, snuggled against her son on the couch, watching Disney movies. Even when she picked up Clayton from his Papa's house and Byron insisted they stay for dinner. She was always alone. No one truly got her, no one wanted to understand her. And that was okay. She didn't mind, truly. But she was ready to move on.

Which is what she'd have to do now that Jaxon was finally kicking her out of the small cottage he had inherited from his dad. Originally, he said it was for them to share. Then he said she could stay, even when he left. The reduced rent was his version of child support, and Emory was thankful in the beginning. Finding a rental was never easy in a town as small as Gardner Creek, especially as a newly single mother who was a known flight risk. Everyone expected her to chase Jaxon back to the city. But she didn't. She stayed because she needed a plan.

And she had one. A good one. Only, finding a new place to live while she finished the last few weeks of her course was not a step she had intended. Evacuating for the impending flood wasn't either. But now she had to do both.

Serves her right for ignoring Jaxon's emails. And for pretending not to hear the phone every time the property manager tried to call. She would have had more time. But now, she had none.

A deep grumble of distant thunder rolled through the house, reminding her of the immediate problems she was facing. Dinner first, then emergency bag packing. And she should call Clayton's grandfather. His house up on his hill would be safe from any chance of flooding.

Emory hated the thought of asking Byron for more help than he already gave, but desperate times and all that. Plus, it was only temporary. It's not like she was asking if they could move in there, even though that would have solved *most* of her problems. She couldn't think of anything worse.

And not because she didn't like her ex-boyfriend's dad, but because she was worried she liked him a little too much.

The phone rang. And rang and rang and rang. Dammit. Emory supposed Bryon was busy, out on the farm doing all the things that needed to be done to secure everything. Moving the cows to a higher paddock, securing all the machinery, and whatever else farmers did before a flood came through. Emory wouldn't know, but she imagined it would be a lot.

With dinner cooking and Clayton still distracted by the TV, Emory had made quick work of packing their emergency bags. A backpack each if they needed to grab something quickly. All Clayton's most precious toys, Emory's most treasured books. And her laptop and its charger. Wherever they ended up for the next two weeks, she was determined not to let the situation stop her from completing her assignments.

Everything else she could think of was crammed into two suitcases. A few weeks' worth of clean clothes, all the library books, the crochet baby blanket she had taught herself to make for Clayton. It wasn't much, and truthfully, she could have used one suitcase between the two of them. But the thought of her entire life fitting into one suitcase made bile rise in Emory's throat. Was that really all she had?

Looking around the worn-down cottage as the phone rang out in her ear, Emory supposed it was. She hadn't really stopped to think about it until now, but everything else in this house held some pretty painful ghosts.

The faded grey couch Clayton now stood on, jumping as the Bluey credits rolled for the umpteenth time, was the very same one she and Jaxon had found at the second-hand markets. The same one they had sat on as Jaxon promised it was her choice, and he would support her either way. The same one she cried on when he left her, eight months pregnant, in a town that still didn't feel like home. Her bed was the same one they used to share. The one she curled up on over sleepless nights with a newborn. The dining table was the one they used to sit around eating dinner, hosting guests. Even the dinnerware and cutlery, all mismatched from bits and pieces they could take second-hand or cheap, once belonged to her old life. She hadn't changed a thing.

And maybe it was because she knew she wanted out. But, okay, maybe it was also because it hurt a little too much when she thought about getting rid of it all.

She didn't still love Jaxon. Truthfully, she now wondered if she ever really did or if she simply loved the *idea* of Jaxon. But it was too hard to look back and admit she was wrong about everything. Maybe she should have gone with her parents when they moved back to New Zealand, but she'd just turned twenty and was drunk on love.

Besides, she wasn't wrong about *everything*.

As hard as each day was, hearing Clayton's laughter

from the living room brought joy into her life, and she knew in her bones that she had made the right choice.

Giving up on calling Byron, Emory dropped her phone onto the counter to focus on dinner. The air fryer sang its song as the chicken finished cooking, and she pulled it out to cut up into small bite-sized pieces before mixing it into Clayton's favourite pasta sauce. It was far from Emory's favourite. All the hidden vegetables blended into a tomato-based sauce that was somehow incredibly bland. But Clayton drank it up like it was ice cream, so Emory kept right on making it for him.

Mixing the chicken and bow tie pasta—also Clayton's favourite—into his bowl, Emory called out to let the three-year-old know his dinner was ready. He leapt over the back of the couch, and Emory held her breath to avoid huffing at her son. She'd bet anything that Byron had taught him that, and she cringed at all the fun Clayton and his grand-father seemed to have. There was nothing wrong with it, but it made her feel bad that *she* wasn't the fun one in Clayton's little life. It didn't matter how hard she tried, how many games she made up, or stories she read, the nagging in her head that it wasn't enough never let up. She shuddered at the thought of seeing the comparison between her and Byron up close. It was one thing to *know* her son had so much fun with his Papa and presumably less fun with her, but it would be another thing entirely to see it play out before her. She could already imagine Clayton rushing to his Papa when he wanted to play, and it stung like needles along her spine.

Even so, she'd have to try to get hold of Byron. She didn't have anywhere else to turn.

After Jaxon left her, Byron was just about the only person in the whole town who didn't somehow hold her to blame. Funny, too, how he was the other person in town who lost the most. His son. But instead of hating Emory for driving Jaxon away, Byron had pulled her under his wing. He *somehow* had convinced Jaxon to let Emory stay in the small cottage. He watched Clayton while Emory worked and studied—even though he wasn't aware of the whole study part. He brought them milk and fresh vegetables from the farm and invited them over for every family event.

At first, Emory had recoiled at every ounce of kindness he offered her. Because really, who would want to be so cosy with their ex-boyfriend's family? Now, she held back as often as she could. Because, hello, who in their right mind would be attracted to their ex-boyfriend's dad? Certainly not Emory. Nope. Her cheeks just burned, and her heart fluttered, and, okay, her insides throbbed a little every time she thought about him. But she wasn't *attracted* to him. Just to the idea of him. The forbidden-ness of it all. And it was all superficial anyway. He was a hot, older man, that was all.

She'd learnt to shove it all aside. To ignore it. After all, she was only attracted to him because he was the only person in town who was nice to her. It had nothing to do with the hint of salt in his hair or the beard she ached to feel against her cheek or his broad shoulders and firm fore-arms. Definitely wasn't those things.

Thunder clapped outside, louder this time. An ominous warning that the storm was about to hit. Clayton jumped in his chair, pressing his hands against his ears. Emory sat down next to him, coaxing his arms down.

"The thunder can't hurt you," she told him. "It's just loud."

It didn't mean much to the young boy. He blinked up at Emory for a while, his wide eyes filled with fear, but when there was no follow-up rumble through the sky, he turned his attention to his dinner.

Bzzzzzz, bzzzzzz, bzzzzzz.

"Mummy phone!" Clayton flicked his spoon out to point at her phone. Tiny specks of red sauce splattered all over the table, a few reaching all the way over to where her phone danced beside her plate.

"Sorry, bud, it must be Papa. You keep eating, okay?"

Emory didn't wait for the three-year-old to respond. She pushed her chair out to stand, grabbing her phone as she went and swiping to answer the call.

"Emory, is everything okay?" Byron's gruff voice had a metallic ring to it through the phone. The reception was all sketchy thanks to the storm that was rumbling through outside.

Emory's breath was shaky as she tried to form her words. "Jaxon is kicking me out of the cottage."

It wasn't what she'd meant to say. She'd *meant* to say something about the flood and how she and Clayton needed a place to evacuate to. But something deep in her subconscious had pushed out her bigger worries instead, as though she knew Byron would have the answer.

CHAPTER 2

BYRON

Byron leant all his weight against the old windmill, urging it to return upright. The late afternoon sky was turning dark, and he'd been out fixing damn fence posts all day. Same ones he'd fixed last summer, and the year before that. The problem with farm fences was that they never seemed to stay up. Maybe because he always half-assed fixing them. He wasn't ready to take the blame, though. He was ready to pack it in, but the farm wasn't. He just needed to secure the supports for his late wife's windmill, and then he and his adult son, Tucker, could finally call it a day.

He strained against the weight of the structure, muscles aching after the long day of hard labour, as Tucker poured a bag of concrete in the hole they had dug around the posts.

"You reckon it'll set before the rain?"

Byron looked from Tucker to the deep grey clouds that hung low on the horizon. "If we're lucky. It's meant to hit worse up north today, down here tomorrow. But I don't like the look of those clouds."

Byron trusted the sky more than he did the weather forecast. The rain would come tonight, and then all he could do was hope the weatherman was wrong about how long it would last. And how widespread it would hit.

The bureau was forecasting weeks of endless rain from here in Gardner Creek right up to the New South Wales and Queensland border. With so much rain on such dry ground, along such a long stretch of the river, they were also expecting a flood higher than they'd seen in almost twenty years. And Byron remembered that flood. Back then, he'd been helping his old man with the farm, learning the ropes because they both knew he'd be taking over one day soon.

Even then, in his twenties, Byron knew this was the way of life for Gardner men. The town was named for them after all. He'd known then, even when his eldest son Jaxon had been no more than four years old, that he'd be the one to pass the farm down and carry on the family legacy. He wasn't sure what he was going to do now, because at forty-five, he knew he didn't have a great many years left of caring as much as he needed to, or working as hard as he did. And sure, he had plenty of men helping him out, and his youngest son, Tucker, helped when he could. But Tucker was only twenty-one and had only just moved out into his own place on the other side of the property. And Jaxon was ... well, Jaxon was gone.

Turned out, that flood in the noughties was the final straw for Byron's dad. Once the waters receded and the stench had cleared, they had fixed all the broken fences and repaired the barn, and then at fifty-one years old, he'd called it quits on farm life. Byron's parents had moved into the small cottage in town, and he had taken over the farm.

Shit, the cottage. He'd have to call Emory when he got back to the farmhouse, make sure she knew about the flood and had somewhere safe to go. He scolded himself for being so rushed to get back to fixing damned fence posts that he hadn't thought to check when she came to pick up Clayton. He'd have to make sure she knew that she and Clayton could stay at the farmhouse. The farm was full of rolling hills, spreading over the hectares Byron called home. The farmhouse took pride of place at the top elevation.

Byron turned to admire the heritage home, way in the distance, up on its hill. Even from here, it was a beauty. He could just make out the steep gabled roof and wrap-around patio against the dark clouds that continued to roll in. The place was huge. Full of empty bedrooms and unused spaces. Plenty of room for Emory and Clayton to come and stay, safe and dry.

The thought made Byron's Adam's apple bob, a firm lump forming in his throat. His heart raced. At his age, he shouldn't feel this way about any woman in her twenties, let alone Emory.

"You right, Dad?"

Byron shook his head, pushing off the now upright windmill and rolling his shoulders out. "Thinking of the flood is all." He didn't need his son's opinion when it came to Emory.

Byron knew what he would say, anyway.

"Not thinking of Mum? Wasn't this her windmill?"

A short puff of air escaped Byron as he held back his surprise at the question. Tucker rarely asked about his mother. He'd been so young when Josie had passed. Byron turned to face the windmill, stretching his neck up to watch the blades spin ferociously against the wind.

"Yeah, she loved this thing. I'd hate for a flood to steal it from her."

Tucker nodded but wrapped one arm around his

middle. His free hand pushed his scruffy sun-bleached hair off his face.

The two men stood, watching the windmill, remembering Josie, for a while. Wildflowers rustled all through the paddock, swaying in the wind. Neither of them gave notice to the way the flowers shook, to the warning in the air. A low grumble of thunder crept along the rolling hills, forcing them to finally look down from the rotating blades.

"Rain's coming," Byron said, breaking the silence that lingered between the men. "Might not stop once it does."

"Does Emory have somewhere safe?" Tucker asked.

Byron gulped at the lump in his throat and willed his heart not to race away like it always did whenever Emory was concerned. Before he could summon an answer that wouldn't give away his true feelings, Tucker stuck his fingers in his mouth and whistled. The sound rang in Byron's ears, but his cattle dog Miff raced over and slipped between Tucker's legs. He ignored her for a moment, planting his hands on his hips to roll his eyes at Byron.

"I'll call her," Byron said when he couldn't think of anything better. "Let her know she can stay at the farmhouse. I've got plenty of room."

"You think that's a good idea?"

No, but he wasn't about to let Tucker know that.

"Why wouldn't it be?"

Tucker sighed, stepping forward.

"Right," he said, drawing out the word.

Byron shoved his son's shoulders. "Right," he repeated, but Tucker stood firm. With a groan that matched the echoing rumble of thunder, Byron tipped his head to the grey sky. "Emory is an attractive woman, and she is also kind and intelligent and a wonderful mother to Clayton. But I'm no bloody fool. She deserves more than this old bloke can offer her." He wasn't *old* old, but he was older than her by a little more than twenty years.

"She's Jaxon's ex. And you're her son's grandfather."

"Exactly."

"But you like her?"

It was Byron's turn to sigh. Because he did, and it was so wrong on so many levels. Even if she wasn't his son's ex, she was young and just finding her feet after motherhood arrived on her doorstep unannounced. There was no way Emory would even look at him twice, so he wasn't about to go kidding himself by getting his hopes up.

"I don't need to have this conversation with you." He didn't need to have it with anyone, really. He knew he needed to hold back his blasted feelings; he didn't need his son reminding him so.

The problem was, he had tried holding them back. He'd been trying for the past 4 years, ever since he'd first laid eyes on her. But they still lingered under the surface of his skin like an itch he couldn't reach. By this stage, he figured that they always would. He'd never act on them, though.

"So, you think her and Clayton coming to stay is a good idea?" Tucker climbed onto one of the quad bikes, clicking the engine on. Miff yapped beside him, her patience wearing thin as she waited for her treat. Her tail thumped against the dry ground as a loud crack of thunder echoed through the air. Byron shivered at the sound. He knew all too well what this much rain could bring. Change. And too much of it.

Byron rummaged through the pockets of his oversized tan jacket to find a jerky treat for the dog. Finding none, he lifted his shoulders. "Sorry," he said, as though she might understand.

She yapped again, but he ignored her, moving to climb

back onto his own dusty quad bike. Miff gave up, jumping onto the tray behind Byron.

"Nope," he called out over the sound of both engines revving, "but it just might be her only choice."

He kicked the bike into gear and sped off up the hill, wanting to get back to the house quickly now, before the rain landed. Even with the house's prime position on the hill, Byron had a list of things to get done in case the roads were closed earlier than they needed to be. There *should* be enough food to last him through a flood, but if he could convince Emory to stay, he'd need almost double what he normally would have planned. Little Clayton ate almost as much food as Byron did during a growth spurt.

It'd be nice, having Clayton around more. Byron would give the whole situation that, at least. He would shove aside his personal discomfort for the sake of his grandson. That little tike lit up Byron's days like nothing else. Made him feel a little less old and a little more lively.

"I'll be back in a couple of days to help get the cows up," Tucker said after they had parked the quad bikes in the back shed and made their way around the house.

"You might not be able to get back across the bridge in a few days, it'll be the first to close."

"I've got the boat."

Byron had forgotten about the little boat his son had bought. He'd thought it stupid, buying a rowboat when they lived so far from any kind of water worth paddling along. But the changing weather patterns through summer had spooked Tucker. As soon as the word 'floods' had been uttered in the local weather forecasts, Tucker had ordered one just in case. Byron wondered briefly if it had been worth it after all. He supposed only time would tell.

"I'll call if I need ya."

"You'll need me, Dad."

As Tucker climbed into his 4x4, Byron pulled his phone from deep inside one of the inner pockets on his jacket.

Fuck. Missed calls from Emory, and a lot of them.

He hit the redial button and jogged inside the house while he waited for her to pick up. The phone rang in his ear, full of static from the storm. He paced the rooms, shucking off his jacket and trying to find the best patch of reception.

He didn't wait for her to speak when she answered the phone. Panic had begun to fester, and he needed to know she was alright. "Emory, is everything okay?"

"Jaxon is kicking me out of the cottage." Her words came out all too quickly, but Byron could hear the way her breath shook as she said them.

He held back his grouchy huff. His damned good-for-nothing, deadbeat son. Byron cleared his throat. He should have known Jaxon would play this sort of game eventually. It took a lot of convincing for him to let Emory and Clayton stay in the cottage. Jaxon had claimed it was 'his inheritance' and no one else's, as though Byron hadn't specifically given it to him as a *family* home.

"I'll talk to him," were the only words Byron could muster up through the rage that had begun to swell in his chest. Never mind the fact he hadn't heard from his son in years, Byron would figure it out. It was beyond him how Jaxon could walk away from not only Emory, but Clayton, too. And it caused a deep pang of regret that settled beneath Byron's lungs. He had raised his sons better than that. Or at least he'd thought he had. Tucker was doing alright, for a twenty-one-year-old in a town as small as Gardner Creek, but Jaxon had slipped through the cracks, and Byron was left to pick up the pieces.

He couldn't say why he felt such a *need* to help Emory.

To protect her like family. Time and time again, he told himself it was just what any other guy worth his grain of salt would do. And time and again, he'd refused to acknowledge the truth that settled deep in his chest and refused to budge.

Emory's voice was distant through the sketchy reception, metallic and crackling. "No, it's okay. You've done plenty, getting him to let me stay here for a while at least. I'll find somewhere else."

She wouldn't. Byron hated to admit it, but it was the stinking truth. Even if there were countless rentals on the market—which there were not—Emory would be far from the top of the ideal applicant list. It wasn't her fault, though. The people of Gardner Creek could be downright mean sometimes, and for whatever reason, they'd all turned on Emory the minute she walked into town. No matter how hard the poor woman tried, the wives and girlfriends of the town never welcomed her in.

He supposed it had something to do with her "stealing Jaxon" from all the eligible bachelorettes in town. Not that Jaxon had ever looked twice at any of them. He'd skipped town as soon as he was old enough, headed for the city to study. They'd all been eagerly waiting for his return, and blamed Emory when she came right on with him.

When Jaxon left again, it had only made matters worse for poor Emory. The whole town seemed to blame her for Jaxon's swift return to the city.

Byron didn't blame her, though. He blamed himself. And Jaxon.

"Emory, I don't want to sound harsh—"

"But there are no properties, and even if there were, I wouldn't get one?" Emory huffed, and Byron heard the shuffling of a chair and the muffled sounds of Clayton running off through the house. "I know, Byron. I do. I'll have to figure out something, though. Preferably before the flood comes, but I doubt that will happen."

"The flood is due in a couple of days."

"I know." Her voice was full of breath, like the acknowledgement had stolen all the air from her lungs.

Byron strode across the den and collapsed into the worn leather couch. His back slouched against the cushion.

"Emory, the cottage is on low ground. Too low."

"Actually, I wanted to call you about that too, but ..." Emory trailed off, lost in her own thoughts. She didn't need to ask, though, not really. Byron knew the question, and he'd been certain of the answer before she'd even thought to ask it.

"Right." He cleared his throat, willing his voice to remain steady. "You best come here, then."

His tone came out sharp, too sharp, but there was no taking it back. No time to reword his response before Emory replied.

"No, it's fine. I'll try the community centre. The SES message said to go there if you had no—"

"Emory, you'll come here. Quickly, too, before the rain sets in. Are you packed?"

"Yeah, we're packed."

"Now, then." He tried to lighten the tone of his voice, but his mild panic rushed out instead.

"I don't want to—"

"Now, Emory." He finally managed to soften his voice, if only a fraction, as he added, "Please, I need to know you're safe."

He heard Emory suck in a deep inhale and let it out slowly. Her breath whooshed against the phone, and he could almost, *almost*, imagine how it would feel if it was ghosting across his neck.

"Tomorrow," she finally responded. "Most of this rain is hitting up north. It'll be a couple of days before the flood hits, at least. I've got emergency bags packed, but I want to clear everything out in case I can't come back."

Byron didn't want her to wait. If he had his way, she and Clayton would leave immediately with nothing more than the clothes on their backs, just so he knew they would get safely across the bridge. He didn't tell her that, though. He understood why she wanted a day. That cottage would have held a lot of memories for her. Just as many good ones as bad ones, he supposed.

One more day would be okay. Even with all the rain expected overnight, she was right about when the flood would hit. The worst of it wasn't due until all the rain up north started flowing down the river and into their basin. If anything, the more he thought about it, the more he realised leaving tonight wasn't the best idea. No point risking the dark country roads while they were slick with the rain that had started to push through the low-hanging clouds.

"Tomorrow," he said. "Before the big storm hits."

Chapter 3

Emory

"Remind me why we're doing this?" Mya's voice was heavy as she sulked.

Emory stuck her head out of her near-empty bedroom. She'd spent all morning fielding her best friend's—her only friend's—questions, and frankly, she'd had enough.

"Because Jaxon is kicking me out and if the flood is as big as they say, this damned cottage will be full of water for a week." She ran her hands through the ends of her hair, gathering it together and looping it through the hair tie she always kept on her wrist. "I need to move everything I want out and at least *attempt* to flood-proof everything else so he can't try to blame me when it all ends up water-damaged."

Making her way down the small hallway, Emory dodged Clayton's plastic bowling ball and paused to help him set up the pins again. Ruffling his mop of blond hair, she swallowed down the unease that had been resting in her throat since yesterday. Living with Byron would be fine. Clayton would love spending more time with his Papa. And she would manage. She'd have to.

Mya stood in the living room with her hands on her hips, twisting her upper body to look back and forth around the room. Two large plastic tubs sat on the coffee table. One full of Clayton's toys, the other loaded with Emory's books and the handful of photo frames she had scattered around the walls. The small TV had been unplugged and was sitting on top of the kitchen bench, and the two suitcases Emory had packed yesterday were by the front door.

"You should really try to take all the furniture," Mya said as Emory entered the room. "The farmhouse is huge. I'm sure Byron has space."

Resigned, Emory flopped onto the couch. Her arm dangled off the side as she groaned. "I have no way of getting it there. I'm going to struggle to fit all these tubs in my car, let alone a queen-size bed and a bloody sofa."

Mya pulled at Emory's legs, twisting them off the couch so she was forced to sit up. Emory had a clear view of her friend's stomach, toned from all the hours she spent helping haul cartons of fresh produce at her parents' store. Emory knew that every morning, without fail, Mya would show up to do all the heavy lifting so her dad didn't have to, then she'd rush off to her job at the community library. Reaching up, she poked Mya in the ribs, then grabbed her wrists and pulled her down so they were sitting together. Mya might as well have been in Emory's lap, they were so close. One of Mya's legs rested over the top of Emory's thigh, and Emory's shoulder was dangerously close to taking out Mya's breast.

Wrapping her arms around Emory, Mya kissed the top of her head.

"You okay?"

Emory felt her whole body droop into Mya's comfort-able embrace. She wasn't okay, she just wasn't really sure how to explain it to Mya. No doubt her friend assumed she was mellow about moving out of the cottage, and sure she was, but it was the least of her current problems. Finding a new place to live in Gardner Creek was so far down the list of her worries, it was barely even a speck on the horizon.

A silent tear forced its way down her cheek, and she batted it away, hoping Mya wouldn't notice. But as the town's most social librarian and therefore the go-to for all kinds of moral advice and support, Mya was well-versed in silent interactions. She caught Emory's hand as it wiped at the tear and clasped it in her own.

"You'll find somewhere."

Emory hiccupped, sucked in a raspy breath, and ran through sentences in her head. She had to tell her friend she was planning to leave town as soon as she could, and now was as good a time as any.

"If you don't," Mya continued before Emory had figured out how to phrase the bombshell, "you and Clayton can come stay with me for a while."

"You don't need to do that."

Mya recoiled a little, scrunching her nose up. "Well, you can't honestly expect to stay with Byron for any longer than you need to?"

"I won't."

Emory pushed herself out of Mya's hold. With her hands on Mya's shoulders, Emory looked up at her friend. The front of Mya's usually styled bob was pulled back from her face in a small, high fountain of a ponytail. A few stray strands framed her face perfectly and Emory wondered how Mya always looked so damned perfect. Even in a pair of faded leggings and an oversized hoodie, she screamed 'put together' and 'I've got my shit sorted.' It was the kind of look Emory always strived for but never felt like she achieved.

"I don't want to find another place in town, Mya. I'm so close to finishing my degree, there's no point. Once the flood clears, I'll find an apartment in the city for me and Clay. Somewhere close to a daycare and schools and *jobs*."

Emory closed her eyes. Under her hands, Emory could feel Mya's shoulders shake.

"I thought I had more time with you."

Emory pulled her friend in for a hug. They wrapped their arms around each other and sat, sharing tears as they both processed the news.

"I did too," Emory said eventually. "But with Jaxon kicking me out, and the flood. The timing feels right."

Emory nodded against her friend. A wet patch started to form on Emory's top, and she felt it bleed through to the skin of her shoulder.

She hated this, feeling like she had let her friend down. It was right for her, though, and for Clayton. No matter how sad Mya was about it, Emory knew she would understand.

As though sensing the rapid change in mood, Clayton burst into the room carrying the plastic ball. It was almost as big as his head, and he held it out in front of him, blocking his view. Emory let go of Mya to grab Clayton's shoulder before he collided with the rough edges of the old coffee table.

"My!" He smiled as he climbed onto Mya's lap. He wriggled against Emory's hold, pushing her back.

"Does he know?" Mya whispered over the little boy's head, tickling behind his ears to further muffle the sound.

Emory shook her head, then tilted it back to rest on the cushion of the couch. Her aching shoulders stretched in pain, the weight of, well, everything, resting heavy. She had a lot to sort out, and thanks to Jaxon's eviction notice and her choice to ignore it for three weeks, not a lot of time to dot her i's and cross her t's. Byron's farmhouse was a stepping stone, she told herself. Nothing more, nothing less.

"I'm hungry."

Clayton popped into her line of sight, climbing across the couch to lean on her. His eyes, such a dark blue they could have been navy, pierced through her own as he waited for her to respond.

"Can you reach the bananas in the fruit bowl?"

The little boy didn't answer, jumping over Emory's shoulder and climbing down the back of the couch. He ran for the kitchen, sliding around the corner on his socks.

"Did Byron teach him that?"

"Climbing over the couch? I think so."

Mya rested a hand on Emory's shoulder, but there was a different energy that charged the touch this time. Emory could feel her icy fingers squeezing too tight by only the smallest fraction.

"Emory, I say this with love, okay?" Mya paused then, waiting for Emory to acknowledge her.

Raising her eyebrows, Emory glanced at Mya through the corners of her eyes. "What?"

"Is moving in with Byron the best idea right now?"

"I have nowhere else to go. If the flood comes as high as they say, we will need to evacuate." Emory spoke directly to the ceiling. She knew where this conversation was heading, and frankly, she didn't even have herself convinced that evacuating to Byron's was the best idea. There was no way she'd be able to convince her friend otherwise.

"You could go to the community centre. They are setting up all the beds now, and they'll have food and toys for Clayton."

"Mya, the only thing worse than being at Byron's would be ending up stuck at the community centre."

Emory hummed. "True. But you hate Byron."

"I don't."

"You do."

Pushing herself up, Emory finally faced Mya. She held her best friend's gaze as she rolled out the kink in her neck. Her heart pounded against her chest, and her ears rushed.

"The problem is not that I hate him, Mya. It's that I specifically *don't* hate him."

She felt her cheeks heat as a blush spread across her face. Wiping at the feeling with her hands, Emory groaned.

Mya squealed and jumped off the couch. Her hand flew up to cover her mouth as she tried to compose herself.

"You mean you ...?"

"Yes."

"But he is ..."

"Yes."

"And you're about to ..."

"Yes. Thank you, Mya. I know, okay? I *know*. It's fucking embarrassing, so don't you dare speak a word of this to anybody, alright? It's just a stupid fucking crush that won't go away, no matter how hard I try to ignore it. And besides, I don't *like him* like him. I just think he's really hot and every time I see him, I wonder what he'd look like without a shirt on."

Mya paced back and forth in front of Emory, her hands flying around her. After a moment, she sat on the coffee table and took Emory's hands in her own.

"Do you *want* to ignore it?"

Emory tried not to shake her head, she really did, but her body gave away her true feelings without her consent anyway. "But it's *dumb*!" Realising she was yelling, Emory dropped her voice into an exaggerated whisper. "He's so much older than me. And he is Clayton's grandfather! And Jaxon's dad. I can't do that. I shouldn't want that."

"But you do."

"Yes, Mya. I do."

Mya's thumbs traced little circles on Emory's palm. She focused on the feeling, trying to ignore the way it hurt to breathe.

"Emory, do you realise that if you go to Byron's and the bridge closes, you'll be stuck there?"

She hadn't thought of that. This whole time, she thought she would just go about her everyday life, but at the farmhouse instead of here at the cottage. She had figured Byron would spend each day doing farm stuff, and she would go to her shifts at the café but just come home to a different house. And, okay, they would maybe eat dinner together, but it would be no harder than all the times before when he insisted they stay to eat before coming home.

But if the bridge closed?

There would be no escape. For either of them.

Emory held her breath. The bridge wouldn't close. Mya was just being overly cautious. That's what friends were for, right?

"The bridge won't close," Emory told her friend, and herself, but her voice shook with uncertainty.

"If the flood gets as high as they say it will, the bridge will close, Emory. I know the community centre would be pretty shit, and I'd offer you my place if I wasn't also evacuating, but are you sure being fully stuck with Byron is the best idea?"

"Where are you going? Can't we come with you and your parents?"

Mya's nose scrunched up, and she looked down at her feet.

"Mya, where are you going?"

In one swift exhale, Mya answered, "My parents are staying with my aunt, and I'm staying with Tucker."

"With Tucker?!"

Mya pulled her hands back and hugged her middle. Clayton came running back into the room with half a peeled banana in his hands. The other half was mushed around his mouth.

"Unky Tuck?"

At first, the cute nickname felt cosy in Emory's ears. It was affectionate, but in half a heartbeat, it reminded Emory of just how much Clayton would be leaving behind when they left. It clawed at her throat, but she had to do this. For her. Clayton would adjust, and he would thrive in a city where he wouldn't be excluded because of who his mother was.

Leaping off the couch, Emory swiped the packet of baby wipes from the coffee table and grabbed Clayton's arm. She pulled him close, before he could spread the banana any further, and wiped his mouth. He squirmed under her hold, wiggling as she set him down on the coffee table next to Mya.

Emory folded her arms across her chest and nudged Mya's leg with her toes.

"Yes, okay. But it's new. Like, *very* new, and this flood could make or break us, so I don't think adding you two to the mix is the best idea."

There was a lot Emory could say about Tucker being five years younger than her best friend or about Tucker's apparent reluctance to get his life together. But she couldn't say any of it when Mya seemed so giddy at the thought of them. The corner of Emory's mouth began to push into her cheek. "I'm happy for you."

"Will you be okay? With ... everything?" Mya waved

her arm between Emory and Clayton, then around the room.

"I'll have to be."

"Let's see if we can fit these tubs in your car, then."

Emory pulled the largest tub over the coffee table and grunted as she picked it up. Mya rushed to open the front door for her, then picked up a box of her own.

Once Emory's small SUV was packed and Clayton was buckled into his seat, Emory turned to face Mya again.

"Thank you for today. And for everything."

Mya scratched the back of her neck. "Thanks for understanding about Tucker."

"What are friends for?"

The two women hugged, rocking a little as they held each other close, neither wanting to be the first to let go.

"What am I going to do when you leave, Emory?"

"You'll have Tucker."

"Yeah, but he's a boy. It's not the same."

Chapter 4

Byron

Byron rolled his eyes, pulling the deep navy blanket back off the bed and folding it roughly before dropping it at his feet. He was overthinking this. He knew it, and looking around the spare room he had rushed to get ready for Emory, she would know it too.

He'd started by simply changing the sheets. No one had slept in the bed since Tucker moved out almost a year ago, but Byron had figured it needed refreshing before Emory settled in for the next week or more. It had been so long since anyone had even been in this room that he presumed everything was covered in a fine layer of dust, bedspread included.

He'd wiped down all the surfaces and across the windowsill, vacuumed the faded grey rug, and fluffed the pillows as best he could. Remaking the bed after stripping off the old sheets, Byron had felt a sudden urge to do *more*.

The off-white sheets he used looked fine, but plain. And Emory deserved far more than plain, even if Byron was not the one to ever give it to her. So, he'd added the deep navy blanket and a few of the throw cushions from the couch in the den. They only got used when he and Clayton built forts and collected every pillow and cushion from the house to be their walls, so he knew they wouldn't be missed. But scattered across the bed, they looked cheap and gave the distinct impression that he was trying too hard to make Emory comfortable. He needed to give an air of nonchalance, not this prissy bullshit.

He yanked the cushions off the bed, throwing them behind him towards the door and turning his attention to the lone bedside table. The lamp was fine, but the books he'd pulled from the bookshelf would have to go. He knew Emory loved to read, but he was kidding himself if he thought he could pick a book out for her. Never mind how downright over the top it was for him to have even attempted it. If she didn't bring books of her own, she could choose from the wall-to-wall shelving down in the den. Most of the books were left behind from the boys' younger years, but there were a few old classics Josie used to enjoy. The ones he still hadn't been able to get rid of might just end up being read again after all.

Byron sucked in a breath at the reminder of his wife. Of how young they both were when she died. It was an age ago now, and Byron had mostly settled into life as a widower. The farm had carried on, and the boys needed him. He'd never had time to dwell, and he preferred it that way. Still, it would be nice to have someone again. To hand him a coffee when he came in after tending to the cows, and to listen to his complaints when the monotony of farm life became all too much. To keep his bed warm on the frosty autumn mornings and to bring light to his otherwise dark and lonely life.

He pictured Emory in that role, and he hated that he did. It looked good on her, at least in his imagination, but it would never do. It wasn't right. And if she was going to stay for the next however long until the floodwaters dropped again and the cottage was clean and safe, Byron figured he would have to rein in this forbidden fantasy that kept popping up.

Shaking the vision from his mind, he removed the fresh flowers he had cut from the garden and propped in a jar from the dresser by the window, too. If everything else was over the top, they were downright excessive.

The sky was a deep grey, a warning of the storm to come. The rain the night before had been nothing more than a pre-game, and the sky was rapidly growing darker as the next pelting inched closer. Byron hoped Emory would be there soon. He'd said before the storm, but he hadn't planned on it hitting so early in the afternoon. These roads were dangerous when they were wet, he knew that all too well, and the thought of Emory driving on them was a persistent itch behind his ears.

Trudging down the hallway to return everything to its suitable, unused place, Byron heard the crunching of the gravel driveway. The sound stirred something unusual inside him, anticipation that flooded his veins with lava and left needles all over his skin.

Lightning flashed outside the windows, sending a burst of light through the house. It was the distant, far-off kind that flashed through the air without any real starting point, but Byron knew it was only the beginning. He started to count, even though he could never remember the proper measurements. All he knew was that the less time between the light and the thunder, the closer the storm was.

He threw the cushions and blanket back over the couch in the den, leaving the flowers and books on the raw wood coffee table. And as he raced to the front door, his heart pounded with that same anticipation, but an edge of something else. Excitement tingled down his spine. God, he was pathetic. Surely at this age, he should be over such immature rushes of emotion. He couldn't help it when he thought of Emory, though.

He got to five one-thousands before the thunder cracked through the air, right as he pulled open the front door. The loud clap shook the branches of the tall gum tree that stood halfway down the driveway. Byron could hear Clayton's cries from inside Emory's small car.

His shoulders dropped. He hadn't realised he'd been holding them so high, but when he saw Emory and finally knew she was safe, an unexpected sense of relief poured over him.

Miff bounded around the house from her kennel out back, barking at the sky. She tangled herself around Byron's feet, squeezing between them and resting her front paws on his toes.

"Alright, inside," he told the scaredy dog. He patted her behind, nudging her into the house.

Seeing the boxes in the back of Emory's car, Byron grabbed a pair of old gumboots that had been propped upside down on the mat, giving them a firm tap on the ground before flipping them up to slide them on. Striding down the steps of the porch, he called out a hello to Emory as she opened her door. She waved, distracted by her attempts to calm the still-crying little boy in the car.

"It was just thunder, Clayton," she said, twisting her body to give him a gentle pat before she got out. "We're at Papa's, hold on." She smiled politely at Byron and pulled two backpacks across the front seat.

Byron rushed over to take them from her, fumbling with the tangle of long straps. His hand brushed against Emory's. Electricity buzzed between them, and lightning lit up the yard once more, only this time, Byron could see the distinct zig-zag pattern as the power surged through the sky.

Just the storm, Byron told himself. Still, he couldn't tear his gaze away from Emory. He counted thousands again, muttering the numbers under his breath as he tried to steady the anxious swirl in his chest. Emory stood, frozen out of fear or shock or unease. He hated feeling like he caused something uncomfortable for Emory, but her nose scrunched up just so, leaving the cutest lines across her freckles. Her long hair had been tied in a loose, messy knot high on her head, with haphazard pieces that flew about in the wind. And there was something about her eyes that Byron couldn't help but get lost in. Before, he might have said they sparkled, but now they reflected the uncertainty in the air. The chocolatey brown of her irises had darkened in the overcast light. God, even in her over-sized grey shirt with the buttons done in the wrong holes, Emory was perfect. So, Byron stared even though he knew he shouldn't, and did his best to fill his expression with something that looked friendly. Caring, even. Until she blinked slowly, breaking the trance Byron had fallen under.

Emory pulled her lower lip between her teeth, and Byron tracked the movement with his eyes. She released it with a slight pop, and her mouth hung open, only by the tiniest sliver.

Byron was captivated.

He stepped forward. No longer thinking. His mouth still counted, but his brain had switched off. Their hands were still touching over the straps of the backpacks. Byron wrapped his fingers around Emory and stepped closer. Her eyes dropped to his mouth. He could tell.

Their chests heaved in time, and Byron swallowed

down everything that was threatening to spill over. It didn't work.

Thunder roared around them. Byron stood his ground, holding down the unsettled feeling storms always brought out in him, but Emory jolted back. She dropped the bags into his arms and raced around the car to get Clayton out. The poor kid was terrified. He clung tight to Emory's shoulders as she picked him up and nuzzled his head underneath her chin.

Emory stared at Byron over her son's head. Her eyes were harsh, and her mouth had thinned into a straight line, and Byron wanted to storm over there and wipe the jarring expression from her face. He took a step towards her, but stopped in his tracks when she shook her head.

"I can help with the tubs once I get Clayton inside."

"Don't be silly. You get him settled. His room is all set up."

It would be good, Byron thought, for Clayton to actually use the room properly for once. He'd set it up as soon as Jaxon had left. He thought maybe he'd take over that fatherly role, and wrongly, he supposed, figured that meant watching him overnight every once in a while. But a grandfather can't replace a father, he'd learnt. And while Emory was more than willing to bring Clayton over as often as possible, she drew a firm line at sleepovers.

As Clayton grew a little older and progressed from an immobile baby to a running toddler, Byron started watching him during the days while Emory worked at the local café. Sure, he'd had his fair share of naps here at the farmhouse, but otherwise, the miniature bed was unused. The toys and books remained too neatly stacked on the shelves. The dresser was never filled.

So yeah, Byron was happy for the room to see a little extra life now that Clayton and Emory had come to stay.

He just wished it would be a permanent change, even though he knew all the reasons why that would never be.

"Thank you," Emory called over her shoulder. Clayton clasped around her neck as she trudged up the stairs and kicked off her shoes.

"You can stay in the room next to him," Byron added as she stepped inside.

Emory didn't respond, although Byron presumed she hadn't heard him over the distant grumble of constant thunder and pounding rain on the horizon. Moving to the back of the car, he threw both backpacks over an arm and pulled the suitcases out of the boot. One was far heavier than the other, but Byron managed to whisk them up to the house and into the entry hall. He dropped the backpacks with them and returned to the car.

All that was left were two large plastic tubs, stacked neatly in the car. Byron double-checked the back seat, sure they should have more belongings than this. Besides Clayton's harnessed booster and a scattering of toys, there was nothing. All that was left were the tubs. Byron hauled them from the car and up into the house.

He stacked them in the living room. One was full of toys, the other books and photographs, and he didn't want Emory to think she and Clayton were confined to their rooms. He wanted them to feel at home here.

Clayton's giggles drifted down the hall, and Byron paused at the sound. It wasn't unusual. After all, Clayton was here most days while Emory worked. But there was a sweet echo to the sound that wasn't usually there. It tickled inside Byron's ears and sent whispers down his spine. It made his breath hitch against his throat and squeezed at his heart.

He stood there, transfixed, and it took him far too long to realise that the sound wasn't coming from Clayton at all. It was Emory. He wondered if he'd ever heard her laugh. Small chuckles? Maybe. The silent 'ha' after a punchline that wasn't quite funny? Definitely. But never this. Never so unfiltered and joyous.

This was light and sweet and laden with syrup. Emory's laugh filled all the little gaps he didn't realise he had, soaking him in a pure kind of warmth. It made his heart swell and his eyes water and twisted at something inside him that he hadn't felt in a very long time.

His brain stopped connecting to his body, and he stood, paralysed in every way, listening to Emory's melodic laugh. It was beautiful, and he could have stood there all night.

He would have stood there all night, too, but Emory stepped out of the room and into his line of sight. She stood, staring at him. A small crease formed between her brows, her nose scrunching. Biting at her lip, she folded her arms across her body before dropping them by her sides and shaking out her hands. Lifting her head high, Emory walked towards Byron, never breaking their locked gaze.

"You alright, old man?"

She was so close to him. So close, all he had to do was wrap his arms around her back, and he could kiss her. He wanted to, but he didn't. Because with two short words, she slapped him with a reality far harsher than the fact that he was actually getting older. It was the fact that she saw him that way.

All this infatuation he was drowning in was one-sided. Byron rolled his shoulders and forced air into his lungs. This was fine. She didn't know how he felt, and she never would.

CHAPTER 5

EMORY

There was something different about the farmhouse. Emory couldn't quite put her finger on it. The same collection of old, fraying picture books was spread on the coffee table. Memories of the boys' youth that Byron revisited daily when he looked after Clayton. The old leather couch was still sunken in the centre, where Miff was curled in a ball. The same cold slate tile floors were covered with the same soft tan rug in front of the fire.

After the distant thunder had eased, Clayton had sprung to life, pulling every toy from the tub Byron had left in the living room. He'd then proceeded to ignore them all and had pulled a box of wooden blocks out from somewhere—Emory wasn't exactly sure where it came from. With blocks all around him on the floor, Clayton was now building the tallest, skinniest tower he could on the big square coffee table. It was time for Emory to get him ready for bed, but with the hustle of a trip to this Papa's and the excitement of going to bed here, Emory doubted she'd have any luck getting him to sleep. She'd let him play for a little longer, then she'd try.

She looked around the room again, trying to put her finger on what was different. After cooking dinner and insisting on doing all the tidying up, Byron had disappeared into the back of the house, leaving Emory alone with Clayton. But it wasn't his presence she was missing, was it? That was silly.

With every ounce of her being, she had tried to ignore the way her stomach fluttered when she saw him stride out of the house. Determination and worry had been written all over his face, and her fingers had twitched, wanting to reach out and smooth away the deep crease between his brows. His hair had been all scruffy, like he'd just got out of bed or he'd spent the afternoon running his fingertips through the ends. Emory couldn't help but imagine it would look the same if it were her fingers getting tangled through the short strands. And then, of course, that made her think of so much more. She imagined what his muscles would feel like under her touch and how his large, calloused hands might feel if they explored her body. How his beard might scratch at the skin on her chin. Or between her legs.

She forced a shudder, desperate to shake off all the inappropriate thoughts.

Byron had been her saviour in many ways over the years. Giving her and Clayton a place to stay was just another item to add to the list. And Emory was grateful, so grateful, for all of Byron's support. She just hated the way her body reacted to his presence. It was hard enough to fight off the heat that rushed through her when they crossed paths as often as they did. When she knew she could escape home and hide her attraction in her bedroom, revisiting it later when she was alone.

But here? Now? There would be no escape. She could squeeze her thighs together as much as she wanted, but she'd never be able to relieve the tension. Not with the man she so desperately wished could be relieving it for her just down the hall. That, surely, would be taking her petty enthralment a step too far.

Emory pushed off the couch, leaving Clayton with his blocks to hunt down whatever it was that was making this place feel so different. She found it in the kitchen. A wide candle with a large, wooden wick flickered on the otherwise empty kitchen bench. Emory had never seen this room so neat. The small breakfast table was usually a dumping ground. Jackets on the back of chairs, a half-drunk coffee sitting atop the local newspaper. Emory was certain Byron was the only person left in town who read the physical copy. Everyone else downloaded the thing straight to their phones. She hadn't noticed any of it was missing when they sat down to eat, but without the bowls of potatoes and chicken wings and veggies spread on the table, its bareness screamed at her.

But that wasn't all. Dishes usually sat drying on the rack by the sink. Crates of fresh fruit and vegetables—Bryon's share from the week's harvest of Tucker's small but mighty produce patch on the other side of the farm—often remained on the bench. But it was all cleared. Even the pots and pans from tonight's meal had been washed, dried and put away instead of being left to air dry overnight. Byron had insisted Emory could play with Clayton while he tidied up after dinner, but she hadn't imagined he would go *this* far. The candlelight danced across the bench, its wooden wick crackling as it filled the air with a fresh, woodsy scent that reminded her of the bush. It looked new. The creamy wax was still high in the jar, the small pool that had started to melt not yet reaching the edges.

"I bought it in town."

His deep, husky voice reverberated through Emory's bones.

"When?" Emory's voice was a breathy whisper. She hadn't meant it, truly, but she couldn't have helped it. Not when her heart did a funny kind of gallop because she thought he was implying he bought it today. For her. He couldn't have meant that, though. That was just her silly little heart thinking. She didn't turn to face him, didn't want him to see the way her cheeks were red hot with her blush.

Byron cleared his throat, and Emory imagined his Adam's apple bobbing with the movement. *Stop it.* She couldn't think like this. Was it too late to go to the community centre? A flash of lightning blinded her, the loud clap of thunder following almost instantaneously. A warning, no doubt, that it was already too late. At least for tonight.

Miff barked, no doubt jumping down from her cosy spot on the couch. The echoing sound of blocks tumbling was followed by Clayton's cries. He climbed over the couch, tiny footsteps plodding along the hard floor with Miff's scampering close behind. The little boy and the dog ran together into the kitchen, colliding with Emory.

She wouldn't have toppled if her heart hadn't already thrown her off balance. At least that's what she told herself. But really, the force of Clayton slamming against her legs and Miff skidding to stop in front of her caught her off guard. She swayed on the spot, unable to throw out a leg for balance because Clayton had wrapped his arms around her and was squeezing tight. They were going down, Emory and her son. All she could do was throw her arms behind her to catch the ground as they fell.

Only, she didn't. She caught something else instead. Firm abs, and then, because she was falling and couldn't help it, her hand dropped lower. Emory squealed when she realised what she'd done, her hand wrenching away from Byron's crotch and dropping lower instead. His thigh was firm, full of muscle, and Emory's entire body was heating up. She needed out of the warm hoodie she'd put on as the sun began to set. Or better yet, out of this room.

Byron seemed unfazed. He huffed, scooping Emory under her arms before she hit the floor. He wrapped his arms around her chest, placing her back upright. But he didn't let go when her feet hit the ground. He stepped closer. Holding her still while she regained her balance, it did nothing to help her composure. Pressed against her back, she could feel him. All of him. And she was hyper-fixated on the part that she shouldn't be feeling. Not when she fell, not now, not ever. But there it was, firm against the small of her back.

Firm!

Ugh, she was never going to live this down. Or be able to forget about it. No matter how many times she told herself it was just his body's natural reaction to being unintentionally groped, Emory was fixated on what it might mean.

She wriggled against Byron's hold, trying to break free. He held her tight and growled, low in her ear.

"Don't."

Emory whimpered as his hot breath caressed the soft pad of skin under her ear.

"You'll make it worse."

She squirmed.

"Emory."

Closing her eyes, Emory took a long, deep breath. The kind she felt right down in her belly. Her exhale was shaky, but she stood, frozen, as Byron loosened his bear hug. She could have sworn his fingertips lingered on her hips. A sharp, whispered gasp escaped her lips, and as if in response, Byron let out a grumbled breath of his own before clearing his throat and stepping away.

Another flash of lightning lit up the room, followed by a clap of thunder that echoed all around them. Still clinging to her legs, oblivious to his mother's crimson red cheeks, Clayton screamed.

"I think we're in for a long night," Emory said, mostly to herself, but from his new spot far across the room, Byron coughed in response.

"From the thunder. Yep." He cleared his throat and left the room.

Emory held in the giant, exaggerated sigh that threatened to escape her. Of course, Byron was less than thrilled at the thought of Clayton crying all night. She wasn't particularly thrilled about it either, but unlike Byron, she couldn't just leave the room at the realisation.

She reached down to scoop Clayton into her arms. Now was as good a time as any to try to get him into bed. He protested against her hold at first, but as she carried him down the hall to his bedroom, Clayton started to relax into her chest, the adrenaline of the day finally wearing off in a big crash of exhaustion. He was half asleep by the time she pulled on his night nappy and tucked him under the tractor-covered blankets. Tiptoeing out of the room, a little bead of hope caught light between her temples. Maybe he would sleep through the night after all. Maybe she wouldn't spend the night curled into his tiny bed, huddled under blankets that would do nothing to keep her warm. She crossed her fingers behind her back as she inched the door closed, holding the handle down to reduce any chance of a click.

When she nudged the handle back into place, her shoulders relaxed. From deep inside the room, she heard the rustle of blankets, Clayton wriggling, no doubt. Emory held her breath, but a deep, breathy snore from the young boy told her he was still sleeping soundly.

"Will he stay asleep?"

Emory jumped a little at his grumbly voice. She'd truly thought Byron had escaped to his room for the night, or somewhere else in the giant house.

Shaking off her surprise and attempting to act natural, Emory turned to face Byron. Any mediocre ounce of coolness she had somehow managed to brush over her disappeared. Standing before her, Byron was ... well, he was a sight. Emory gulped, then squeezed her eyes shut. She shook her head involuntarily.

He'd gotten changed. Now dressed in a pair of low-hanging grey sweats and a tight black tee, Byron leaned against the wall with one leg propped up behind him. With his arms folded across his chest, his biceps threatened to bust out of the arms of his tee.

What Emory wouldn't give to just reach out and touch them. To run her fingers along the veins that protruded from the muscles. To feel her way down to his large hands and wrap his arms around her. She let out a shaky breath. Because fuck, Byron looked good no matter what he wore, but this? This was on another level. She equally hoped that he wore this around the house *all the time* and never again.

She let her eyes creep open and figured his feet were the safest place to look.

Byron cleared his throat.

"Emory?"

She blew air through the tiny gap between her lips and ran her hands over her face. Slowly—because now that she was looking, she simply couldn't help but *look*—Emory ran her gaze up Byron's body. Over his thick legs, and where his sweats clung to the bulge between them. Past the abs she could make out through the tight tee and across his arms again. Until finally, with a deep throbbing in her core, she found his face.

Beneath his beard, the corner of Byron's mouth was tilted up, and a deep crease was set between his brows. But his eyes were molten. She didn't know what colour they usually were, beyond the way they reflected the gold in the sun when they were outdoors. Now, they were black as night, but somehow sparkled. She was drawn to them, she got lost in them. Heat spread from her core, up her chest and over her cheeks. Her breaths turned heavy, and her mouth dropped open, just a fraction.

Byron grumbled. No, he downright growled, from a place deep in his chest, and Emory couldn't help but imagine how it would feel against her skin. His hot breath vibrating against all her most sensitive spots. Behind her ear, between her breasts, at the apex of her thighs.

She cleared her throat, squeezing her eyes back shut and shaking her head. Again. As though she could just forget any of it had happened. This was bad. Very bad. She should not, under any circumstances, be thinking these things. About Byron. Her ex's dad. Her son's grandfather. Nope. Not happening. *Please.*

"I'm going to bed," she squeaked out.

Pivoting on her heel, she turned back and forth, not knowing where Byron had put all her stuff. He'd said it was next to Clayton's room, but there were doors in both directions. She chose one blindly and hoped for the best.

"Other way," Byron laughed.

Standing a little taller, Emory switched direction. She looked straight ahead, not daring to be caught checking him out again.

"On the left, next to—"

She didn't stop to let him finish, rushing into the room and hastily pulling the door closed behind her. It was going to be a long night after all.

The room was quaint, similar in layout to the one next door where Clayton was now sleeping, but with a large king-size bed in place of his toddler one. It took up most of the room, but Emory didn't mind. She didn't need anything else anyway. All she wanted to do was curl up under the covers and pretend the past five minutes never happened.

Hell, she wanted to pretend the past hour never happened. From the moment she found the candle, everything went downhill. Except for her pulse. That was still racing. With embarrassment and anticipation and need. It throbbed in her temples, and under her chin, and deep in her belly.

Her back still resting against the door she'd swiftly shut behind her, Emory let out a long puff of air. How the hell was she supposed to last here? Outside, the rain was finally pouring, never-ending sheets of water thrashed against the window so ferociously she couldn't see the paddock that extended beyond the back of the house. She bet against herself that it wouldn't stop for weeks now that it had started, and wondered just how long she'd end up stuck here with Byron.

There were worse people she could end up stuck with, she supposed, but she doubted she could ever look Byron in the eye again after tonight. The image of him, looking all smug and downright fucking sexy was ingrained behind her eyes. And her back still tingled at the memory of Byron's dick, pressed up against her. He could have done anything, could have let her fall, could have held her at arm's length when he set her back on her feet, could have turned away instead of stepping closer. It was almost as if he *wanted* her to feel his reaction to her accidental touch.

Had he?

It was ridiculous to think, surely, but Emory's imagination got the better of her. Lava pooled out from her galloping heart, spreading across her skin. She groaned, wishing she could do something to ease all the built-up tension and craving that flowed through her veins. She couldn't, though. She wouldn't. Not here.

Except, over the persistent patter of rain against the window, she heard a noise from the room next to her. Not Clayton's, the one to the other side. A shower clicked on, the clanking as someone—Byron, clearly—stepped through the glass screen. If Byron was in the shower ... could she?

It was that final thought that tipped her over the edge. Byron, naked, under the stream from the shower. She pictured rivulets of water coasting their way across his shoulders, down his front and over his abs. And even though she tried not to, she imagined what his cock might be like. Large, at least that's what she assumed from the feel she accidentally took and the bulge she couldn't help but notice in his sweats.

Pulling her lower lip between her teeth, Emory gave in. She collapsed onto the bed and dipped her hand beneath the waistband of her leggings. Her pussy was hot and needy, moisture pooling in her panties. Dipping a finger between her folds, she used her other hand to push her pants down, taking her wet underwear with them.

A gasp escaped her, then a moan as she pinched her clit and sunk two fingers deep inside her. She rode her own hand, imagining it was Byron's, wishing it was him. Hooking her fingers against her walls, she stroked her orgasm free. And as she toppled off the cliff, she forgot where she was and who was on the other side of the wall. She was so caught up, she never noticed the shower turn off. She never heard his heavy breathing on the other side of the wall.

"Byron," she moaned as she spiralled down from her peak.

And only then did she hear him.

"Emory."

CHAPTER 6

BYRON

The hot water took an age to flow through the pipes. So much so that Byron contemplated stepping under the ice-cold flow. It might have done him good, a cool shower. Truthfully, he needed it. His balls still ached and his cock still hadn't got the message that nothing, *nothing,* was going to happen with Emory.

Still, her sweet laughter and bright-as-sun smile had infiltrated his mind and body even more now than they ever had. He couldn't get the thought of her out of his head. Couldn't shake the feeling that being flooded in was both the best and worst thing that could happen to them.

The rain pounded outside, but it wasn't this storm he was worried about. This storm would flood the creek and spread water across some of the lowest paddocks. But that was nothing. That was a regular thing this time of year when the blasted air currents flowed whichever way they were. Sure, the cows had a little less breathing room, but the bridge was still open, and life went by just as it always did.

So, nah, it wasn't the sheeting rain that kept coming

and going as the storm swirled around them that worried Byron, it was the rain up north. That rain would fall, and it would have nowhere to go but down. It would flow down the river, an endless stream of too much water, and where the creek turned narrow just out of town, it would be forced to stop. It would dam. And when, not if, it did, the bridge would close.

Byron stuck his hand into the shower, flinching as the now-burning water hit his arm. Turning the tap down, he stepped under the waterfall and tipped his head up. Big droplets hit his face, and he closed his eyes as he let the water rush over his body. It tingled on his skin, washing away none of the dirtiness that invaded his thoughts of Emory.

They might have one more day before the SES would be forced to close the bridge to his property. They would be trapped. It hadn't even been twenty-four hours, and already, the tension was thick. Each blistering moment was another weight on his chest, and Byron wasn't sure how many more he could take.

Maybe he should have bought a dinghy boat when Tucker did. At least then he'd be able to get away to breathe properly every now and then. If things kept going the way they were, he doubted his weary lungs were going to survive the pressure.

His mind raced as he carried out the motions of his shower. He did his best to keep his mind off the woman in the next room, but everything circled back to her.

Did he need more food? He might, now that Emory was staying.

How would he entertain Clayton when they couldn't go further than the small section of manicured lawn? Hopefully, Emory had some ideas.

What would he do all day when he had no farm to

tend to? What would Emory do when she couldn't get to her shifts at the café?

Emory.

Always Emory.

His hands skated down his front, rubbing soap over his abdomen and lower between his legs. His cock hung, still half hard, and the soap that trickled over it tickled at the tip. He tugged at it, contemplating, but eventually thought better of the idea. Not when Emory was *right there*, on the other side of the wall. His cock protested, but he was determined to do the right thing. If there even was a right thing anymore, now that he was so hopelessly gone for the one woman he could never have.

He'd been alone a long time, but not for lack of options. Just about every woman in town had tried her luck in the years after Josie passed. They didn't really want Byron, though, they wanted what he stood for. The young widower, alone in his farmhouse, raising the boys that would carry on the Gardner name. Generations ago, Byron's ancestors had called this land home, and the farm had been in the family since. The whole damn township was named for his great-great-great—however many greats —grandfather. So yeah, the women didn't want him so much as they wanted a claim to the town.

Byron had tried for a while. Not to replace his late wife, because no woman could ever do that, but to open his heart to love again. Nothing, no one, ever felt even close to right. None of the women he tried dating made his heart sing or made the farmhouse feel like a home again. So, eventually, he'd stopped trying.

It was a cruel twist of fate when Emory arrived in town on the arm of his son. Byron didn't believe in love at first sight, but just seeing her started to chip away at the icy walls he'd built around his heart. He'd been fighting to keep them built ever since, and it became increasingly hard when Jaxon left her, alone and pregnant, a little over three years ago.

Now, it seemed the walls were melting down faster than he could refreeze the bricks. Having her here, not being able to leave, was going to test him.

He rolled his shoulders and stood, still under the water as the soap washed free.

Turning off the tap, Byron heard something from the room behind the wall.

Frantic movements.

Laboured breaths.

He swore under his breath. He hadn't meant to hear Emory, truly, but the walls of the old farmhouse were thin and her room was right on the other side of this one.

He couldn't say he was disappointed that he had, though. If anything, he was glad. Of a few things.

Firstly, he was glad he hadn't rubbed one out in the shower like he had done so many times before. All those times he'd imagined Emory's lips wrapped around his dick or her bouncing in his lap while he pumped himself dry. He'd wanted to tonight, too, he rationalised, but something had stopped him. Maybe it was knowing she was in the next room because it had felt wrong, somehow. He'd hesitated, and he was glad he did because if he hadn't, he would have still been in the shower.

Then, he was glad of the small lull in the storm that came at just the right time. He stepped out of the shower to the sound of Emory's heavy breaths, the slight creaking of the bed, the wet pumping as she fucked herself with ... well, he imagined it was her hand.

His cock sprang to attention. Never mind the fact it had been halfway ready ever since Emory had fallen on him in the kitchen. It ached, his balls hanging low between his thighs. And so instead of grabbing a towel, he reached below his waist and grabbed his cock.

Just a small adjustment, he tried to tell himself, but his hand lingered.

He stroked his firm length lazily at first, listening to the sounds Emory made, appreciating the little whimpers and the heavy moans. But the pressure continued to build until his insides ran hot and his heart was racing. Byron spat into his palm and rubbed the moisture up and down his shaft, collecting the bead of precum that was spilling from his tip. A groan rumbled in his chest, and he dropped his head against the wall. So close to the woman he craved, yet so far away. Always so. Far. Away.

With every tense stroke, he hated himself a little more, but he couldn't stop. The desire, the wanting, was too much.

Emory's pumps hastened, her breath turning shallow, and Byron imagined her falling to pieces in his arms. He imagined how her lips might tremble and her legs might shake. Licking his lips, he imagined how she might taste on his tongue; musky and sweet, like the honey of her laugh and the earthy scent of the candle he lit in the kitchen. The one he'd seen in the small boutique in town and just *knew* she would love. He pumped his cock furiously to the sounds of Emory's orgasm, ignoring the tiny voice in his head that said he shouldn't, that it was wrong.

"Byron."

As the sounds from her room slowed, she whispered his name. It was as quiet as a summer breeze, but with his forehead against the wall, Byron heard it as clearly as though he was lying over her. He never, in all his wildest imaginations, thought it might have been him she was picturing as she made herself come. Knowing then that it was him in her mind, his orgasm hit him hard and fast.

Spurts of his cum lined the tiled wall as he stroked every last drop out.

"Emory," he whispered. And fuck, he hadn't meant to say her name but then again, maybe from some deep part of his subconscious he had. Maybe he wanted Emory to know that he was thinking of her, too. That this, whatever *this* was, was shared between them.

Later, after he had cleaned the wall and the room beside his had long gone quiet, Byron lay atop his bed with his hands behind his head. Staring at the ceiling he couldn't see through the dark, Byron listened to the rain as it pummelled against the old tin roof.

He didn't want to think about tomorrow. When there was every chance they might wake up and realise they couldn't leave. What would they do then?

And how should he act?

Should he pretend it never happened, or should they try to talk about it? But what would he say?

'Hi, Emory, yes, I made myself come while completely breaching your privacy and listening to you pleasure yourself. Sorry, but I heard you say my name, did you hear me say yours?'

His cheeks burned at the thought, and a concrete slab found a place on his chest. Turning to his side in a futile attempt to throw it off, Byron curled his face against his pillow and closed his eyes. It was going to be a long few weeks. And not just because they were going to be stuck together.

But also because maybe, being stuck together was exactly what they both needed.

Byron huffed, pulling a pillow over his face. That was his heart talking, or his balls. Either way, it definitely wasn't his head. It didn't matter that he heard Emory masturbating or that she probably heard him too. It didn't matter that they had called for each other from beyond the wall and through whispered breaths. Byron could pretend it meant more than it did because he so desperately wanted it to. But the cold, hard truth of the matter was that it meant nothing. It had to.

Byron was too old for Emory. She deserved a chance to forge her own path, not be tied to the family that caused her so much pain. So, even if she did fantasise about him, he couldn't, wouldn't, let either of them get carried away on a dream.

CHAPTER 7

EMORY

The smell of breakfast woke Emory, stirring her from her slumber. She yawned into her pillow and rolled over to stretch her arms above her head. Streaks of light broke through the gaps around the curtains, pasting bright lines on the high ceiling. Blinking the dryness from her eyes, she wondered how long she'd been asleep on the couch for.

For three years, she'd been woken by Clayton. Every morning. When he was younger, he would cry from his cot, demanding attention and love she was more than willing to give, no matter how tired she was. Lately, he'd climb into her bed before the sun rose and play with her hair until she gave up trying to get him back to sleep. Back at the cottage, she used to read him a book while her coffee brewed and play games on the floor while the bitter liquid slowly brought her yawning body back to life. This morning, though, she'd been too afraid of waking Byron with the whirring of his fancy espresso machine. So, she'd scooped Clayton up and hobbled, eyes half closed, to the living room, turned on some TV show that was probably *terrible* for his development, and snuck in a few extra precious moments of rest.

For a while, as she lay with Clayton curled between her legs, she'd forgotten where they were or who she had to face when the rest of the world finally woke up. The fluffy cushions she'd assembled into a nest on the couch sank beneath her head, and for a second, she contemplated staying there. Clayton was no longer nestled in her lap, and without his weight and warmth, all she could think about was last night.

Byron had heard her; she was sure of it.

More than that, though, she was fairly certain she'd also heard him. As she rode down the wave of her orgasm, her senses sprang back to life, and the distinct sound of heavy breaths and low moans could be heard through the wall.

And then he'd said her name.

Embarrassment had flared through her when he had whispered those three syllables. Emory had snapped her legs shut and cowered under the blankets as though he could see her, and her heart had raced on long after the pulsing in her core fizzled into nothing.

She couldn't figure out what it meant, the way her name was all gravelly on his lips and the panted moan that followed. God, she felt her cheeks burning again as she thought about it. As she thought about him, coming undone over her.

Biting the inside of her cheek, she pulled the blanket over her head. She thought about hiding under there and sleeping the morning away to the dull tune of high-pitched nursery rhymes. She imagined waiting until Byron had long since left the house, off to do whatever farm-related tasks needed to be done before a flood. But she couldn't do that.

With Clayton absent from the couch, she knew he must have found his Papa.

So, she would have to leave the room and face Byron. She just had no idea how she was going to muster up the confidence to do it. Sinking further into her nest of cushions and blankets, she allowed herself ten deep breaths before she tried.

It took twenty.

Twice.

Finally, in one swift flick, she threw the blankets off the couch. The sudden rush of air from the room hit her bare legs and made all her tiny hairs stand on end. It made her shiver even though it wasn't that cold.

Rolling over, Emory had to drag her body over the edge of the couch and force her feet down onto the floor. Pulling the tie of her dressing gown tight, she tucked the fabric around her body. She wanted to hide under as many layers of comfort as possible. Maybe if she didn't look at all appealing, Byron would go along with her plan to *never* mention the events of the previous night. Ever.

That would be the ideal, but Emory wasn't kidding herself enough to think it was likely. Not with Byron.

He was always so forward. Full of sarcasm and jokes and the kind of banter that tugged at her inner romantic, even if he never meant it to. She could just imagine the puns he had probably been planning all morning.

Her worn-down Ugg boots dragged along the tiled floor as she made her way to the kitchen. The smell of bacon guided her, but she held her breath as she stepped toward the large archway that connected the rooms. Clayton laughed from around the corner, his squeaky giggles and claps warming the chill that had settled in Emory's bones.

Byron's husky voice cut across the giggles. "We might have to take breakfast to Mummy if she isn't awake soon."

"I get her!" Clayton, she assumed, clapped as he squealed.

A chair scraped against the tiled floor, followed by the sounds of Clayton jumping down and the distinct crunch of an egg cracking.

"Shit!" Byron grunted as Emory took a deep breath and stepped into the chaos of the kitchen.

Clayton, the little parrot, stared wide-eyed at the egg he'd knocked to the floor. His mouth dropped open as he gasped. "Shit!"

"No, Clayton, don't say that," Byron corrected him.

He was crouched on the floor, wiping up the eggy mess with a paper towel. Looking between the floor and Clayton, he hadn't noticed Emory enter the room. She wished it could stay that way, even if only for a moment longer.

With his knees bent low to the ground, Byron's faded jeans pulled tight across the muscles of his legs. Thick thighs stretched the fabric. It sat flush against the round of his ass and heavens help her, Emory had never thought of herself as an ass and thighs girl but if *this* was the view, maybe she was after all.

It wasn't just Byron's legs that had her heart rate spiking, though. It throbbed under her ear and deep in her belly as she watched Byron scoop her son into his arms. Clayton's lower lip had started to tremble, only a little, but enough to show his remorse at repeating the word. Byron had, quite literally, taken Clayton under his wing. With one arm supporting the young boy, he wiped away the last of the mess with the other hand.

Emory stood, transfixed, unable to look away as her heart melted into a pool of goop that oddly resembled the egg whites Byron had just finished cleaning up. This was why she had been terrified of staying here during the flood. Her heart was not going to be able to cope.

She had mostly convinced herself that until this moment, her feelings for Byron had been entirely physical. She didn't *like* the man, she just dreamed about how it would feel to come apart in his hands, under his touch. She just swooned a little when the muscles of his strong arms bulged under the weight of whatever farm-related item he happened to be carrying at the time. It was a perfectly normal, biological feeling to have. Especially around a man like Byron.

There was no denying he was an attractive man; his chiselled jaw and the sprinkle of salt and pepper in his beard were enough to make any woman drool. Emory had overheard the gossipy bitches in town talking about it many times. So, okay, she imagined sharing his bed, and maybe last night wasn't the first time she made herself come while thinking about him. But that didn't mean her attraction was anything more than a physical one.

Except that in a small way, it was. Byron was more than just the attractive older man to Emory. He was the generous man who welcomed her in when everyone else shut her out. He was the caring man who always made sure she had what she needed. He was the loving man who stepped up when Clayton needed a fatherly figure. Seeing Byron with her son did nothing to quell the emotions that had been slowly rising since the day she met Byron. Even back then, still clinging to Jaxon's arm, she saw something in Byron that made her heart flop and her insides spin. Being alone only made the storm of emotions stronger. She'd been fighting them off ever since, holding her breath at every passing, every shared family dinner because she knew it was so wrong. So, any time that flicker of emotion had started to swell, she'd shoved it away and told herself it was all physical. Only, if he kept up this happy family act while they were all stuck together, her ovaries might not cope. Her heart definitely wouldn't.

Emory held her breath, biting her lower lip. She would do well to remember that Byron was only including her because he wanted to include his grandson. She closed her eyes, still holding her breath as she reminded herself that Byron was only acting this way around Clayton because he had a personal investment in the boy's life. It was *normal* for Byron to want to be involved in Clayton's life. It had nothing to do with Emory. She was nothing more than the baggage in this scenario.

Knowing it didn't help, though. No matter how many times she repeated the words in her head, she still couldn't shake off the memory of how Byron had whispered her name. *That* had nothing to do with Clayton, she was more than sure of it. But even so, there was no logical way he felt the same way that she did. Last night was simply an anomaly, nothing more. A physical reaction to what he heard. Just like how she'd had a physical reaction to the feel of his cock pressed against her back. That was all.

She had to get a grip on herself or the next few weeks were going to be excruciating.

Byron stood, and Clayton wriggled in his arms. Emory knew she should announce her presence sooner rather than later. She'd been watching them for a while now, and it was getting a little too close to the creepy line for her liking.

She cleared her throat, bouncing on the spot and shaking her arms like it might quell the sudden burst of whatever was racing through her.

Hearing his mother, Clayton wrestled free of Byron's bear hug and jumped to the floor. His bare feet landed with a *thwack* on the cold tiles. Emory stepped forward and scooped him up. She cradled him high in her arms, blowing a raspberry on his tummy.

Byron coughed. Cleared his throat. Turned back to the stove and started pushing bacon around the pan.

"Morning," Emory mumbled. She didn't trust her voice with anything more than that. It was a good thing, too, because Byron just huffed in response.

Maybe—and this was the hopeful part of Emory thinking—they'd be able to forget about the previous night's escapades after all.

"Papa made breakfast." Clayton giggled in her arms.

"I can see that. Should we get some plates?"

Emory sucked in her breath, holding the tension tight in her shoulders. The reminder of exactly who Byron was to her was a good thing, even if it stung a little. Clayton scrambled to the floor and over to the cupboard Byron had flicked open.

"Thought you might be hungry," he mused. His deep, rumbling tone pitched upward, and although he didn't turn to face her, Emory knew. She just *knew* that he was having a go. A blush rose over her chest, and the breath she had been holding in started stabbing at her lungs.

She could do this. She could fake nonchalance and serve Byron up a slice of his own cake. She could. She would. If only she could breathe.

"You ..." She stumbled at her attempt, but sucked in some air, straightened her shoulders, and tried again. "You must be, too."

As soon as the words darted past her lips, she wanted to pull them back in. Emory flung her hands over her face, hiding behind her embarrassment, even though Byron *still* hadn't turned to look at her.

Byron froze over the pan. Clearing his throat, he

turned the knob off and stepped back. He dropped his hands to his knees, shaking his head a little. Emory did nothing, she didn't dare *breathe* in his direction. Was he going to tell her off? Was he going to ignore the whole thing and pretend their little jabs—and last night—never happened? Was he going to stalk over and demand more from her? She had no idea what was happening or how to act or even how she *wanted* the whole scenario to play out. God, she was useless.

An age passed. Clayton clanged plates together as he chose his favourites, bacon sizzled in the cooling pan, toast popped out of the toaster. Emory did nothing, said nothing. She couldn't have found the courage even if she'd tried. She'd wasted all the oomph she had in her on that one, shaky line. Her shoulders ached as she continued to force her body to stand tall, but her heart hammered against her chest. *Do something,* she willed Byron. *Say something.* Anything would have been better than this horrid, unknowing silence.

When Byron finally pushed his hands off his knees to stand, he moved slowly, turning on the spot and bringing his arms up to cross them over his chest. The golden amber of his eyes met Emory's, and all the bravado she had maintained crumbled. She felt every inch of his burning gaze as he took in her daggy grey dressing gown and her bright red cheeks.

"I slept like a baby," he said with a wink.

And if she had thought she was a puddle before, she definitely was then.

Choking on her saliva, Emory dropped her head and rushed to take the plates Clayton was pulling out of the cupboard. She dropped them on the bench without a word and scurried away to hide behind the kitchen table. It was futile, she realised, as she collapsed into a chair.

Futile to hide from Byron this morning, futile to even attempt at pretending that last night never happened.

Byron had definitely heard her, and he knew she had heard him too.

Never again, she told herself, even though she knew she was lying. Because at the end of the day, Byron was still the one man in all of Gardner Creek who made her heart race in ways it shouldn't. He was still the man she was going to continue picturing every time her loneliness got the best of her. He was always going to be the one man she knew she could never actually have, and that made the fantasy *so* much better. So, okay, again was a given. But not for the next few weeks, at least. Not until the flood cleared and she could escape this farmhouse and this town, and she was far away from the man she was imagining.

Cowering in her chair, Emory faked enthusiasm as Clayton showed her the latest of his stick figure drawings. They were all head and long legs, and the only thing that differentiated the pictures of her from the pictures he drew of himself was the little line of scruffy hair that dangled where her ear should have been. The first pictures had made her heart swell, the second made her feel all warm and cosy, but the third and fourth and hundredth were getting a little repetitive. But she grinned and clapped and 'awed' all the same, praising her son for all his hard work.

She pulled him onto her lap. Hiding behind her son was, possibly, the most pathetic thing she had ever done. But she couldn't help it. Not when Byron kept looking at her as he plated up their breakfast and carried all three plates to the table.

Emory shifted Clayton onto the chair next to her, mumbling a thanks as Byron placed their plates down and took his place opposite them.

They ate breakfast in near silence, broken only by

Clayton's epic cheering and the beating of Emory's heart. She was sure Byron could hear it from his place across the table. If, by some miracle, he couldn't, she was certain he noticed the subtle way her hands shook as she cut into her perfectly runny yolked egg. And she was certain the burn in her cheeks was still glowing bright red.

Byron leaned back in his chair after finishing his meal, stretching his arms behind his head. Emory caught one glimpse of the way his triceps and biceps—and all the 'ceps, really—stretched out the arms of his plain tee and swallowed the toast in her mouth whole. It caught behind her tonsils, and she gulped at her coffee to force it down. The hot liquid proceeded to burn her throat, but that was easier to manage than the burning in her chest.

He stared intently at her, and if only it were night, she could have wished on a shooting star for him to stop. Instead, she wished on the surprisingly clear sky she could see through the window. She needed to compose herself somehow. She needed to get out of the house.

CHAPTER 8

BYRON

"I don't want you leaving today," Byron said as he stood from the table.

He could read the thoughts racing through Emory's brain all through breakfast. She wanted out. And he didn't completely blame her.

She pushed out of her chair, slamming her hands on the table, but instead of the gusto of rejection at his statement that he had been expecting, she remained silent. Her mouth had fallen open, and the tie from her gown had come loose. It parted down her front, revealing the thin satin nightie she wore underneath. Silky green fabric clung tight to her curves, the spaghetti straps disappearing into delicate lace that hung low on her chest.

Low.

So low.

Byron squeezed his eyes shut and turned away before his erection pressed too firmly at the zipper of his jeans. Fuck.

There was silence from the table, but Byron couldn't turn back. Not yet. He needed to get a grip. He listened for the ruffle of fabric as Emory pulled her gown back around herself, but it never came. Instead, he heard the distinct scraping of a chair and Clayton's scrambling as he ran off. No doubt heading for the living room to squeeze in every last minute of screen time he could get. They'd have to turn the TV off eventually, Byron figured, but a few more minutes wouldn't hurt the kid.

But still, no rustle of soft cloth, no movement from Emory that Byron could hear. He stood, dirty plates in his hand, waiting for her to do something, say something.

He wanted her to at least acknowledge what he'd said. It was important. With all the rain yesterday, he had no idea how high or how fast the floodwater would come in. Even with the clear sky today. Until he got a better idea, it was safest for them all to stay in the farmhouse.

He growled. He hadn't meant to make such a guttural sound, but some protective subconsciousness stirred in him and ached to be let out.

"Emory, I mean it," he warned.

She huffed behind him, and that was all he could take; the low sound that came from her was so similar to the sounds she had made the night before. The sounds he wasn't supposed to hear, but he'd heard anyway, and he'd enjoyed.

He dropped the plates into the sink and spun around, and he was ready to stride back over to the table and tell her to cut the crap but when he saw her cowering in her chair he couldn't. Her cheeks were that vibrant shade of crimson red again, and all he wanted to do was pull her close and tell her that she didn't need to be embarrassed. About last night, about her dressing gown, about anything.

Byron's arm twitched to reach out for her, but he held it firm as he returned to the table and sank into his chair.

"Look," he started, but he stopped to shake his head when the word came out all rough and hasty. "Emory," he tried again.

Her arms were wrapped tight around her middle, and her chin was on her chest, but she raised her eyes to look at him.

"We can either talk about it, or we can pretend it never happened, or we can acknowledge that it happened and just move on." He tapped his knuckles on the table.

"I don't want to talk about it."

Byron nodded. "Got it."

"I can pack our stuff back up. We'll go to the community centre. I'm sure they still have space. Or they would have to make space." Her words were shaky, and she dropped her gaze back down to the table.

"You can still stay here, Emory," Byron insisted. "I'd prefer it, honestly."

"But—"

"There's no but. We aren't talking about it."

Emory took a long sip from her coffee, grimacing as she swallowed. It was probably cold by now, but she kept her hands clasped around the mug as she set it back down.

"Okay," she said with a sigh. "But I'd like to head into town today. I'll take Clayton, we'll go to the park and the library. We'll get out of your hair while we still can."

That protectiveness in Byron stirred again, pulling at his chest until it hurt to breathe. "Can't," he choked out.

Emory's brow furrowed. She tapped her trim nails against the mug in her hands. "The bridge?"

"Not yet, but up north had a lot of rain last night. We can't risk crossing the bridge until we know we'd be able to get back." If they had no rain for twenty-four hours and the bridge stayed open, they'd be safe to head into town if they needed. But if it started raining again, they'd have to stay.

Emory didn't question Byron's judgement. Her nod was short and curt, and she didn't say a word as she stood from the table and returned her mug to the sink.

"Byron," she said before stepping back into the living room. "I don't think I can just pretend it never happened, but I still don't want to talk about it."

Byron chuckled, moving towards her and caging her in against the wall that formed the elaborate archway between the rooms. "I can't pretend either, Emory. But we don't have to *talk* about it."

He lingered longer than he should have. There was an inch of air between their bodies, but he felt every bit of it as he hesitated. Emory gasped and pulled her lower lip into her mouth.

"I'll check the bridge. If it doesn't rain today, you can head into town tomorrow before the next storm hits."

Byron spent most of the day hidden in the den. He could try to tell himself he was just giving Emory the space she needed all he wanted, but there was no denying the truth. Shortly after breakfast, Emory had taken Clayton to play on the old slide outside, and Byron had attempted to do the washing up. Truth was, he kept getting distracted, staring at Emory out the window.

So, as soon as the dishwasher was loaded and the pans were drying by the sink, he'd run down to the back end of the house like an embarrassed teenager. He liked it down here, honestly. The brick walls and dim lights made the room feel cosy and warm, even in the dredges of winter.

Relaxing on the couch to do the word puzzle from the paper or read a book was calming enough that he almost forgot all his worries. Down here, he wasn't overworked from long days fixing fences and herding cattle. He wasn't stressing over the wheat fields or whether it was time to pull the bull from the field of heifers. Heck, down here, he didn't even care if they *were* heifers or not. All he cared about was his peace.

And down in the den, with its wall of books and faded pool table, peace is what he found. Even today, after a night like the last. Byron was able to forget it all for a moment.

Most days, he would have trudged back through the house by now. Although truthfully, he probably wouldn't have been down here so early in the day. It felt more than a little odd, not finding *something* to do outside. But the threat of the storm and flood had been too much for him in the week prior. He'd worked himself to the ground getting everything sorted, and there wasn't much else that could be done.

Sure, he still had to move the cows to higher ground, and all the chickens would have to deal with being in one coop instead of two, but Tucker was due tomorrow to help with all that. Byron had sent the other farmhands home two days ago, telling them to prepare their own properties and not worry about his.

As he stared at the book in his lap, Byron found all the words were beginning to blur. He was certain he'd read the same paragraph three times now, and he still wasn't sure it had sunk in. With a huff, he gave up. He took the flap of the dust jacket and tucked it between the pages to hold his place. From down the hall, the rest of the house had turned still. No distant sounds of nursery rhymes on the TV, no muffled voices as Emory read Clayton a book, no giggling as they played. Tapping his phone to check the time, Byron realised the young boy was probably napping by now. He'd skipped lunch. No wonder his eyes were dry.

Standing and rolling his neck out, Byron dropped the book onto the couch. He was still thinking about what he could whip up for a quick meal when a gentle tapping caught his attention.

Emory was standing in the doorway to the den, one foot still in the hall and the other hanging over the step down into the room. She'd gotten changed at some point. The accidentally revealing dressing gown had been replaced by another oversized jumper. This one was a faded blue, with writing on the front that Byron couldn't make out in the dull light of the lamp beside the couch. It was so big he couldn't tell if she was wearing anything underneath—which he tried his utmost best to ignore— and she'd rolled up the sleeves, the folded cuff sitting tight across her wrist. She held her hand at shoulder height, resting her knuckles against the old door frame. Byron couldn't remember there ever being one.

"Am I interrupting?" she whispered, although Byron wasn't sure if it was because the room was so silent or because Clayton was asleep.

He shook his head. "Nah." At first he whispered back, but he hated the way it made his voice so unintentionally seductive, so he cleared his throat and started again. "I was just reading. You know you can take any you like, if you need."

He waved his hand at the book he'd left on the couch, then up over the wall. Emory's gaze followed the path of his arm, her mouth falling open a fraction when they reached the overflowing bookshelves. She seemed to hesitate a little but stepped down into the room and towards Byron's personal library.

Although it wasn't his. Not really.

It had been his mother's first. Then his teenage books had begun to fill out the shelves. When Josie had moved in, she brought with her the rest of the collection that now sat on the shelves. Being down here, reading books that were years old, made Byron feel a little closer to the women he'd loved and lost.

Emory squeezed herself behind the couch to inspect the books and reached high above her head to pull one down. It made her jumper pull up, revealing a pair of tight black bike shorts. At least she had something on, Byron figured. Although knowing they were so tight didn't help his imagination much.

She snickered, and at first, Byron thought maybe he'd made some embarrassing comment or sound out loud. But she was enthralled by the book she'd pulled down. Byron couldn't blame her.

The book would have been one of his mother's. If the well-worn edges and faded corners weren't a giveaway, the cover surely was. It showed a couple, which sounded innocent enough, except that the man was shirtless. The woman was leaning into him with a look of longing and awe. Deep red writing swirled across the bottom half.

"This one of yours?" Emory laughed. And there it was. That sweet-as-honey melody that warmed his insides.

Byron wanted to laugh back, but he couldn't. Not when he'd read the book. And it wasn't half as funny as Emory was making out. Actually, it wasn't half bad.

"Technically," he said as he stepped forward to grab it from her, "it was my mother's. Although this one is pretty good."

He flicked through the pages, soaking in the way the paper smelt like home. Emory stepped one foot over the back of the couch, climbing across it until she was standing on the cushion. The book he'd dropped—a thriller, he read widely—teetered towards her feet. From up there, Emory was at least a head taller than Byron, and she leant over him to pluck the book from between his fingers.

"You know, in all these years, I never imagined you as a reader," she said with a smirk. "But if you say this one's good, I'm reading it."

For the second morning in a row, an eerie silence woke Byron from his slumber. On any regular day, he would wake to the cows mooing from their paddocks, and Miff barking to be let outside to contain them. Spread across the higher paddocks on the other side of the farm, the cows were too far away to be heard, and Miff had disappeared somewhere in the house, no doubt enjoying her lazy morning off. Even so, Byron woke just as the sun was rising.

He'd barely slept the past two nights, tossing and turning in his bed as he tried to figure out how in the blaming hell he was going to survive being stuck in the house with Emory. He'd come up with nothing, and even as he stretched his arms above his head with a yawn, the answer to all his worries still eluded him.

There was nothing to be done. There would be no hiding his attraction for the bright-as-day twenty-four-year-old. Because no matter how many times he told himself he had to stop, he just couldn't help himself when it came to Emory.

From the day he met her, Byron had known she was special. She'd skipped into town on the arm of his son, and

Byron had been reining in his burning attraction—well, trying to at least—ever since. It had been wrong, so wrong, to feel so strongly about a woman near half his age. Never mind the fact that she was dating his son. And it had been even more wrong when they announced she was pregnant, and worse still when Jaxon skipped town and Byron was hopeful, even if only a little.

From that day, he'd done everything in his power to be the rock she needed, the man she deserved to help her raise her son. He'd done everything he could to keep his thoughts to himself. He wasn't naïve enough to think she might feel the same. Until now. Until he heard her two nights ago and until they spent all day yesterday sharing glances and intentionally *not* talking about the fact they'd masturbated over each other.

Byron pushed himself to stand and peeled back the curtain. The sky was blood red as the sun rose through the stormy clouds. The rain had held off all day yesterday, and all night, but he doubted it would stay that way for long.

Pulling on a pair of jeans and a deep grey flannel, Byron planned out his morning. Tucker would be over after breakfast to help herd the cows into the high paddock, and the time had come to cart all the chooks into one coop. Beyond that, there wasn't much to do. Nothing could be done to salvage any of the wheat crops. It was too early in the season to harvest, and the fields lay too low between the hills. If they weren't already covered in water, they would be soon. The lack of current rain didn't fool Byron. The creek would keep rising as more rain hit the north and west, feeding water into their basin faster than it could drain back out.

He supposed he should do a quick check of the water levels over the bridge, too. If they could, one last trip into town for extra supplies wouldn't hurt. Nappies for Clayton, another candle for Emory because he saw the way her eyes lit up and her shoulders relaxed when she spotted the one he had been burning the past two nights. He didn't like the thought of her leaving the safety of the farmhouse, but he couldn't keep her hostage, and she deserved one last trip into town if they could make it happen.

Miff caught up with him as he walked out the back sliding door. She pounced around his feet until he bent over to scratch behind her ears.

"Come on then." He whistled as he climbed onto the quad bike.

The dog chased after Byron as he took in the current state of the farm. As suspected, the lowest fields were already covered with a thin layer of water, so he didn't risk running the bike through the valley for a closer look. From his vantage point halfway up one hill, he could see them huddled under the trees scattered along the hillside. He shot off a message to Tucker, asking for a hand rounding them up later in the morning, even though they'd both known all along that Byron was going to need Tucker's help. The water would never get as far up as the high paddock, and that way, even if the gates did blow open, the cows wouldn't be going anywhere once they were surrounded by water. Sure, they could swim, but they typically weren't dumb enough to try it.

Byron steered the bike back towards the house, not stopping as he pulled onto the driveway and headed for the bridge. It was still clear, and from the looks of it, they had time to run into town if they needed to. The water hadn't even hit the first marker yet, but Byron knew it was only a matter of time. He gulped, thinking again about being trapped in the house with Emory for a week or more. It wasn't a terrible thought, and that was part of the problem.

Rolling his shoulders, Byron whistled to get Miff's attention. "Oi, Miff, let's go."

The dog's ear pricked up, but she kept her focus on the flowing water of the creek. She wanted to swim, most likely, and Byron didn't blame her. The air was hot and sticky, but he knew how fast the undercurrent would be as the creek continued to rise.

He revved the engine on the bike, and Miff raced back towards him to jump on the small back tray before he took off.

The house was still quiet after he'd parked the quad bike around the back and snuck back in, and he thought, for a moment, that Emory and Clayton must have still been in bed. But light flickered from the living room. The TV was on, but the sound was down low, flashy cartoons bouncing over the screen. Clayton sat just as he had yesterday, nestled in his mother's legs, cuddling his teddy and watching intently. He seemed oblivious to the fact that his mother was sleeping. Her dressing gown pulled tight around her shoulders, she was curled up on the couch, facing away from the TV. Byron could only just see the side of her face, the way her nose pressed up against the cushion she was using as a pillow. The book she borrowed from the den lay open across the arm of the couch. Byron took in the sight, for longer than he probably should have, appreciating the moment of calm.

He could get used to spending his mornings like this. Checking on the farm, then coming home to Emory sleeping on the couch. The thought pulled at something in his chest.

Not wanting to wake Emory, Byron ducked back out of the room before Clayton saw. He moved to the kitchen and started fixing breakfast. Bacon, eggs, mushrooms, muffins. Byron knew how to cook a few good meals, and this was one of them. He hoped the smell would draw Emory back from the land of nod, just like it had yesterday. If it didn't, he was unsure how he would go about waking her. He *wanted* to tuck her hair behind her ear and press a kiss to her temple. Whisper in her ear to coax her awake. But he couldn't do that.

In the end, it was Clayton who woke Emory. He smelled the breakfast, or heard Byron's cooking, and jumped from the couch with a squeal.

"Papa! Breakfast!"

Emory stretched her arms over her head as she stood. Her dressing gown dropped off one shoulder, revealing the thin spaghetti strap of the same satin nightie she'd had on yesterday morning. Byron did his best to ignore the lump in his throat, swallowing down the heavy sigh that got caught with it.

Turning slowly, Emory tugged her robe back into place and tied the cord around her waist. The thick fabric cinched in at the knot, highlighting the gentle curve of her hips. Byron swallowed again, ignoring the blood rushing to his cock. *Fuck*, this was going to be … difficult.

Chapter 9

Emory

"You made us breakfast again?" Emory yawned, a big, exaggerated one as she stretched her arms out again. She was trying to distract herself from the current vision in the kitchen, and it wasn't working.

In faded jeans and a deep grey flannel, Byron stood holding two heaped plates of food. A tea towel was thrown over his shoulder, and his hair was all messed up from sleep. Emory could get used to this, waking up to a hot as fuck man who cooked her breakfast. But then, she couldn't, could she? Not when this arrangement was only temporary. Not when she was only here because her cottage was about to flood, although maybe it already had. And definitely not when she still had plans to leave town as soon as she secured a job in the city.

So, okay, she couldn't get used to it, but she could enjoy it while it lasted.

Byron smirked, the corner of his mouth tilting up as he gave a slight nod. Emory could have sworn he swayed his hips a little as he moved around the bench to position the plates on the table. He turned back to the kitchen and stretched over the counter to grab the third plate. Emory held back her gasp. She shouldn't be looking. She certainly shouldn't be *admiring* the way his jeans pulled tight against his butt. Or the way his shoulders threatened to bust his shirt as he reached forward.

But then again, she'd spent all day yesterday doing exactly that, hadn't she? After their awkward-as-*anything* breakfast and their agreement to never speak of the night prior again, they'd spent the day pottering around the house. It appeared Byron had gone out of his way to make space for Emory and Clayton, and she'd done her best to take up as little of it as possible. She'd tidied away Clayton's toys the second he moved on to the next activity. After his nap, she'd taken him outside, and while he played on the old rickety slide, she read the book she'd borrowed. It was better than she thought it would be. The heroine had just met a truly scrumptious prince, and Emory was certain they were going to fall in love in the most delicious way.

And all day, she had stolen glances at Byron every second she could. She'd caught him doing the same, and each time, her heart had started racing faster than the quad bike he jetted off on in the afternoon.

Before she had a chance to turn away, Byron stood from the bench and pivoted on his heel. The movement was so quick, Emory was certain he was *trying* to catch her staring. And he had. His eyes turned dark, but he kept them on Emory as he placed the small plate of food in front of Clayton.

Emory's breath was caught in her throat. Her mouth hung open as she exhaled.

"Thank you," she whispered on a shaky breath before clearing her throat and trying again. "Thank you, Byron. Clayton, say thank you to Papa for breakfast."

Instead of waiting for Byron to respond, she sat down at the place he had set for her and gulped at her coffee. The hot liquid burned her throat, matching the heat that flared through her body.

They were going to have to talk about that night. It would kill her, though. She would die of embarrassment, but they couldn't continue this dance. The stolen glances and lust-filled looks were too much. It was one thing to imagine Byron hovering over her while she came, and another to realise he was imagining the same thing. But the air had been thick with need ever since, and they had to do something or they would suffocate from it.

They ate mostly in silence, just like they had the day before. Clayton chewed loudly, blissfully unaware of the tension that sparked through the air. Halfway through their meal, rain began to patter. Nothing like the previous storm, at least not yet, but big fat droplets that clanged against the tin roof. Emory lifted her gaze from her plate to look out over the back paddocks. Beyond the kitchen window, the sky was dark, and big puddles began to form over the lawn. It stopped almost as soon as it started, but Emory knew it was just a teaser of what was sure to come.

"Thanks, Papa," Clayton cheered after they had all finished eating, and Byron cleared the plates away.

Byron ruffled the little boy's hair as he passed. Clayton climbed off his chair and disappeared into the living room. The sound of wooden blocks tumbling echoed through the house.

Byron stood unmoving in the kitchen, still holding the plates. "The bridge is still clear, if you want to head into town for anything. Might be your last chance," he said.

Emory's heart sank again at the reminder that soon, she would be stuck here. But Byron was right, she should head into town while she had the chance. A few extra night nappies for Clayton probably wouldn't hurt. Nor would a dozen or more bottles of wine. She was going to need them to get through the next couple of weeks.

"Do you need anything? I'll head down now so we can be back before Clayton has to nap."

She took the plates from Byron's hands, sucking in a breath when her fingers brushed against his. Electricity zapped between them.

Byron cleared his throat. "Nope, we should be good. I bought a few weeks' worth of stuff before you got here, it's all in the freezer. Why don't you leave Clayton with me? Stop at the library for some more books and toys for him."

"Are you sure? Don't you have work to do before the water peaks?"

She lined the dirty plates into the dishwasher and turned the tap on to wash the pans stacked on the stovetop. It was the least she could do, given Byron was hosting them for the immediate future and had cooked them breakfast twice now.

"I need to get the cows into the top paddock, but Clayton can come. I'd rather you not be distracted on the drive down."

She was elbow deep in hot, soapy water, but glared at Byron over her shoulder. "I've driven that road plenty of times with Clayton in the back. He's not going to distract me."

With an eye roll, she turned back to the sink and got to work on the dishes. Byron had some sort of magic pan because all the bacon grease was washing off with more ease than she was used to, but she scrubbed away out of habit. She was so focused on making sure the pan was *spotless* that she didn't hear Byron moving until he was right behind her. His hands dropped to the edge of the sink, caging her in, but he kept a small gap between their bodies.

The breath that whispered along the back of her neck was shaky. "Please, Emory. This is important to me."

"Why?" She shouldn't have pushed his buttons, but she snapped at him anyway. Who was he to suddenly tell her she couldn't drive with Clayton in the back? Against her better judgement, or maybe because of it, she dropped the sparkling pan onto the drying rack and turned around.

They were so close. So goddamn close that Emory's breast skated across Byron's front. With every breath she took came a searing heat that spread from the contact. She had to tilt her head up to look at him, holding her breath as she did so. What she saw had her mind reeling.

From this close, she first registered that Byron's eyes were no ordinary brown. His irises were laced with gold and surrounded by a deep rim of chocolate. She could get lost in them. She would have, too, if they weren't so wet. His tears overflowed, clumping his eyelashes and spilling down his cheeks.

Emory squeezed her hands up between them to cup his face. It was well-meaning; she'd wanted to wipe away the moisture. Only her hands were still wet from the sink, so instead she only added more. Byron chuckled, batting her hands away and stepping back.

"Thanks for that," he mumbled. Picking up the hem of his shirt, Byron wiped his face.

Emory did her best *not* to look at his abs while he did, but it was a futile attempt, really. Who could resist looking at such a fine specimen? It reminded her of the hero from her book. Abs on abs, with a truly edible V of muscles that led below his belt. She squeezed her eyes shut until she heard the rustle of his shirt as he dropped it back down.

"Wet roads are dangerous, Emory. This family knows that all too well. I don't like the thought of you driving on them at all, especially not with Clayton in the back. You forget that I've driven with him, too. I know how he squeals." Byron had folded his arms across his chest and was talking mostly to his feet. Every now and then, he glanced up at Emory, and she caught a glimpse of his eyes, welling with tears again. She reached for the tea towel on the bench, drying her hands.

"What do you mean, you know it all too well?"

Byron's chest heaved as he sighed. He shook his head, and for a moment, Emory thought she might have prodded too deep. Clayton started imitating a siren, *nee naw*-ing from the lounge room as he ran around with two little cars. But Byron and Emory ignored the sound, trapped in a silence she thought neither of them was going to break. After a few more heavy breaths, Byron ran a hand over his face and finally started to speak.

"I guess I never told you about Josie, did I? Tucker and Jaxon's mum."

Emory mirrored his stance, tucking her hands under her arms. She shook her head. It stung behind her eyes a bit, the mention of Byron's late wife. Sure, she'd known about Josie. Small details that she'd gathered up here and there. Mostly from Mya, though, if she were honest. Jaxon had never mentioned his mother, and maybe that should have been the first red flag, but Emory had always ignored it. But the thing with small towns is that everyone knows everybody else's business. So sure, after Jaxon had left, Mya had told Emory that his—and Tucker's—mum had died when he was little, but she'd never gone into detail. That same stinging feeling behind her eyes started up in Emory's throat. She should have cared more, should have been a better friend to Byron after he had shown her so much kindness all these years. He'd always seemed so closed off, though, and she'd never been one to pry. Didn't stop her feeling bad about it now she could see the hurt in his eyes though.

"Tucker would have been about Clayton's age, Jaxon a bit older," Byron started. Emory had never heard his voice sound so grim. It burrowed into her until she wished she could take away his pain. "Night before, the rain came down like nothing else. Different to now, though. It didn't flood because the ground was already so wet, and there was no rain up north. Josie took Tucker into town and I was fixing fucking fence posts like I do every day."

The next sound from Byron was inconsolable. He sank to the floor with a sob that shook Emory's bones. She followed him down, crawling across the floor to wrap her arms over his body.

"I had Jaxon with me, and I should have told her to leave Tucker with us, too, but she took him." Byron spoke to the ground, hugging his knees. "They think he distracted her, and when she tried to correct her steering, she went into the ditch. If he'd been with me, she never would have lost control."

"It's not your fault," Emory whispered. Other people had probably told him the same over and over, but she had to say something.

Byron sniffed and wiped his eyes with his shirt again. As he began to compose himself, Emory slid back, unsure of what he needed.

"I know," he said when they were no longer touching. "It took a few years of therapy, but I know. Still, if I could do something different, that would be it. I'd take Tucker with me to fix the fence."

Emory understood then why he needed her to leave Clayton while she went to town. Maybe even why he helped with Clayton as much as he did. Byron's hand found hers on the rough, tiled floor.

"That's why," he whispered. "Please."

She squeezed his fingers and whispered back, "Okay."

Grief was still flooding Emory's veins as she pulled into the crowded car park at the small independent supermarket in the centre of Gardner Creek. She wasn't sure what it meant that Byron was opening up to her after all these years, but it seemed like everything about their relationship had changed in the kitchen this morning. They shared something now, an understanding. It made all the little nuances of how Byron acted around her and Clayton make so much more sense. For a while, especially recently, Emory had been fooling herself into thinking maybe he acted the way he did because of her. But it wasn't that at all. He acted the way he did because he was trying to atone. He clearly held a lot of guilt, even if he said he had moved past that, and looking after Clayton was how he made up for it. It had nothing to do with Emory at all.

She did three laps of the overflowing, tiny supermarket parking lot before giving up and pulling out onto the road. She had more luck at the school across the street. The kiss and go parks on the side of the road were all labelled for five minutes only, but being the Saturday before a flood came through, Emory doubted it mattered. She wasn't the only one; three cars pulled in behind her as she exited her car. If the ticket inspector did care to come past, he would be chuckling. Emory took the risk and headed for the supermarket.

Nappies, she reminded herself. And something for Clayton to do that didn't involve reruns of Bluey and Play School.

Her basket full of Play-Doh tubs, cheap paints, a few sticker books, and a ream of paper, Emory juggled the packet of pull-up nappies under her free arm. Clayton still needed one most nights, and although he occasionally woke up dry, Emory wasn't ready to risk night training him just yet. That was a Future Emory problem.

Making her way through the aisles, just in case, Emory added plenty of snacks and chocolates into the bright green basket. *You can never have enough snacks* might as well have been her life motto, and she wasn't about to run out while stuck at Byron's farmhouse.

In the next aisle, she froze in her tracks. Body wash in a thousand shades of pastel lined one side, a variety of medications on the other. But it was the handful of small boxes in deep colours, navy blues and steel greys, that got her attention. High on the shelf to her right, the condoms screamed at her.

Did she need them? The old her would have laughed at the thought. But she wasn't on the pill, and after everything between her and Byron, maybe she did. She could still hear the way he moaned her name through the wall and see the way he looked at her when he thought she wasn't looking. Plus, there was that weird thing her heart kept doing after he opened up to her in the kitchen. Didn't matter what her head said, her heart was convinced it *meant something*.

She chose not to overthink the condoms, considering that the worst-case scenario, if she did buy them, would simply be them not getting used. They could sit, hidden in the bottom of her suitcase, until the floodwaters receded and she moved to the city. It wouldn't be the end of the world. And that way, they would be there if they did need them. And *God*, she hoped they did.

Without pausing to check the boxes, she grabbed a

pack and tossed it into her now overflowing basket. She cringed at herself and raced towards the front of the store to pay.

"Emory?"

Her heart sank. She'd recognise that voice anywhere. It was the sound of all her hopes and dreams falling through the floor. It was the crashing of her heart, breaking into a million tiny pieces. The song of solo parenting and long nights in a town that still felt far from home.

Emory sucked in the deepest breath her lungs would allow and pushed her shoulders back. She tipped her chin up as she turned slowly towards the man who broke her heart, but not her soul.

"Jaxon." Her tone was firm, all pleasantries for the man having fled along with him three years ago.

"I went by the cottage, but you weren't there."

Jaxon reached for her then, stepping forward with an arm outstretched. Emory shied away from his touch. She didn't need his false concern, and she didn't want it either.

"We evacuated for the flood. After it's all safe, I'll go back in to remove the rest of my stuff." She shrugged her shoulders in a way she hoped screamed indifference. She wasn't sad about leaving the cottage. In fact, she just hated that she would have to go back to clean it out. "Before the lease ends, don't worry."

Jaxon ignored her promise, looking around her feet. "Where's Clayton?"

"He's safe." *Thankfully,* she didn't add. Clayton didn't know his father, considering Jaxon had left before he was born. She didn't need to worry about their first meeting in the middle of a crowded supermarket when she was pressed for time. "Why are you here?"

"Same reason you are, I suppose. Stocking up before the flood."

Emory couldn't hold back the way her eyes rolled at how blasé he was acting. "Yes, but why are you here *in town*? Why are you back?"

"A guy can't come back to his roots?" Jaxon held his arms out wide, nearly knocking over an old lady with the basket he flung around. She scowled at him and hurried on, but he either didn't notice or didn't care. Either way, it was another good reminder for Emory that he really was a pathetic waste of space.

"Sure, but considering you've run away from your *roots* twice, it's a little odd, don't you think?"

He scoffed at her jab. "I have finally realised city life is not for me. And why should I waste my dime paying someone else's mortgage in the city when I have a perfectly good house that *I* own right here in Gardner Creek? I'm staying at the motel until I can move back in."

Emory could read between the lines. His money was running dry, probably from all the overseas holidays and excessive parties. It wasn't like she stalked him or anything, but any mother worth the title would keep an eye on what the father of her child was doing. Mostly, she was just trying to make sure he wasn't planning to do exactly what it was he appeared to be doing. Coming back. The timing was gross, but if she could survive the flood, she'd head off for the city before Jaxon could try to wiggle his way into their lives.

"I thought I could meet Clayton," Jaxon added. He dropped his arm and scuffed a foot along the floor. And Emory could at least give Jaxon credit for looking sincere, even if she didn't believe it.

"Look, I have to go," she said instead of answering him. "Things to do before the creek rises any higher. I've got a bridge to get across."

Emory turned on her heel to head towards the checkout. Her basket flung around her, loose on her arm.

"Wait, where are you staying?" Jaxon called behind her.

"It's not your business, Jaxon."

"So why do you need condoms?"

Emory felt a cracking in her chest, followed by an intense heat in her cheeks. Ants crawled through her skin as half the people in the queue for the checkout stopped to look at her. With no gap between snacks and craft items in her basket, the deep purple box sat on top of the bags of chips, ready for them all to see.

Closing her eyes, she did her best to shut out Jaxon's pestering question and the curious glances everyone continued to throw her way.

When she opened her eyes, Jaxon was standing right in her face. "What bridge, Emory?"

She shook her head. He knew all her tells when she lied, it wasn't even worth trying. She opted for silence instead.

"What bridge?"

A register—self-serve, to her delight—opened up in front of her, and Emory took her escape. Still, she felt Jaxon's eyes on her as she scanned all her items and raced back to the car. The back of her neck tingled as she rushed to the library. Mya wasn't there, no doubt already safe and sound at Tucker's house, and Emory would have missed her if she hadn't been so rattled. Instead, the town's other librarian, a greying woman with an arm of beaded bangles and a brightly knitted cardigan, helped her find a selection of toys for Clayton.

The tension in Emory's shoulders eased a little when she walked past the new homeware store that had popped up in town just a few months ago. It must have been where

Byron bought the candle. The thought soothed something in her, like a soft reminder that maybe he wanted all the things she wanted, too. She ducked inside. The candle had been a lovely addition to Byron's manly farmhouse, and she'd appreciated the subtle crackling as the wooden wick burnt down. It would be nice to have more. There were so many scents in the store, from subtle linen to the sweetest florals. Emory lost herself as she smelt them all and tried to decipher which one Byron would appreciate most. It shouldn't have mattered, really. She was buying it for her, not him. But she cared all the same. Hastily, because she was desperate to get back now, she picked one.

Anticipation and hesitation swirled in her, never letting up until she crossed the bridge towards Byron's farm.

As the farmhouse came into view at the end of the long driveway, something else replaced all her concerns. Thrill.

Sure, getting into bed with her ex-boyfriend's father could get messy. But she was leaving town soon anyway. Seeing Jaxon had stirred a long-forgotten fire in her, reminding her of how she used to go after what she wanted instead of huddling in the corner and waiting for her dreams. So, why not give in to the temptation that was spun through the house and enjoy herself while they were flooded in? Because if nothing else, it would be fun.

CHAPTER 10

BYRON

The last of the cattle were dragging. Protesting against Miff's incessant barking, the way she ran up close then backed off for another round. Normally, the cows would hustle under her lead, but today, Byron was surprised none of them had given her a swift kick to the face. Especially Betty. She was the feistiest dairy cow Bryon had ever come across, and her deep mahogany coat stood out against the herd of black and white Holsteins, but Byron had all but fallen for her at the auction two years ago, and it had been a love-hate relationship ever since.

Especially now, when the Aussie Red was ever so slowly creeping away from Miff's herd. The cattle dog hadn't seen her yet, but Byron had. Determined to get all the cows secure in the high paddock, then back to his farmhouse before the rain started up again, Bryon jumped down from the quad bike. Making sure Clayton was steady on the seat, he pulled the key from the ignition and shoved it into his pockets.

"Clayton drive?" the little kid asked, and Byron agreed, tapping the handlebars. Clayton always loved 'driving' the quad bike. It was the easiest way to keep him occupied when Byron had work to do. It reminded him of all the times he had spent riding around the farm with one of his own sons on his lap. Emory always praised Byron with thanks for looking after Clayton so often, but honestly? Byron enjoyed it more than he cared to admit. Having Clayton around brought a little youth and light back into Byron's otherwise monotonous life. And helped him feel like he could make up for lost time.

He hadn't meant to get so emotional when he asked Emory to leave Clayton with him this morning, but once the tears began to flow, he couldn't stop them. It was the chance to right his wrongs, even if therapy had him convinced it wasn't ever his fault. Still, he wasn't about to risk it all happening again. In the end, opening up felt cathartic, and he was glad he'd done it with Emory. Truth was, he wished he'd done it sooner. Maybe it would have eliminated all the times she brushed off his help or thanked him a few too many times. The past three years of looking after Clayton had brought a little joy back into Byron's life. If anything, he should have been thanking *her*.

With one eye still on his grandson, Byron ran through the grass towards the wandering cow, arms wide like he was going to wrap her in a bear hug. He nearly did. He would have, if she hadn't seen him coming and pranced away.

The little—well big, really—fucker thought it was a game.

"C'mon, Betty." Byron huffed as he circled around her.

Tucker moved away from his position holding the gate, rounding to corner Betty off and help guide her into the paddock.

With Byron on one side, Tucker on the other, and

Miff barking her way closer, Betty's only choice was to go the way they wanted. Her tail dropped, and she turned in a wide circle, padding her way to the gate and joining the rest of the herd in the high paddock. Now at Byron's feet, Miff barked to show her agreement. A paw propped up to tap Byron's knee.

"Hold on," he mumbled. The blasted gate latch always caught. It was never a big deal because they never used this paddock. It was too high on the hill, and a fraction too small for the more than two hundred cows who now huddled around the scattered trees. Byron wished he could have secured them in the barn, but it was on low ground. It wasn't worth the risk.

Tucker shoved his old man out of the way, throwing all his weight onto the gate until it dropped down and he could latch it closed. "Never got around to fixing this one?"

Byron huffed. "Never needed to."

"I'm going to inherit a run-down old farm that's more work than it's worth, aren't I?"

Byron didn't respond. He left his son's side and walked back to the quad bike. Clayton's helmet was a fraction too big, sitting lopsided on his tiny head. Lifting the boy off the bike, Byron unlatched the strap and pulled the heavy head protection off.

"Unky Tuck!" Clayton barrelled towards Tucker with his arms wide. Mud squelched under his boots, but that didn't stop Tucker from hoisting him up.

"Who says you're the one inheriting it?" Byron jabbed. It was rhetorical, really. Everyone in the whole town, probably the whole state, knew that Tucker Gardner would inherit the family farm.

There may have been a while there when the boys were young and Byron thought he might have to choose between his sons, but Jaxon made it clear he wasn't interested long before he decided to skip town.

The harsh reminder of his son's incompetence as a father burned at Byron's throat. He'd raised his sons better than that, but sometimes, it seemed, a bad seed could grow from even the cleanest of crops.

"Besides," Byron added, ignoring the way all this talk of inheritance made his head pound, "I may be getting older, but that doesn't mean I'm ready to pass the farm on. I'm only forty-five."

He felt every year of his age, too. But he wouldn't tell Tucker that. Didn't need the chirpy twenty-one-year-old knowing his old man was on his way to just that, being old. That thought burned through his insides even more.

"Wasn't grandpa in his forties when he passed the farm to you?"

"He was forty-nine."

"Well, you're in the right decade then." Tucker sighed, crossing the muddy path to stand next to his father. He shifted Clayton onto one hip and placed his free hand on his father's shoulder. Byron's resolve collapsed under the calming gesture. "Look, I don't mean to come across like I'm shoving you out, I swear. I just want us both to have realistic expectations, and maybe we can come up with a plan. I reckon I'd need more than five years to figure out how to run this place anyway. So maybe we should start."

Change. Byron could feel it. He knew the flood would bring it, he'd been waiting for it. He just hadn't expected it to hit so soon. Or for it to feel this ... easy. "You're right," he admitted. "But you've got a better understanding of the whole thing than you give yourself credit for. And besides, we need to get through the flood first."

He climbed onto his quad bike and reached his arms out. "Come on, Clayton, let's drive."

Clayton squirmed out of his uncle's hold and toddled back through the mud. After hoisting Clayton up, Byron tucked the helmet back over his head.

"Can we address the other elephant in the room?"

Byron held in his grunt. He didn't want to. He knew exactly what Tucker was referring to, and it was one thing to 'not' talk about it with Emory and another for Tucker to inadvertently bring it up. Or figure it out. Byron appreciated the friendship he and Tucker had grown into over the past few years, but there were some lines that definitely didn't need crossing between a father and his son. "We're not in a room."

"In the bloody paddock, then. Fuck, Dad, stop being so literal." Tucker climbed onto his own quad bike but made no move to turn it on. "Where's Emory?"

"What makes you think she isn't back at the farmhouse?"

On cue, Clayton clapped. "Drive, Papa!"

"Not yet, kid," Byron said, resting his chin on Clayton's helmet. "What if I just wanted to bring Clayton out with me? Wouldn't be his first time out on the farm and it sure as shit won't be his last. Does Emory have to *be* somewhere for it to happen?"

Clayton appeared to hear none of what Byron had said, except for the swear word. He proudly repeated it.

"You're in trouble," Tucker mused. With a leg on either side of the bike, he hoisted one foot up onto the front of the seat and rested an arm against his knee.

"She went to town," Byron admitted. The acknowledgement of how far away Emory was pulled at something in his chest. That protective beast was grumbling, ready for her to return, so he knew she was safe.

"What could she possibly have needed in town?" Tucker questioned. He might as well have been talking directly to Byron's untamed beast. "Café's closed for the flood, so she's not working. Mya's not at the library, so she won't hang around there, and last I checked, you had enough food to last a small army a whole winter. Why would you let her leave? What if the bridge closes?"

"It won't," Byron growled.

"It might."

"She'll be back before it does, just like you'll be gone before it does, too. I can't force her to stay when there is a clear way out, no matter how much I might think it's the best for her. She ... ah ... needed to get away." Byron stumbled over the words, immediately realising he'd said too much without saying much of anything.

Tucker ran a hand over his face, his fingers lingered in his beard, scratching at his chin. "I don't think I want to know the answer to this question," he started.

"So don't ask it." Byron's tone was flat.

Nodding, Tucker turned the key, and his quad bike revved to life. "Don't fuck it up, old man," he called out as he sped off down the muddy track that led back to the farmhouse.

Emory's tiny bright green hatchback was parked next to Tucker's truck when the men returned from the paddock. Clayton cheered in Byron's lap, clapping for his mother, but he didn't wriggle or squirm out of the seat. He waited, just like Byron had always shown him, until the quad bike was parked safely in the back shed and turned off before climbing down. He ran for the back door, pushing it open and storming into the house.

Byron cringed at the thought of how much mud his

little gumboots would be traipsing through the house. It was a problem for later, though, because Tucker stood with his arms folded across his chest, staring at Byron. He raised an eyebrow, and Byron felt every piercing stab of his son's disapproving gaze.

"I thought you didn't want to know the answer to whatever question is brewing inside that brain of yours."

Tucker snorted. "I don't, I'm not asking it. There are some things a son does not need to know about his father."

Byron cleared his throat and turned away. Even if Tucker asked the question he clearly wanted, there was nothing to tell. There was nothing between Byron and Emory other than a fleeting attraction and a temptation they had to resist.

"You should get back across the bridge. Stay safe."

In response, Tucker only nodded and climbed into his truck.

Walking inside, Byron tried to ignore the way each breath felt like knives in his lungs. The house smelled like … Emory. A candle was lit on the kitchen bench. Not the one he'd bought, but one that smelled fruity and fresh, like baked pear and lemonade. It reminded Byron of the subtle hints of Emory's shampoo he always did his best not to fixate on.

There was that change again.

Only this one, he thought maybe he could get used to. Some tiny part of him began to imagine what it would be like if being forced to stay together for a few weeks became the start of something more between him and Emory. The *more* he never allowed himself to picture because it still felt so *wrong* to want it, but he was realising he wanted it nonetheless.

But he couldn't try to convince her to stay with him

after the flood receded. He knew what it was like to be thrown into a life you never had a choice in, and he couldn't ask that of her. Not when just being in Gardner Creek was enough of a change for her.

Besides, Emory was in her twenties. Of course she wouldn't want to move in with a middle-aged man, and of course she wasn't going to fall in love with him. Knowing that didn't turn off the sheer attraction he had for the woman, but it was an icy dose of reality.

CHAPTER 11

EMORY

The house was empty as Emory trudged all the groceries inside. For a moment, she had wondered where Byron and Clayton were, but after lighting her new candle she'd found the box of condoms deep in one of the shopping bags and her neck had rolled with relief. At least Byron wouldn't have to see them.

She could still feel the embarrassment on her cheeks. She hadn't exactly said where she was staying, but there was only one house within a two-hour radius she could have been referring to. The town might have sat along the banks of a creek, but it and the main road were spread on one side of the waterway. The only bridge in Gardner Creek led to one place: Byron's farm. Jaxon had to have known where she was going. And thanks to his outburst, everyone in the supermarket knew too. And they knew that she was buying condoms. It was only a matter of time before that juicy bit of gossip was spread down the phone tree.

Emory supposed that she should tell Byron. That his son was back in town, sure, but also that the whole town knew she was staying at Gardner Farm, and she thought she would need condoms.

Leaving the food and art supplies and books and toys spread over the kitchen bench, she held the condom box under the hem of her jumper. If she just raced it to the bedroom, she could try to explain the whole situation to Byron before he saw them. She side-stepped around the bench, holding the box hidden.

Byron and Clayton weren't in the house, but Miff and the quad bikes were also missing. And despite his oversized ute in the driveway, Tucker was also not around. No doubt the men were taking the last chance to check the farm before the water rose. As Emory traipsed awkwardly toward the hall, she wondered how high it would get, how much of the hill surrounding the farmhouse would be left uncovered.

"Mummy!"

Shit.

She was too far from the hallway to make a mad dash, but she couldn't exactly pull the box out now. Clayton would probably be fascinated with the almost secret box. His little mind might assume its a packet of lollies. Thinking quickly, Emory tucked the box into the waist-band of her leggings. The sharp edges dug into her hip bone, but the baggy hoodie she wore hid its harsh square shape.

She threw her arms in front of her just in time, catching Clayton before he rammed into her legs. His muddy boots left brown footprints across the tiles, and as he jumped in front of her, dirt splattered off the soles and onto the flooring.

"Clayton, shoes."

Rolling her eyes, she bent down and carefully peeled the gumboots off his feet. The condom box poked her, sliding lower in her leggings. She wasn't sure how long it would hold. With the boots at arm's length, she tried to stand, but Clayton clung to her leg, and she wobbled on her feet.

"Here, I'll take them." Byron surprised her, although she wasn't entirely sure why. Logic told her that he would have entered the house with Clayton, but she hadn't exactly thought that through. She jumped at the sound of his gravelly voice, making Clayton giggle against her crouched legs. He cheered and clapped, bouncing himself as though this were a game. Emory lost her balance. She dropped the gumboots in a desperate attempt to stay upright, but it was no use. She toppled backward until she landed on the floor with a thud. Pain shot through her back.

Before she could stop him, Clayton leapt onto her, worming his way up her body until he could throw his arms around her neck. Relaxing her head back against the cold tiles, Emory hugged him tight until he stilled, and the piercing pain in her butt began to ease. There was no stopping the burn of horror at the fact she'd fallen on her ass twice now.

For a second, and only a second, she forgot what she was trying to keep hidden under her jumper. She didn't think about it as Clayton's wriggling made the hem ride up. It wasn't until she heard Byron's little chuckle that she remembered. She scrambled to get Clayton off her chest so she could pull the grey hoodie back down, but it was too late. Byron had seen.

"Clayton, you want to get the cars out? We'll race 'em once I help Mummy, okay?"

Clayton pushed off Emory as he stood. She coughed as his weight dropped onto her chest, but he ran away into the living room. Toys crashed as he tipped out the tub in search of the small die-cut cars. Emory made no such move to get up. She'd stay there, on the floor, thanks. Maybe if she was still enough, the faded black of her leggings and deep grey of her hoodie would camouflage into the colour of the tiles, and Byron wouldn't see her. Again, obviously.

"What's all this?" From across the room, Byron's voice was the perfect mix of light-hearted and guttural. It stirred just about everything in Emory, and she pressed her hands into the tiles to get away. The floor was cold against her skin, the chill seeping through the thin fabric of her leggings.

When she opened her eyes, she saw that Byron had dropped Clayton's shoes in the basket by the back door and was now returning to the kitchen. The corner of his mouth was pressed into his cheek, and he walked with his hands in the pockets of his jeans and his head high. He didn't look at her, still lying prone on the floor.

Sighing, Emory got up. She tugged at her hoodie.

"I already saw them," Byron said, clearing his throat. So maybe he could see her through the corner of his eyes. "Can't imagine the box is particularly comfortable shoved down your pants."

Emory could think of things she *did* want shoved down her pants. None of them were box-shaped. But also, *stop*. Why was she like this? Why couldn't she keep her cool around this man? She'd spent three years pining over him from afar, so why was it that the second she had to live in the same house as Byron, all her cool went out the window? No, further. It was all the way down the creek with yesterday's rain.

She kept her eyes down as she pulled the box from under her clothes and dropped it onto the counter. It bounced, landing next to the cheap watercolour palette she'd bought for Clayton.

"For what it's worth," Byron added. His voice dropped an octave, and the grovelling tone made Emory whimper. "I don't think it was a bad idea." He knocked his knuckles on the bench.

Sweeping up the books she'd collected from the library, Emory added the box of condoms to the stack. It teetered in her hands, but she steadied the pile with her chin. "I'll get these out of the way, then come back to help with the groceries."

"Where are you taking them?"

Emory scrunched her nose. "Ahh, my room? You don't need all my books taking over the house. Clayton's toys are bad enough."

"I wasn't talking about the books, Emory."

Her cheeks burned. Of course he wasn't.

Turning on her heel, she steadied the books again and raced away. This was going terribly. First, she'd been caught *buying* the condoms, then she'd been caught trying to hide them like some teenage kid. She wouldn't have blamed Byron if they never got used. The whole thing was probably a giant red flag to him. A blinding reminder of their differences. He always seemed so sure of himself, so steady even when things went awry. Emory was nothing like that. She flinched away the second things got awkward or uneasy. It was probably an age thing, she mused. And that should have turned her away, but it didn't. It only made her want it more.

Byron was twenty years older than her, for heaven's sake. And sure, all the moral parts of her could see why that meant she shouldn't feel this way about him, but the immoral parts? The part that enjoyed romance books that took morally grey a little over the line, or had heroes a little too broody? That part was positively giddy at the thought of her and Byron giving in. It was forbidden in all the best ways, and that's what made it so alluring.

Dropping all the books and the box of condoms on her bed, she hesitated. She figured she had two choices here, only she wasn't certain she was capable of pulling either of them off.

She could, if she could manage it, walk out there with her head high, her shoulders back, and her breasts out. She could sway her hips and lean right into the seduction and let Byron know exactly what she had been thinking when she bought the condoms. She could knock him off his feet, leave him speechless, and make the evening drag as they waited for Clayton's bedtime.

Or—and this was the more likely scenario—she could walk out there with her usual slightly hunched posture and act as though nothing had happened. She could put away groceries without giving Byron a second glance, then head into the living room to play with Clayton as though it were any other day. As though nothing out of the ordinary had been bought at the shops. She'd just have to control the constant lump in her throat and ignore the tingle that was still creeping down her spine.

She hadn't made her mind up yet about which option she would attempt when a loud clap of thunder shook the house. Her heart froze, and adrenaline raced through her at the shock. Clayton's cries followed almost immediately after, and she raced out of the room. All thoughts of Byron and how she should act had evaporated.

Byron arrived in the living room at the same time she did. From the kitchen, she presumed. Clayton stood, surrounded by cars, in the middle of the room with his hands over his ears. Emory navigated her way around the furniture to reach him, but Byron wasted no such time. He vaulted over the back of the couch and landed next to the coffee table. His arm reached out, and Clayton fell into his Papa's embrace.

"Shh," Emory heard Byron whisper into Clayton's ear. "Papa's here. And Mummy. Everyone is safe. Thunder is scary when you aren't ready for it. I know."

All his calming reassurance was lost on Clayton's whimpering, but it meant the world to Emory. He hadn't told Clayton to stop crying, or that he was okay, or that it was nothing to be scared about. No. Byron had acknowledged Clayton's feelings, just like Emory always tried to do.

She sat down on the floor next to them and placed her hand on Clayton's back. Feeling her touch, Clayton climbed onto his mother's lap, but he kept a tight hold of Byron's arm. He forced the two together until they were sitting in an awkward three-way hug.

"Thank you," Emory said after Clayton had settled in her lap.

Byron huffed. "I used to be terrified of the storms when I was younger. I would have been older than Clayton, but I remember hiding in my room, jumping at every crack of thunder. I'd lie awake all night listening to the rain, too nervous to fall asleep."

He sank into himself a little then, curling his shoulders down. Emory felt the movement beside her, it pressed Byron's side into her own. She didn't know what made her rest her head against Byron, but she did. The pounding in her head remained. Her ears still burned because of the whole condom situation, but the steady rise and fall of his chest calmed her a little. The silence between them was broken by Clayton's residual whimpers against her, but the whole thing felt comforting and ... perfect.

"That must have been hard."

"It sucked," Byron scoffed. "But if I ever told my dad,

he'd say a storm was nothing to be scared of and I needed to grow up. It wasn't his fault; it was the generation. But I knew then I'd never let my boys feel that scared without helping them through it."

"But Clayton ..."

"Clayton's my boy. Just as much as Tucker and Jaxon. It's not his fault his real dad fucked off."

Right. That changed things, Emory figured. She just wasn't sure how. Or what, exactly. Her immediate thought was of how selfish she had been to think she could just leave town as soon as she finished her degree. She still wanted to go, she still would go, she thought, but she'd have to come up with a better solution to letting Byron know. He was the closest thing to a father Clayton had. And clearly, her son meant more to Byron than she had realised.

It also made the pounding between her ears start up again. Could she really dive into a week-long fling with the man, knowing he considered Clayton his boy? It reminded her of all the messy details and excess baggage the two of them held.

"That's making you think of the box, isn't it?"

She held her breath. How did he know?

"As far as I can see, Em, we're both adults. We both know whatever this is between us is just for now. I'm too old for you, and you have too much life ahead of you to get stuck living on a farm. If it comes to it, what's the harm in letting off a little steam?"

If that was all it was to Byron, maybe it could be a fun idea after all. Emory could ignore that itching part of her heart called hope. She knew, for all the reasons Byron mentioned and all the ones he didn't, that they couldn't be anything more than a good time. And it had been such a long time since she'd enjoyed herself.

They were stuck here, after all. Releasing the tension was probably a good idea. But then, if they did, what would happen to that little piece of her heart? Would it grow? Would she be setting herself up for heartbreak? She'd had enough of that to last her forever. She didn't need any more.

Stuck in her own spiralling thoughts, Emory shook her head. She bounced between thinking it was a good idea and *knowing* it was a bad one. If they were going to do this —and it was a big *if* because she still wasn't sure they should—she'd have to build a big, cushioned wall against her heart and hope for the best.

Rain pelted against the tin roof, breaking the silence but doing nothing to slice the tension between them. Byron shuffled against her, clearing his throat. Right, he was probably expecting an answer. Some sort of recognition for his proposal. Emory hummed, but still couldn't find the right words to say.

CHAPTER 12

BYRON

The storm raged, on and on and on. From that moment they shared in the living room as the first of the rain hit the roof, it continued to pour well into the night. Byron held back his fear as much as he could, but the truth was, he was scared shitless. He'd been telling the truth when he opened up to Emory, but he left one crucial piece of evidence from the story. The storms still petrified him.

It was different now than it had been when he was younger, though. He was no longer afraid of the deep rumble of thunder, and he no longer jumped in terror when lightning sent flashes through the house. He didn't have to hide under his covers with his hands over his ears, but every hour of nonstop rain still acted like a hammer to his chest. The hairs along his arms stood tall from the second the rain started, and he knew there was no chance of them falling any time soon.

As an adult, he understood the weather. He knew thunderstorms were a simple part of the cycle, especially in his part of Australia. It was all part of the parcel, really, and he'd grown to accept it over the years. But there was something unnerving when a storm like this hit, and he'd never been able to shake off the fear that crept down his spine every time the wind rattled the roof.

It was no longer the storm he feared, but what came next. The change.

Each wretched moment in his life could be tracked against a storm. His father retiring after the flood in the noughties, the storm that played a key factor in Josie's tragic passing, the rain that poured for weeks on end after his mother died.

He didn't tell Emory that, though. Didn't need her pity, for one thing. For another, she had enough on her plate as she tried to calm Clayton. She'd spent the afternoon with her son clinging to her. Byron didn't want to be a burden with his rattled emotions. He'd survived many storms in the farmhouse, alone, and he'd survive this one too. It was the afterwards he was most concerned with.

Waking in the morning to survey the damage, to see just how flooded in they were, and hear just how long the SES expected the flood to stick around. How long would he be able to keep Emory before she ran?

He spent the evening watching her from afar. He'd offered to help at first, but in the depths of his fear, Clayton had latched onto Emory's chest and seemed determined to never let go. Byron didn't blame the boy, and he didn't try to force his way in when he could see he wasn't wanted. He did other things, though, as much as he could. He cooked Clayton's favourite bland pasta and sang songs while they ate. He'd blasted nursery rhymes and Spider-Man cartoons as loud as the TV could go to drown out the pelting on the roof. But still, the boy clung to his mother, and Byron could do nothing to help ease the fear. Three nights of storms was apparently the little boy's limit.

Long after the last of the thunder had torn through the sky, the wind and rain hung around, still pounding. Clayton never settled, and Emory had fallen asleep, huddled with the boy under his blankets.

When she'd never returned from putting the boy to bed, Byron had assumed as much and crept his way along the hall to check. He watched them now, sleeping soundly in the tiny bed.

With her back to the door, Emory's legs were curled around Clayton's tiny frame. The hoodie she'd worn all day was dropped on the floor beside them, revealing the pink tank she'd worn underneath. Byron had caught a glimpse of it earlier that afternoon, in the kitchen, but he'd never stopped to imagine what it might be like. Why should he have? It was just a simple undergarment after all.

Only seeing it now, he realised it was so much more than that, even though it wasn't, really. It was tight against her curves, and the thin lace straps dropped low on her back. With his eyes, he traced the deep U shape the fabric made against her skin. He imagined how the lace would feel under his fingers, how she might react if he gave in to the temptation and kissed the centre of her back. He wouldn't, though. Regardless of the looks they'd been sharing all day, and the silent agreement they'd almost, maybe, hopefully, come to. He wouldn't wake her from her sleep, and he wouldn't take her from Clayton when the boy clearly needed his mother's comfort.

He couldn't let her sleep all crouched up in that tiny bed, though. It was miniature, made for a toddler, not a woman. Definitely not made for them to share. He had to move them to Emory's bed in the room down the hall. Only, how?

Byron was a fit man, even for a forty-five-year-old. He knew that. He was proud of it, even. It wasn't by chance, though. He continued to work hard out on the farm, every day, to make sure he maintained the level of fitness he'd grown to expect of himself. He was strong. But strength wasn't always all he needed. He could pick Emory and Clayton up, no dramas. Combined, they probably weighed less than the hay bales he was used to throwing around. The two of them together, though, while they slept, it would be awkward, to say the least. There was no chance he could cradle them close without waking them.

He'd have to move one at a time and hope they didn't wake when he pried them apart. He tapped his fingers against his thigh as he thought through the best course of action. Thankful he never wore shoes in the house, he eventually tiptoed into the room. Clayton's favourite teddy was squished between the boy and Emory, but neither of them seemed to be holding it. Inch by inch, he tugged it free, then held his breath as Clayton whimpered at the sudden gap. Emory responded in her sleep, scooching herself closer until the boy could nestle against her chest.

Right, step one was done.

Byron took the teddy into Emory's room and tucked it into the middle of the bed. He pulled the blankets down and arranged the spare pillows to create a low wall along one side of the bed so that Clayton wouldn't roll off.

Back in Clayton's room, he scooped the boy up and held him tight. He wriggled in his sleep, stretching out his limbs before relaxing in Byron's hold.

Step two, Byron thought as he carried his grandson to the next room. He sighed in relief as he placed Clayton in the centre of the bed and pulled the blanket around his tiny body.

Now for the hard part.

Emory needed a little coaxing to roll over and allow

herself to be swept into Byron's arms. She protested, gripping the blankets and holding them tight. With one arm around her back and the other supporting her ass and legs, Byron did his best to think innocent thoughts. He was just taking the woman to bed, that was all. Fuck, not like that.

She was asleep, and he still found her irresistible. There was an urge that started deep in his chest and spread into every corner of his bones to carry her past her room and take her straight to his. He wanted to see her sleeping in his bed. To be able to see the way she might curl against his pillow. Nothing more than that. He was a gentleman, and he had no desire to attempt anything while she was still asleep. But maybe, just maybe, she would find comfort in his bed and in the morning, his pillow would smell like her.

He didn't, though, because no matter how strong the urge was, he knew where she was needed most. The rain outside had eased a little, but there was no doubt that it would be up again soon before the night was through. Clayton would stir at the pounding noise it made against the tin roof or as sheets of water rammed against the windows. And he would need his mother.

That was more important than Byron's fantasies.

In her own bed, Emory reached instinctively towards Clayton and pulled him close. The teddy was once again squished between them as Byron pulled the blankets up and tucked them in. A small piece of Emory's hair fell across her face. Byron's hand shook as he tucked it away. His fingers lingered on her cheek, tracing her jaw and settling right where her dimple always gave away her smiles.

He left her then, near ran from the room when he realised the new emotion that was swirling. This one didn't start in his balls, it started in his heart. And it scared the shit out of him.

It was quiet again when Byron woke after yet another restless night. It had taken him an age to fall into his unsteady sleep. Pins and needles had spread from his heart until his entire body was shivering in his bed. He lifted his arms over his head, stretching out of the blankets as the morning sun pierced its way into the room from the gap in the curtains.

The rain had stopped then. But for how long? And at what cost?

Byron didn't wear pyjamas, so in nothing but his briefs, he felt every degree of the chill in the morning air as he stepped out of bed. The fire must have burnt down overnight, and without it, the house had become cold. Served him right, he supposed. That's what you get for letting yourself get carried away on a dream. After tucking Emory into her bed and realising the deep feelings that settled in his heart, he'd retreated to the kitchen and poured himself a double shot of his finest whiskey. The amber liquid had burned at his throat as he gulped it down, but he savoured the pain. Maybe, with enough of it, he could melt away the sudden lump of emotion.

He wasn't kidding himself. There was nothing sudden about his feelings for Emory. He was just finally, for whatever reason, letting himself feel them. He'd have to stop, though. He needed to rein himself in and remember just how this whole situation was bound to play out. How it had to play out.

His bare feet padded across the carpet of his bedroom to

open the curtains. The floor-to-ceiling window looked out past the back yard and into the paddocks beyond, and although the sky was now clear, the signs of last night's storm were glaring. Thick branches and leaves were scattered across the yard, and the old gum tree looked more than a little lighter. Beyond the shed, where the yard started sloping down into a valley, Byron could see the water beginning to fill. It was a shiny glaze over the grass, but it spread wide. All the way through the valley. Past it, the high paddock stood on its hill against a backdrop of deep grey clouds. A new storm was brewing up north, sending more rain down the river.

If the gate had blown open in the wind, it didn't matter anymore. The cows were officially flooded in, and all he could do was hope none of them tried their hand at going for a swim. Cows did well enough in water, but a flood that spread as far as this one was a hell of a lot different to the dam by the far paddock.

Byron pulled on a pair of grey sweatpants and threw the first shirt he could find over his head. It was a deep navy that, in hindsight, was probably an inch too small, but it was stretchy and comfortable. The silence of his room was broken as he opened his door. The high-pitched squeal of cartoons echoed down the hall, and although the TV was turned down low, the repetitive tune burrowed into his eardrums. He'd be humming this song all day.

Just like the past two mornings, Emory lay curled up on the couch, with Clayton between her legs. Byron wondered how long they'd been there. And how often this was the morning routine. He could get used to it, seeing the two of them all cosy in his living room every morning.

He thought the same thing as he ducked out to the henhouse for eggs. And again as he pulled bacon out of the fridge.

It was a worrisome thought because he knew he *shouldn't* get used to them being there. He knew that no matter how much it might please him, things between him and Emory were never destined to be anything more than whatever the next week brought. Temptation was rising faster than the floodwater, but even if they did give in, it would be temporary. She hadn't said as much, but Byron couldn't see Emory wanting to stick around in Gardner Creek forever, and he wasn't going to be the one to try to convince her she should. His son had tried, and look where that ended up.

With his head down as he whisked up the eggs, Byron didn't notice her enter the kitchen. Not until she yawned. He looked up to find her balancing Clayton on one hip while covering her mouth with her free hand. But he could still see that cute as anything dimple on her cheek. She plopped Clayton into a chair.

"Can I help?"

He shook his head and turned to pull the breakfast muffins out of the toaster. "Nearly done."

"I feel bad. You've cooked breakfast every morning, and all I've done is sleep on the couch."

Byron cleared his throat. "You're looking after Clayton," he said plainly. "That's enough."

Leaning over the kitchen bench, Emory grabbed Clayton's small plate of food. Her breasts pressed against the counter, pushing up until her cleavage was spilling out of her dressing gown. Byron caught a glimpse of the lace trim on her pink tank. A lump quickly formed in his throat, and desire pulled at his balls. He swallowed back the sensation and shifted on his feet.

She didn't do it intentionally, don't be a creep, he told himself. But he didn't miss the twinkle in her eye as she stood back up and turned away. And there was an added sway to her hips as she took a step towards the table.

"Thank you," she said with that same sultry smile once they were all seated with their food. "For moving us to my bed."

"It was nothing," Byron mumbled. He was having a hard time focusing on the meal and not staring at her chest. She hadn't pulled the cord around her waist tight, so her gown hung open, revealing the front of her tank. The pink lace dropped to a deep V between her breasts. Byron found he had to constantly remind himself that Clayton was *right there,* so he didn't do anything ... crazy. Uninhibited.

"Well, my neck and back appreciate it all the same." Emory arched her back against the chair and rolled her neck.

Did she know what she was doing to him? She had to know.

Byron felt blood rush. South. He shifted in his seat, dropping a hand below the table to adjust his rapidly growing length. He hissed at the contact. The friction of the fabric sent a shockwave through him. She'd bought condoms, he reminded himself. She wanted this just as much as he did.

They just needed to decide what, if anything, they were going to do about it.

CHAPTER 13

EMORY

Something glistened behind Emory's eyes. Maybe not literally, but she could feel it. The spark, the heat, the excitement. It flared out of her as she watched Byron from across the table, struggling to focus on his food. He kept stealing glances at her when he thought she wasn't looking. And she loved it.

She might not have needed to stretch her back out in a way that pushed her breasts forward and made her dressing gown fall open, but she did it anyway. Just to see him squirm. She snickered to herself when his hand fell underneath the table, and she just *knew* he was adjusting himself. The thought was wild and daring. Emory had to press her thighs together when her core grew hot.

Clayton—bless the little three-year-old and his completely innocent brain—didn't seem to notice the way the air grew thick. Emory shivered, trying to shake off her thoughts. She'd been doing a lot of that lately, shaking off the temptation. Reminding herself all the reasons why it was not a good idea.

"Cow!" Clayton jumped to stand in his seat and pointed out the back window.

Byron didn't even turn around to check before responding. "Nah, buddy, all the cows are in the high paddock, we can't see them today." He shook his head with a short laugh. "We always go for a drive to see the cows. Might take him a little while before he realises we can't just up and go right now."

Emory would have agreed, but Clayton wasn't pointing to the shed where Byron kept the quad bikes. And he kept jumping with excitement. His little arms flapping around but always returning to the same point out in the flood-covered fields. Emory grabbed one of his hands, not quite stilling him, but offering a little extra support so he wouldn't bounce right off the chair and onto the hard floor.

"No, Papa, cow!" he said, jamming his little arm out as far as he could.

"Not today, Clayton," Byron said with a sigh.

Emory might have been annoyed he wasn't listening to her son, but there was so much sympathy in Byron's voice. It cracked a little as he looked down at the table. She wondered if this was one of the few times he had to turn his grandson down. Surely not—she knew how often Clayton begged for snacks, after all—but maybe this was one of those moments where he really wished he could say yes instead.

"Show me," she said, with the little lilt she often added when talking to her son. Wrapping one arm around the still bouncing child, she leant her head close to follow his line of sight.

There was so much water, already. When she had peeked out the window this morning, the lowest parts of the valleys had a shiny coat that she assumed was the flood, but now there was no denying they were covered. She couldn't have said from here how deep it was except that the tall posts of the old windmill seemed a lot shorter. Emory choked on her inhale. The view was as breathtaking as it was concerning. She looked out, following Clayton's pointed arm, to the high paddock way off in the distance. It was crazy to think that Byron owned so much land. Crazier still knowing that he owned so much more, too. Byron had never said as much, but Tucker was quite the town gossip and had never been shy about the investment portfolio he was bound to inherit one day.

But all that was no matter, because there, a long way from the paddock and playing in the floodwater, was a deep red cow.

"Shit, Byron," Emory gasped. She would have scowled at herself if she could, because of course, Clayton repeated her. "Shit, Papa!"

That got Byron's attention. He dropped his fork, briefly looking up at Emory before turning slowly in his chair. She wished he'd hurry up because she didn't know much about farming, but surely one of his prized cows being *in the floodwater* was not good.

He stood with a start as he finally realised that Clayton wasn't asking to go see the cows, he was showing them that one was right there.

"Fucking Betty," he exclaimed. The chair tipped from under him as he raced towards the door.

Emory hoisted Clayton onto her hip and followed him out. She kicked her slip-on shoes over a few times before sliding them onto her feet and running down the hill.

"Byron," she called out, but he just lifted his arm in a wave without turning back.

She was just starting to wonder what exactly he was going to do about a rogue cow swimming about in the floodwater when Byron stopped short just before his feet hit the water. He took a step forward, then a quick one back. He turned to look up at Emory or the house, but pivoted before she could catch his eye. And he let out a groan that echoed through the hills.

She could see the indecision as he shook his head.

"Maybe we could call Tucker?" she offered. He'd bought the boat after all, maybe now was the chance for it to come in handy.

Byron huffed. "He'd take too long to get here. She could swim down to the next county and we'd lose sight of her."

Walking tentatively forward, Emory shifted Clayton onto her back. He clung tight to her neck as she held him in a piggyback, for once not demanding to be put down so he could walk. He probably sensed the urgency and panic of the situation.

When she came up beside Byron, Emory stood a step back so there was no chance of the water hitting her feet. It was still, but murky. And Emory had no idea how quickly the water was rising. It was higher now than when she first looked out in the wee hours of the morning, but she couldn't really have said by how much. She didn't know how much more they were to expect.

"Is she okay? Swimming?" She reached an arm out to rest on Byron's shoulder. It shook beneath her touch.

Maybe it was the chill in the morning air, or maybe it was because one of his cows was in danger. Certainly wasn't just because of Emory, though. At least that's what she told herself.

"Technically," Byron said as he ran his hands through his hair and down over his face. "I mean, yeah, she can swim, but if she doesn't turn back soon, she's going to tire herself out."

"She'll turn back before that, won't she?"

Emory did her best to ignore the way Clayton was beginning to tug at her ears. Whatever kept him occupied up there would do for right now. The longer the situation went on, the more she was sure that a cow swimming in floodwater was *not* ideal. But she knew so little about farm life. She had no idea what to say or how to help, and from the way Byron was still scratching his beard and stepping back and forth, Emory was willing to bet he didn't know either.

"Honestly," he said, not taking his eyes off the cow, "any other, I'd say they'd figure it out. But with Betty, all bets are off. She's gonna do something dumb."

"How do you know it's Betty?"

Clayton pulled at her ear, leaning down and speaking directly into it. "Betty red, Mummy." He gave her hair a small tug for good measure. Her son was right, even in the water, Betty's coat shone a deep orange-red.

"She's the only bloody red one," Byron added. "Still not sure why I bought her. She's brought me nothing but trouble."

"Why do you keep her then?"

Byron looked up to the overcast sky, and Emory watched as his chest rose with a deep inhale. When he brought his head level again, he was looking at Emory, not the cow.

"There's just ... something about her. She's feisty and determined, and for all the grief she gives me, I don't think any of the other ladies have shown me the kind of care she has. She always comes to say hello when I open the gate and follows me around as I'm fixing fences. I think she's as connected to me as I am to her." As he spoke, his eyes continued to dart back to where Betty was still swimming happily in the floodwater.

She'd moved closer to them, much further away from the high paddock where all her herd-mates seemed unfazed. Emory saw then that all of the rest were black with varying amounts of white splotches. In all the times she'd been at the farm, she'd never noticed. Although she'd never really paid attention to the cows either. Her experience at Gardner Farm was completely restricted to the farmhouse and its immediate surrounds.

"Ugh," Byron groaned as he saw the path Betty was taking, then turned swiftly on his heel and started stalking up the hill toward the house. "Keep an eye on her. Maybe call out her name and see if she gets closer."

Emory turned to protest, but he was halfway back to the house. She returned her attention to the swimming cow. It was an odd sight, but it filled her belly with amusement.

"You want to help me?" she asked Clayton as she turned her head back. "I'll count to three and then we'll yell *Betty* as loud as we can."

Clayton cheered in response, and Emory could only take that as a yes.

"One ... two ... three," she counted before they called out together.

The cow didn't seem to notice them. Probably their voices weren't loud enough to reach as far away as she was. Or she just didn't care.

All Emory could do was watch as she frolicked about in the muddy water and wait for Byron to return with whatever plan had sprung to mind.

It wasn't long, thankfully, before he returned. He skidded to a halt beside her and dropped a long rope at his bare feet. Without a word, he ripped his tight T-shirt over his head. It fell to the ground beside the rope. Emory forgot why they were standing on the edge of the floodwater all together, completely distracted by a now shirtless Byron. A fine layer of hair covered his chest, and there were those edible ab muscles again. She was so fixated on them that she didn't realise he was stepping out of his pants until he kicked them to the side. His briefs clung tight to, well, everything, and Emory let out a faint whimper. She bit her lip and willed her body to chill *the fuck* out.

But Byron paid her no mind. He was anything *but* distracted as he grabbed the rope from the ground and hung it over his neck and shoulder.

"What ... what are you doing?" Emory managed to ask.

"What does it look like I'm doing, Emory?" Byron was already knee deep in the water. "I'm getting her."

"Is that safe?"

He turned back and shrugged. "Only one way to find out!"

And then he was gone. Waist deep in the water, he dove and began swimming. Every now and then, Emory heard him call out to the cow. Her name, gentle coos, and maybe the odd click of his tongue—although that might have been bugs. Emory shuddered at the thought. Byron seemed unfazed; he swam through the water like it was a beachside pool. Emory marvelled at the sight, transfixed by his strong arms and the muscles on his back. With each stroke, his shoulders tensed, delicious lines forming and moulding across his upper body. Again, she wondered what it might be like to feel his muscles from underneath him. To move in sync with his body. She would have lost herself to the thought if Clayton hadn't pulled her hair.

"Papa got Betty!" he cheered.

And sure enough, there Byron was, chest deep in floodwater on the other side of the nearest valley. He was wrestling with the stray cow. Or hugging her. Emory couldn't quite tell from such a distance. Soon enough, he had the rope looped around Betty's neck. Emory expected him to turn back, but instead, he seemed to frolic in the water. He swam around with the cow, and across the otherwise still water, Emory heard his bellowed laughter and the soft mooing from the cow. Eventually, Byron began to coax Betty along. They moved slowly towards the house. Holding tight to the rope around Betty's neck, Byron paddled through the water.

Emory watched them for a while, marvelling at Byron's dedication to his herd. Everything she'd read about floodwater said never to get in. Even when it looks still, it could have a fierce undercurrent. But Byron had leapt right on in to save Betty from swimming away. His commitment and care were second to none, just like his commitment to supporting her after Jaxon left.

He was more than halfway back before she realised she was of more use elsewhere right now. He'd swum through the gross-looking water to save Betty, and all she'd done was watch. Correcting her grip on Clayton, she headed inside to fetch a towel.

Only, she was halfway up the hallway when she realised she had no idea where the linen closet was. Byron had left a stack of clean towels in the bathroom, and she'd hung them up to dry after her past couple of showers—and the ones she'd used for Clayton—so she hadn't needed a new one yet. But Byron would be back on their dry patch of land soon.

With Clayton still on her back, she grabbed a towel off the bathroom rack and raced back outside. At the door, she kicked Clayton's shoes over a few times before placing him down and helping him slip them on. He ran off as soon as she let him go, right down to where Byron was now strolling from the water.

Because there was no other word for it. He guided

Betty up the slope like he wasn't knee deep in a flood. The cow stopped to shake, much like a dog, spraying water all over Byron.

"Wait there, Clayton," he called out.

And to his credit, the little boy did what he was told. Maybe spending all that time with Byron at the farm had taught him a little discipline. Sure, he was only three and Emory could forgive him for not listening to most of what she asked him, but it was good to see him following instructions here. It was important on a farm, she knew that much.

"You gonna pass me the towel or ...?" Byron said before he reached the edge of the water.

His shoulders shook a little as he took the towel. Emory did her best to keep her eyes on his face, really, but it was impossible not to see everything else. His bare chest, his thick thighs, and, fuck, the way his briefs now clung tight and revealed literally everything. She pulled her lip into her mouth and bit hard. Focusing on the pain, she willed herself not to get flustered. Byron held the towel at arm's length and raised an eyebrow at her. He let his eyes drop down over his body, then slowly brought them up to Emory. She was still drinking in the whole thing when Clayton stepped between them and started cheering.

"Papa save Betty!"

Byron gave a little chuckle, tucking the towel under one arm and ruffling Clayton's hair. Betty nuzzled her large head against Byron's shoulder, then moved back to shake again.

Fat droplets of dirty water splattered over the trio, shocking Emory out of her trance. The water hit her face, dripping down over her eyes.

"We might need more towels," Byron laughed as he wrapped his around his waist and headed up the hill.

BYRON

Byron was growing used to the sound of laughter echoing through the house. It made him smile at the man he saw in the mirror when he stepped out of the shower. Maybe he was seeing things, but he could have sworn the wrinkles on his face were changing. He'd never really cared about the frown lines forming on his forehead. After all, it was just a part of growing older. But they seemed less so now. Instead, small lines darted out around the corners of his eyes.

He was smiling more—and frowning less—and his face was beginning to show it.

Drying his body in a rush, he pulled on clean clothes. He needed to double-check the rope he'd used to secure Betty. Earlier, he'd tied it off in such a rush. He hadn't cared when he first stripped down to his underwear and leapt into the floodwaters to save the blasted cow. More focused on the fact she was bound to float away to the next town over, the thought of being near naked around Emory hadn't even crossed his mind. But walking out of the water, he felt her eyes taking him in more than he felt each rivulet of muddy water that trickled down his skin.

It wasn't bad, he supposed, to be ogled. But he'd felt exposed and a little awkward. Plus, with Clayton running around their feet, he'd been careful not to say anything too crass. Better to act like he was completely unfazed by the whole situation. Thinking back, he was sure he'd pulled it off.

But his mind had still been elsewhere as he tied the rope around one of the poles along the pergola, and he wasn't sure he trusted his muscle memory that much. Now she'd had a taste for swimming, he could just about guarantee Betty would want to give it another go.

Stepping into the hall, Byron noticed the laughter was coming from Clayton's room, rather than the living room. The door was open a little, and Byron poked his head in. Just to see what they were doing, nothing more. As much as he was enjoying spending so much time with Emory and Clayton, he knew that it wasn't always his place to step in. They needed time alone. They deserved it, even when they were staying in a house that wasn't their own.

Sitting on the tiny bed, Emory read Clayton a book. Byron couldn't see what it was, not that it should have mattered. But through the silly voices she was putting on, Byron could piece together the basics. A witch and a broom, and a frog that wanted to hop on.

Clayton laughed at almost every line, even the ones Byron didn't think were meant to be funny. But the little boy was enjoying it all the same, clapping at his mother's exaggerated inflection and the way she pointed at the pictures as she read.

Something in Byron's chest began to ache. Nothing painful, but a longing. A pulling towards Emory and Clayton he had to fight to ignore. The picture of them, cosy and happy on the bed, was searing itself into Byron's mind, and all he wanted was to join them. To be a part of that picture. To be a part of that family.

But he couldn't do either. He couldn't disrupt their time together. Sure, they'd probably welcome him with open arms, but he was mindful not to overstep and was certain there was a line around here somewhere that he dared not cross.

And more importantly, even if he did join them today, he couldn't be part of their tiny family.

Emory had been through enough heartbreak at the hands of a Gardner man, and Byron wasn't going to add to that list. Not that he thought he would break her heart. Quite the opposite, actually. He was beginning to learn that, given the chance, he would spend the rest of his life loving her with every fibre in his body.

And how did that old saying go? If you love someone, let them go? Byron thought that was it, and he believed now that was what he had to do. He had no idea what Emory's plans for the future were, but he doubted it involved sticking around with her ex-boyfriend's dad. She thrived in the hustle and bustle, not in the busy solitude of farm life. That much was clear. Byron had been in the café on more than one occasion, and even when the women who seemed to hate her barely gave her a second glance as they ordered their coffee, Emory always had the biggest grin on her face as she did her best to make small talk. Being around people was what she needed more of, not being around one lonely and grumpy farmer.

Resigned to stay lonely a while longer, Byron backed away from the door on tiptoes. He didn't return to his normal gait until he had cleared the hallway altogether.

Through the kitchen window, he couldn't miss Betty grazing on the manicured lawn he considered his backyard.

It was a small space, really. Just enough flat ground for Byron to feel like the farmhouse was any other home. Beyond the turf, the slope fell toward the valley, now covered in water and the paddocks beyond. A gum tree, not quite as tall as the one along the drive but still decades old, towered over the yard, and in its shade, he'd set up a small set of play equipment for Clayton.

It had been his, once, that's how old it was. The wooden cubby was faded, and a few of the wall panels had fallen off over time, but the ladder was still secure, and the small slide still worked, even if it was more than a few shades lighter than it once was. Byron had found it in the back corner of the shed when Clayton was still a baby. He'd pulled it out, full of memories from his youth, and Clayton had been using it ever since.

He hoped Clayton would keep using it for years to come. Even if Byron couldn't have what he wanted—meaning, Emory and Clayton moving in with him permanently—he still wanted to be there for them both. He needed Emory to know that watching Clayton was so far from a hassle. It was the opposite; a joyous, wondrous thing that Byron would love to continue with for as long as Emory needed. It was the closest Byron would get to being part of their immediate family, and it would have to do.

Rolling out his shoulders, Byron tipped back on his heels and whistled. Who knew a brooding countryman could be so soppy and emotional? Having Emory in the house had really done a number on the safe he tried to keep his emotions locked away in.

Outside, Betty mooed. The sound didn't exactly shock Byron, but it did remind him of the task at hand. He stepped outside as Betty stretched her tether as far as she could. Byron raced forward to grab the rope as the cow pulled the knot free.

See, distracted minds do shitty work.

This time, Byron focused as he tied the knot, looping the rope around the pergola post and back over itself. Once he was certain his second attempt would hold Betty secure for the next week or more, he followed the long lead to the cow's neck and gave her a good scratch. What was he going to do with this blasted animal? She was more pain than she was worth. He still didn't understand what kind of voodoo had washed over him when he purchased her. Truth was, she stuck out like a sore thumb in his herd of Holsteins. And for all the affection she gave him, times like now, she caused just as much grief. Like the fact she was here, not over in the paddock with the rest. He couldn't bear the thought of selling her on, though.

Still, he couldn't have her eating his small patch of actual lawn dry. With the rope now securely tied, he trudged over to the shed and hauled out a bale of hay. The dry stalks scratched along his bare arms, but he welcomed the familiar sensation as he carried the bale back towards the house. The *thud* as he dropped it to the ground by Betty's post echoed across the water. As she wandered over to check out his offering, Byron gave his beautiful red cow another scratch before heading back inside.

The house was quieter now. Clayton's door was pulled closed, and through the cracks, Byron could hear the soft sounds of lullabies. Emory hummed along to the tune.

There was that pulling again.

Byron rubbed his palm across his chest, as though he might erase the feeling that lingered there. He rolled his eyes at himself, then carried on down the hall to his den.

His book was sitting on the coffee table, but instead, he reached for a puzzle from the stack on the shelves underneath. He grabbed the first one, not looking at what it was until he was tipping the pieces out on the green felt of the pool table.

The image on the box was a mix of deep blues and greys. The Sydney Opera House took up almost half the picture, with the harbour and bridge in the background. Byron couldn't remember when or why he'd got this puzzle. Probably some Christmas present from some distant relative once upon a time. Although there was a chance it used to be Josie's. Or his parents'. That was the thing with this room, there was so much history if you knew where to look.

Despite the cityscape not being what he had in mind when he decided to do a puzzle, he got to work hunting down the flat edge pieces all the same. Turned out the picture itself didn't matter. His mind was racing around as he began to assemble the border of the puzzle. He needed to figure out a way to *stop* thinking about Emory. To stop thinking about how perfect she was. To stop hoping she was also thinking about him.

Okay, she'd bought the condoms, and he'd heard her whisper his name when she was alone in her bedroom. But that only made his dilemma worse. He could no longer convince himself that his attraction to the woman was purely physical. But as far as he knew, that was all she felt. It would have been so easy to give in to temptation and taste the forbidden fruit, but what then?

What would he do when the flood receded and the bridge reopened, and Emory took her leave?

Would it be fair for him to ask her to stay?

Byron knew the answers to both questions, and they hurt.

He was still mulling over how exactly he could stop

himself from loving Emory the way he did when she hopped into the room.

"Thought I might find you down here." She hummed, holding the book he'd lent her loosely in one hand. "I came to return this."

Byron leant his hip on the edge of the table and tried *not* to look like he'd just spent the afternoon dreaming of a future where they could be together.

"You read it already?"

She nodded with that gorgeous smile of hers and hummed. "It was better than I thought it would be."

"There's plenty more where it came from. You're welcome to borrow as many as you like." Stepping forward, Byron gestured towards the top right section of the large bookshelf. "Now and after the flood."

That had Emory stopping in her tracks. "After the flood?"

"We won't be stuck here forever, Emory, and you're welcome to stay as long as you need, but I'm sure you can't wait to be back in a place of your own."

Her face dropped a little, but as quickly as she blinked, Emory pasted the smile back on her face. Byron saw it all, though, and wondered what it meant.

"Thank you," she said when she reached the shelves. She slid the old romance novel back into place and began tracing her finger along the fading and sometimes broken spines until she stopped to pull out another book. Byron watched as she read the blurb, her face lighting up. "Ooh, a woman who falls into bed with her ex-boyfriend's dad? Sign me up." She tucked the book under her arm.

Byron held back his chuckle. Josie had been the same. Just because Emory liked the thought of reading about a love so forbidden didn't mean she was interested in it for real life.

He turned back to his puzzle, but all the pieces blurred under his vision. He couldn't focus knowing Emory was right there, in the room.

"You want to help me?" he called over his shoulder.

She was there in a heartbeat. Less than, given the way his heart was acting all funny. Skipping beats and then racing around all willy-nilly now that she was near. Emory's hand dropped to the table so close to Byron's, and when she turned to talk to him, he could feel her breath on his neck.

"Never pegged you as a puzzle guy."

Byron nudged her with his elbow. "It's good for your brain."

His hand fell back to the table, and he hadn't meant to, but his pinky finger brushed against Emory's. He slid his hand away, then froze and held his breath. It was nothing, right? There was no need to act like a bloody teenage boy with his first crush over it. But his finger still tingled all the same.

Forcing his attention back to the puzzle, Byron sifted through pieces, separating the greys from the blues and trying to find something of a strategy here. Truth was, he wasn't *much* of a puzzle guy. He did one every now and then, mostly when he had too much on his mind and couldn't focus on a book instead. Beside him, Emory was completely enthralled in placing the border pieces. She at least hadn't seemed to notice the way his finger had brushed against hers. Or had she? Because in the corner of his eye, Byron saw her flex her hand against the table. She kept it in place, but he swore she inched it closer.

"Will Betty be okay tied to the house?"

Byron took his eyes off the puzzle to look at Emory properly. Her hand was still there, on the edge of the table between them, but she'd turned her upper body towards him. The long strands of her hair hung loose around her shoulders, but she'd pinned her fringe off to the side. It framed her face like she was a piece of art, and Byron supposed she was. Beautiful, unique, and he could stare at her all day. He did, for a second, until she pinched her eyebrows together.

He cleared his throat. "She'll be right. I got some hay out for her, and she might complain, but there's nothing else we can do about it."

Emory looked pleased. "Clayton seems to like her."

"He does. He always marvels at her colour, and she loves the attention. They'll be fine together when you take him outside to play, but I can show you how to shorten the lead while you're out there if she gets annoying."

"Please, even if it's just in case." Emory looked away, down at the puzzle. She picked up a piece, secured it in place, then dropped her hand back between them. Only this time, Byron was certain it was closer to him.

She looked up again. "And the other cows? Will they go for a swim too?"

"I doubt it," Byron chuckled. "None are as brave as Betty. But I messaged Tucker. He'll come past in the boat and secure the gate."

"Good. That's good." Emory's voice was soft, like a whisper, but ... breathier. It floated out from her and coasted its way along Byron's skin.

He moved his hand along the edge of the table, over the leather pocket. "Emory?" he said on a whisper of his own as his hand reached hers. Pinky fingers first, and when she didn't pull away, he hooked his finger around hers and covered her hand with his own.

Her hand was soft and smaller than he'd imagined. But their fingers fit perfectly together. The touch spread through him like warm honey, oozing into his blood-stream and wrapping around his heart. Emory whimpered.

And then Clayton cried, calling out to his mother as he woke and found her gone.

Emory and Byron jumped apart at the sound. She stared at him for a while, unmoving, before Clayton called down the hall again. Emory's mouth dropped open, and Byron thought she might have said something, but instead she turned on her heel and raced toward her son.

CHAPTER 15

EMORY

Groaning, Emory dropped her head into her hands, then lower until it rested atop the books she had spread over the dining table. Instrumental tunes blasted into one ear, but it did little to drown out the clanging of Clayton's toys as he occupied himself in the living room. She felt as though they were taking up the whole house.

If Byron was still down this end of the house, she might have felt awkward, pulling out all her university texts. It wasn't as though she had tried to hide her studies from Byron. They'd just ... never come up in conversation. She was always honest when she picked Clayton up, so he knew she spent a lot of time at the library, but Emory was always quick to change the subject, and Byron had never prodded for more information. He either wasn't interested or was too afraid of the answer.

But if Emory had any hope of getting her last assignments finished while they were trapped here, she might have to ask for help. Clayton continued to use the toy cars and blocks as musical instruments, and the noise made it impossible to concentrate. Her second earbud was *right there* on the table in front of her, but she didn't dare put it in. For something so small, they did an impressive job at blocking out surrounding noise, and she did actually need to hear Clayton in case he called for her. She took the one in her ear out, dropping it next to its sibling.

Byron had escaped down the hall shortly after breakfast, and she hadn't seen him since. She thought they might have shared a moment down there, the previous day. But an odd silence had lingered between them all afternoon and long into the night. And although Byron had cooked breakfast again, as was becoming the norm, it seemed all the things they left unsaid and undone still hung about in the air.

It was probably her turn to cook a meal by now, but every time she came close to starting, Byron was already there. Chopping vegetables or frying bacon, and every time she offered to help, he would shoo her away. It was nice, being looked after for once. She could get used to having her meals cooked for her.

But then again, she couldn't. She shouldn't. The books spread around her were a glaring reminder that no matter how trapped they might be right now, this whole situation with Byron was nothing more than a temporary hiccup. She'd have to remind her heart of that. The silly little thing was getting all racy now. Anticipation flooded her veins, and even though Byron wasn't in the room, she knew it was his house she was making herself at home in. Her body remembered the searing heat that coursed through her at all the not-so-subtle glances he threw her way. They'd made an unspoken agreement, in a way. Both of them well aware of the attraction they shared. It seemed like it was a matter of when, not if, they gave in to the temptation.

Leaning back in her chair, Emory stretched her arms

high above her head and rolled out her neck. The hard wooden chair was making her butt numb. She wriggled in her seat, scooping her legs up underneath her before picking up one of the heavy texts she had laid out. The bright cover was deceptive. It made the book seem appealing, but it was mind-numbing. 'Marketing Principles for Social Media Management'; even the title made her yawn. Mya had ordered this one and the rest of the books on the table, down from the state library in Sydney, just for Emory, but that didn't make it any easier to digest. If anything, it made it worse because Emory knew her friend would remember. She was sure to get a message any day now. "Hope those books are helpful," it would read, and Emory would be obliged to say thanks, again.

She was thankful, truthfully, but that didn't make it any easier to find them useful or entertaining. All she wanted was to be done with the last of her assignments so she could start applying for graduate programs. Then a trip to the rural university a few towns over for her final exams and … done. She would graduate and finally, *finally*, have her ticket out of this town. The thought thrilled her. Not just the moving to the city but the *finishing*. She'd started her degree a year out from school, but two years in, she'd been swept away by Jaxon's charm. That thought had bile rising in her throat. But no matter. After the hardest, earliest months of Clayton's little life, Emory had realised returning to her degree was what she needed. She applied for a remote—and part time—tuition, and thankfully, most of her credits were still valid, so she didn't have to repeat too many units. It was all coming along nicely.

All except this final essay. Emory ran a hand through her hair, pulling at the knots slowly forming in the split ends that were far overdue for a trim. She just needed one more solid reference to help her argue her point. Because

God forbid someone completing an undergraduate degree should have an original thought. Flicking through pages, she looked for any cues that the author might, maybe, almost, agree with her that social media was an ever-changing, always moving beast that a business could never really keep up with.

Words blurred on the page as Clayton's banging and shouting droned on. She had no idea what he was playing, but he still hadn't demanded her attention, and a quick glance—she didn't dare attempt anything more than that—showed her his mess was still contained to the living room. So, it was fine. Just noisy and annoying.

She gave up, throwing the book back on the table with a *thud* of her own. Clayton didn't even look up as she huffed, he just continued right on using the coffee table as a drum and a toy car as his drumstick.

Emory moved quickly into the kitchen, opening the pantry door and hiding behind it. There had to be something good in there. Scanning the shelves, she found it. Perfect. Well, almost perfect. She'd have to remind Byron that chocolate belongs in the fridge, but the packet of Tim Tams on the highest shelf was practically calling her name.

She moved slow as she opened the packet, peeling the crinkling fabric gently as Clayton continued to bang away in the living room. She pinched the biscuit between her fingers and took a delicate bite. The chocolate melted on her tongue and warmed her soul. Stretching up, she placed the packet back on the shelf, but made no move to leave her hiding spot. If Clayton saw her, all hell would break loose. He'd demand chocolate, and she'd eventually end up giving in, and then he'd go on a sugar high. It was an inevitability she was hoping to avoid.

But the clanging from the living room had stopped. Tiny footsteps padded into the kitchen, and Emory shoved the rest of the biscuit in her mouth. She chewed as fast as she could, but Clayton was too quick.

"Choccy?" he asked, with his little puppy dog eyes and precious smile.

Ugh, even at three, he knew right how to play into her weakness. Emory didn't even try to resist, but she did break the next Tim Tam in two before giving Clayton his piece. She kept the other half for herself.

They stood in the kitchen, enjoying their little late morning treat. Emory closed the pantry door and slid her back down it until she was resting on the floor. Clayton climbed onto her lap, as he always did. She held him close, smelling his hair a little. When she hugged him like this, she still wondered how he ever managed to fit inside her. How she managed to *create* him.

She was still marvelling at her own maternal abilities when Byron reappeared.

He rapped his knuckles on the table as if to get their attention. Clayton jumped out of Emory's lap, running to hug Byron around the legs.

"Papa!" he cheered. "We got choc'late."

Byron ruffled the boy's hair and gestured to the table. "What's all this?"

"Oh, sorry. It's just some uni stuff. I'll clear it up." Emory stood and rushed over to the table.

She hastily stacked all the books into a pile. When she moved her hand to close her laptop, her fingers connected with Byron's as he reached to do the same. She pulled back from the zap that sparked between them. *Was he permanently charged with static electricity?* It sure felt like it.

Byron removed Emory's hand from the laptop and held it against his chest. Clayton, maybe sensing the weird tension that had begun to sizzle or maybe just having the attention span of a three-year-old, shoved the last of his biscuit in his mouth and ran off towards the living room.

Looking down at the table as she used her free hand to gather the last of her things, Emory felt Byron's intense gaze on the back of her neck. Her fingers burned where he held them, but she didn't try to fight against his hold. She did take her time turning her attention to him, though, thinking—hoping, really—it would allow her a moment to compose herself.

It didn't.

When she finally dragged her eyes up to meet his, she gulped. Visibly. Byron's eyes were dark, his usual whisky-coloured irises were nothing more than a thin, rich brown rim around his wide pupils. A strange pulling tugged behind Emory's lungs. No, deeper. In her core. Still, he held her hand against his chest, and she could feel the way his heart raced underneath it.

She cleared her throat. "I'll move it to my bedroom. Sorry."

"What is it?"

"My uni work. I have an assignment to finish, and I figured since we'll all be stuck here, I might as well make good use of the time. It won't be as quiet as the library, but I'll make do."

"No."

Emory scrunched her brows together. *Excuse me?*

"You can use the study. When you need it, you can close the door, and I'll keep Clayton occupied. So, you can finish your assignment in peace."

Byron relaxed his grip on Emory's hand, turning to the table. He stacked Emory's computer on top of the large pile of books, then picked them all up. Without another word, he carried them through the house and back to the small room off the entry. Emory had never paid it much attention; the double barn-style doors were usually closed. Byron pushed one side open with his foot and walked in to place the pile of texts on the large desk that stood in the centre of the room.

The study was exactly what Emory expected it to be—after she found out there was one. The room was small, with a large wooden desk that commanded the space. A sophisticated leather armchair sat in the corner by the window, and a respectable office chair was behind the desk. Emory had a sudden vision of herself at that chair, between Byron's legs. Her eyes closed as she held back the tiny whimper that made her lip tremble.

Byron froze, still facing the desk. Emory wondered if he was imagining the same thing she was. But if he was, he didn't act on it. Instead, he rolled his shoulders back and tilted his head to one side to stretch out his neck.

He didn't speak as he left the room, but Emory was certain she could hear the increased raspiness of his breath as he passed.

CHAPTER 16

BYRON

Byron sat, cradling his coffee between his hands as the rain poured. After clear skies all day, it had started as a sprinkle a little after lunch, fat raindrops leaving a melodic clatter on the tin roof. Clayton had dropped the monster trucks Emory had borrowed from the library to stare up at the ceiling, and as if on cue, the crashing intensified. It was so loud, Byron could barely hear his own thoughts, although that was probably a good thing. He needed a break. Needed to stop thinking of Emory in the study.

He barely used the room. Maybe once a week, he'd been in there checking off the admin for the farm and keeping an eye on his investments. He'd grown quite the portfolio over his years of running this place, always keeping his options open in case farm life suddenly wasn't for him. So, he was glad the room was getting a bit more use.

That, and he couldn't stop seeing Emory behind the desk. She was nestling her way into his home, his life. And he loved it almost as much as it hurt to know it was temporary.

With the rain coming down as heavy and as often as it was, they were going to be trapped in this house for a while yet. Maybe even longer than the week he had planned for. But it was all going to end eventually.

Clayton dropped a monster truck onto the couch beside Byron's lap. "Papa?"

Carefully, Byron shifted the coffee mug into one hand and away from Clayton's grabby fingers. "This one for me?" he asked, picking up the deep purple truck. Paint had chipped away in more than a few places, and the plastic roof had collapsed. Such were the joys of borrowing well-used and much-loved toys from the community library. Byron figured his own sons might have played with this small purple truck, once upon a time. Tucker and Jaxon had loved racing anything with wheels around the house.

He shrugged off the thought of his eldest son. Byron didn't want to think about what Jaxon might think if he had any inkling of what Byron and Emory wanted to do. Of what they were *going* to do if Byron got his way.

Nothing filled the empty pit in Byron's gut when he thought of his estranged son. He'd grown used to it, for the most part, but it still gnawed inside him. Even so, it wasn't worth stressing over Jaxon. He made his bed a long time ago, and Byron had hardly heard from him since. Chances are, he'd never even find out about the flood, let alone the sleeping arrangements of his ex-girlfriend. Didn't make it easier for Byron, though, to give in knowing what was at stake. Whatever minor chance he had of reforging a relationship with his son down the track, Emory was going to be a wedge between them. No matter what happened in the next week.

Jaxon had done her wrong, and Byron was realising more and more how much *right* she deserved.

Byron gulped at his coffee, letting the liquid wash away his reckless thoughts. Once the mug was empty, he dropped it to the table and stood up to play in Clayton's game.

Following his grandson around the room, Byron steered his toy around the obstacle course. Clayton cheered as the trucks crashed together in one final heap. The two continued playing as the rain got heavier and heavier. The sky grew so dark, Byron got up to turn the lights on.

Emory's silhouette in the doorway shocked him. *How long had she been watching them?*

"You're good with him, you know? Better than me." She held back her tight smile, pressing her lips together. Byron wanted to reach out and press his thumb between them, forcing out the smile she fought against.

His fingers twitched, but he resisted, reaching beside her to turn on the overhead lights instead.

"*Much* better than me," Emory continued, still watching her son. She hadn't looked at Byron yet. If she had, she might have noticed the way his eyes were trailing her collarbone or the way he pulled his lower lip between his teeth.

"I doubt it."

Emory looked at him then, and shoved his shoulder with her tiny hand. "I mean it. I *hate* playing with him like that. It's so ... monotonous. Boring. God, that makes me a terrible mother, doesn't it?"

"No," Byron said, giving in to temptation and cupping her cheek. "It makes you human. It's pretty boring to me too, but look at the smile on his face. That's worth it."

"Yeah, it is."

Byron took a chance and stepped closer, right into her space. Emory's breasts coasted along his chest as she inhaled.

"You know what else is worth it?"

"What?" Her breath was raspy, but then again, so was Byron's.

"You."

Fuck everything else.

Leaning his body over hers, Byron tilted Emory's head up. The movement caught her by surprise, and her mouth dropped into a tiny 'o' as she gasped. Byron stole the sound with his lips, planting a kiss on her lower lip. He felt Emory's shoulders slacken into him, and he pulled her closer, until their chests moved as one.

She took an age to kiss him back, but just as Byron was about to pull away, Emory stretched up on her toes and held their mouths together. She sucked Byron's lip into her mouth, and he reached behind her to tangle his fingers in her hair.

Something pulled inside Byron's chest. He groaned into Emory's mouth, teasing her with his tongue. When she opened up and let him in, he sighed with something that felt like relief.

The rain flurried outside, and their kiss turned frenzied as their mouths collided in a storm of lips and tongues and teeth. Byron tilted Emory's head to deepen the kiss, and she wrapped her arms around his neck, holding them close.

With one hand in her hair and the other on her waist, Byron turned them so her back was pressed against the wall. Inhibition flew away with the storm outside. He bent his knees and thrust against her core, the thick fabric of his jeans and the thin material of her pants creating a barrier that burned his skin.

He wanted more. He needed it.

His fingers danced under the hemline of her thin shirt, and he felt goosebumps erupt over her skin. Emory whimpered as Byron pulled away from her mouth to kiss his way down her neck. He nibbled at her pulse point and stretched his hand under her top to palm at her breast.

"Fuck, Emory, I've been thinking about this for a very long time."

She hummed, the sound echoing through his veins and pumping blood into his cock. Byron groaned and thrust himself into her again.

"Feel how hard you make me, Emory. Feel how my cock aches for you."

"Fuck," Emory whispered, pulling away from Byron's grasp. "Is this wrong?"

Byron tightened his grip on the back of her neck, turning her head back towards him.

"If it's wrong, Emory, I don't want to be right," he growled. "But honestly, I don't think anything has ever felt this right before."

Tears welled in Emory's eyes. Byron brought his hands to her cheeks and wiped the trickling moisture with his thumbs. Emory nodded, her head bobbing in his grasp. "Okay."

He leant down until his forehead was resting on hers. "I'm going to need more than 'okay', Emory. I need you all in."

Planting a kiss right in the centre of her mouth, Byron released his hold on her. He stepped back, reaching down to adjust the way his dick now strained against the zipper of his jeans. Fuck, it was uncomfortable, but he couldn't do much about it right now. Not with Emory standing right there with her doe eyes and fucking perfect ... everything. Not with the way she hesitated.

Byron would convince her they were right, he had no doubt. He didn't blame her for her hesitation. Hell, he'd felt it too at first. But there was an undeniable attraction between them, and Byron had a feeling that a couple of weeks being trapped in the same house was exactly what the two of them needed. He could forget all about the future she deserved if it meant spending two weeks enjoying every fucking inch of her.

Clayton crashed two trucks together in the living room, shocking both Byron and Emory fully out of the moment and into reality. Lightning burst through the front windows, filling the otherwise dark hallway with light. Emory pulled at the hemline of her top, ran her dark gaze over Byron, and raced to Clayton. She swooped him into her arms just as the thunder crashed.

The lights flickered overhead, and expecting the worst, Byron headed for the entry table. Three torches rolled about as he yanked open the small drawer on the unit. He never knew why he kept three. Couldn't have explained his logic to anyone if he tried. But at that moment, he understood exactly. He fished them out but froze when his gaze stretched past the open study doors. Emory had left a lamp on, and a multitude of massive books spread around her laptop.

He wondered what she was studying. And why they'd never spoken about it. All those times she said she'd stopped at the library before coming to collect Clayton, Byron had assumed she had just wanted a few moments of peace. Or that she was visiting Mya. Or maybe collecting more toys for Clayton. He never thought there was anything more to it, but seeing it now, this made perfect sense.

How soon would she be finished with her degree? And what did she plan to do after? How much longer did he have with her?

Sighing, he knocked his head with the largest of the three torches. He couldn't think like that. He had no right to try to keep her here. His throat turned dry. It ached more than his balls did after that kiss.

Byron never expected his heart would end up on the line, but with every little moment they shared, he was realising he had more at stake in this than he first thought. He should have known, really, that Emory was so far under his skin that she'd burrowed straight into his soul. Should have been able to feel her presence in every breath that he took. But it had taken him so damn long to realise.

He dropped his head against the torch again.

Fuck.

It wouldn't be fair to Emory. She deserved so much more than he could give her. Byron wasn't about to let his own bloody feelings get in the way of her dreams. He should never have kissed her.

Only he had, and now that he had done it once, he fucking desperately needed to do it again. What was it she'd said? Something about having a little fun while they were stuck? He could do that. He'd enjoy it. A lot. And she would too.

He could fool himself into thinking that getting all the sexual tension out of their bodies would help ease it, but he'd have to keep his heart under lock and key while they did.

CHAPTER 17

EMORY

It was late by the time Emory had convinced Clayton it was time to go to bed. He'd spent his entire bedtime routine protesting, and her patience wore incredibly thin, but she persisted until he finally fell asleep as she dragged out a made-up lullaby for the fifty-somethingth time.

Her thick socks were soft against the carpet of the hallway as she crept out of the room and snuck down the hall to her own bedroom before Byron could see her. She wasn't hiding from him, but she wasn't ready to face him yet either.

Every sense had been heightened, and she'd been on edge all day, but it had become exceptionally worse after Byron had kissed her in the hall. She let out a shaky breath at the memory. Kissing Byron had been everything and not enough. If he had intended it as a mere teaser for what was to come, it had worked. Emory had spent the rest of the afternoon and all evening with the memory of his lips on hers, and she was ready for more.

But she needed to shower first, to douse herself in cold

water so she could back off just a fraction. Maybe then she wouldn't come off quite so needy.

She gathered her things and snuck across the hall to the bathroom. Dropping her towel on the floor, she pulled off her clothes. The water was still cold as she stepped in, but the shock was exactly what she needed.

With soapy hands, she let her fingers roam over her body, and her imagination ran wild. She pictured Byron, in the shower with her, getting her all sudsy and slick. She thought of his hands exploring her body, and she remembered that this was no longer just a fantasy. This could be her reality.

It was wrong, wasn't it? To want Byron in this way. Wasn't that what she had told herself so many times over the past few years?

But even with those years of trying to force away her sexual attraction for the man, it still blossomed deep in her belly. As the water streaming over her warmed, so did the desire. It pooled in her core, and she realised that this was it now. There would be no turning back.

She was suddenly determined to see this through. After all, she'd earned herself a little fun, hadn't she?

The rest of her shower passed in a blur, she was in such a rush to finish. To find Byron. To claim what she'd wanted for so damn long. She was just rinsing the conditioner from her hair when the lights turned black. A half second later, before she'd really had time to process the lack of light, the water turned icy. She yelped at the chill. Reaching behind her, she fumbled to turn the tap off. A little excess conditioner in her hair wouldn't hurt. She could wash it off tomorrow when the power came back on.

As she stepped out of the shower, the bathroom door swung open and torch light shone into the space. Byron's figure was silhouetted by the bright beam, which blinded her. Dropping to the floor, Emory scrambled to find her towel. But Byron had jolted the torchlight away, and her eyes were still flashing anyway. That was a top, her leggings, until finally she felt the soft fabric of the towel and hastily wrapped it around herself.

She was unsteady as she stood, both hands grasping at the towel, holding it against her dripping body.

"Fuck, sorry," Byron mumbled. He'd half turned away but left the torch shining against the ceiling. "I heard you yell. I worried you'd fallen when the lights went out. I'm sorry."

He thrust the torch towards her, shaking it around a little. "Take this," he added. "I've got another in the den."

Emory pulled her lower lip between her teeth. She wondered if she should be embarrassed, but she wasn't. She was ... thrilled. Excited, even. Her pussy throbbed and she felt a wetness that had nothing to do with the shower beginning to pool.

Holding the towel with one hand, she reached her other out to grab the torch from Byron. There was nothing accidental about the way her fingers brushed against his, or the way she held her hand over his instead of pulling the torch away.

"Byron," she whispered. Her exhale was shaky, and the sliver of courage was waning. She needed him to turn around. To look at her, to see her. To feel it too.

His eyes were closed as he turned his body back to her. Emory watched his Adam's apple bob in the shadows from the torch. She waited, and waited and waited until she couldn't hold herself together any longer.

"Open your eyes."

Her chest heaved, and something deep rumbled from Byron's.

"Can't," he groaned.

Oh. *Oh.*

"Why?"

Please don't say you don't want to. God, if he had changed his mind about this, she was going to crawl into a tiny ball and hide right here inside the bathroom until the flood receded and she could escape.

"Because I saw you." Byron let out a shaky sigh and brought his hand up to scratch at his jaw. He shook his head. "I didn't mean to, Em, but I saw you and if I see you again, I'm not going to be able to stand here like a gentleman while I hold the light for you."

Her mouth dropped open with a gasp. She could feel her heart racing in her chest. It pounded in her neck and throbbed in her core.

"Good," she whispered. It was shaky and quiet and not at all the confidence she wanted to portray right now, but it was all she could muster.

"Emory," Byron warned her, hesitating.

She pulled her lips into her mouth to wet them and let her bottom lip out with a faint *pop*. "I said good," she managed to say. "Open your eyes."

He might have, but if he did, he moved too quickly for her to notice. One second, he was a foot away from her, squeezing his eyes shut, and then the next, he was standing over her with a hand behind her neck. The torch hung at his side as he backed her against the shower screen and crashed his lips into hers.

He moaned as she opened her mouth, inviting him in. Emory kept one hand to her chest, holding the towel around her, but she let the other hand feel up his arm and loop behind his head. She grabbed at the short hair on the nape of his neck and pulled him closer. His tongue explored her mouth, running against her own while his lips held her close.

It was all frenzy and wild and fucking hot. Byron must have put the torch down because he ran his hand up her inner thigh, ducking under the loose ends of the towel. He traced his fingers higher, pausing when he reached the little dip.

His featherlight touch tickled Emory, and she gasped. Byron pulled back from their kiss, his hand unmoving.

"Emory?"

She hummed. She didn't trust herself with words anymore.

Byron's forehead rested against her own. "Are you sure?"

She nodded.

His thumb inched closer to the apex of her thigh. He was so close. So. Close. She pushed her hips forward, but he held her still.

"Use your words, Em."

Emory pulled in a deep breath, letting it out with a shaky sigh. The word was caught in her throat, but she knew she needed to voice it. "Y-yes," she stammered.

Byron caught the word with his lips. He kissed her like his life depended on it and dipped his hand to her core. His thumb pressed against her clit as his fingers stroked through her folds, spreading her wetness all around her.

He moaned into her mouth. "You're so fucking wet for me, aren't you? So fucking ready for me."

Emory whimpered. She could do nothing more than kiss him and hold him close. When he pressed two fingers inside her, she gasped against his mouth and dropped her towel. She felt so full, more so than her own hand had ever made her feel. Her head dropped back against the cool glass of the shower screen, and Byron kissed his way down her neck. While his fingers pumped in and out of her, he pulled her breast into his mouth.

His tongue flicked her nipple, and her knees began to shake.

Popping off her breast, Byron stilled his fingers. "Not yet," he warned her. "Not until I've had a chance to see how good you taste."

Nodding her head, Emory held her breath. Byron pressed his thumb against her clit but kept his fingers still.

"You'd like that, wouldn't you? To come all over my tongue? Your pussy is fucking aching for it."

"Please," she whispered.

"Oh, Em, it will be my fucking pleasure."

Byron dropped to his knees in front of her and hoisted one of her legs over his shoulder. His breath was warm against her cunt and Emory reached a hand above her head to grab the top of the shower door. Bryon growled against her core, and she felt it vibrate through her bones.

When his tongue flicked against her clit, she melted against him. She pulled him closer, grinding her hips against his face in an act of pure need. There was no other way to explain it.

He licked her pussy, devouring her like she was his last meal until her legs began to shake again. Her chest heaved as her release soared nearer. Byron dipped his fingers back between her folds and thrust them into her. He curled them against her inner walls and grazed his teeth against her clit and Emory was nothing but a puddle. With one hand holding her weight, he drew her orgasm out until she was gasping for breath and shaking all over. He continued to suck on her clit until every tiny spasm eased.

Standing up, Byron wrapped his arms around Emory's waist and lifted her into his arms. She pulled his face towards hers, kissing him as she caught her breath. The taste of her desire on his tongue was more than enough to fuel the fire in her veins.

"The condoms," she moaned against his mouth. "My room."

Byron carried her across the dark hall, barely breaking their kiss. Hazy, cloud-covered moonlight bled into the room through the open curtains, giving them just enough light to find the bed. Emory crawled across it, reaching for the bedside table and pulling out the box.

She pinched at the plastic wrap that still coated it and cursed herself for not thinking to open it before *right now*. She didn't want the moment to pause any longer than it needed to. But the damned plastic was tough, and she was still pulling at it with her nails when Byron grabbed the box from her.

Emory rolled onto her back. Her eyes widened, and she pulled her lower lip into her mouth. Byron had pulled off his pants and shirt and was kneeling over her. His cock hung firm between his legs. She'd been right. He was big. She didn't know if he would fit, especially not after so long, but she wanted desperately to find out.

Byron kept his eyes on her as he brought the box to his mouth and bit a hole in the plastic so that he could rip it off. He wasted no time pulling out a foil packet, bringing it to his mouth, too. Emory watched with her lip between her teeth as he rolled the condom over his length. Once it was on, she reached for him, sure she was supposed to do *something* here other than just lie there aroused, wanting and waiting. But Byron grabbed her wrist before she could touch him. He placed her hands above her head, but he didn't hold them there.

Moving at an aching pace, he trailed his hands down her body. He palmed at her breasts, pinched her nipples, then continued lower to grab her hips. Pulling her towards him, he spread her legs wide and leant over her. He smirked at her, then spat on her pussy. The saliva hit her clit and she gasped, *again*.

She'd always imagined sex with Byron would be fucking amazing, but this? This was extraordinary. This was more.

He ran his shaft through her folds, spreading his saliva in with her own need. Once she was soaked, he pressed the tip against her entrance.

Leaning down, Byron held himself over her and kissed her.

"Em," he warned. "Are you sure?"

She shook her head. "I don't think it will fit."

"It will fit if you're sure."

Emory kissed him, wrapping her arms around his neck and pulling him closer. "I'm sure."

Byron pushed in slowly, and Emory felt herself stretch for him. Her breath caught in her throat as she adjusted to his size.

"That's it, Em, a little more. You can do it."

It was those words that had her coming undone. His praise, his encouragement. She let her legs drop open a little further, and Byron thrust into her. He paused, moaning.

"Fuck, Em, you're so fucking tight."

She bit his lip. She wanted him to *move*. She needed him to move. She rocked her hips against the bed, then back into him.

"Fuuuuck," he moaned, the word dragging out on his breath. He moved slowly at first, pumping in and out lazily until Emory was desperate for more.

When he finally started to pick up the pace, Emory's head fell back against the pillow. Byron held her close, and he thrust into her over and over again. She was full and whole, and her body ached to feel everything that Byron could give her. Her breaths quickened to short gasping intakes of air as her second release built and built and built.

"Byron," she murmured through her raspy breaths. "I'm going to ..."

She wasn't able to finish her sentence. He kissed her as her orgasm ripped through her, thrusting deep into her until she couldn't breathe. Stars filled her vision, and tears filled her eyes. She trembled underneath him. Byron groaned with his last frenzied thrusts as his own orgasm had him shuddering.

He rolled them together until they were on their sides, and then he kissed her. This one was nothing like the frenzied explorations of before. This one was slow and sensual and ... loving. Emory kissed him back, but she brushed off the thought.

Don't get silly, she told herself.

It was just the post-orgasm endorphins.

She told herself that's all it was, even after he took her to the bathroom to wash up and after he got her a drink. She even told herself it meant nothing when he curled into bed with her.

And even in the morning, when Byron stirred early, slipping out of bed with a gentle kiss on her forehead before Clayton came to find her, she still told herself it meant nothing.

But she knew she was lying.

CHAPTER 18

BYRON

The house was alive again. Byron had sensed it from the minute he'd dragged Emory and Clayton's suitcases through the front door, but it was undeniable now.

It wasn't just last night that had shifted everything, although he didn't doubt it had something to do with the added spring to his step. Nah, this was something more.

Clayton's toys had spread beyond the living room, a few stray cars scattered the hallway, and a plastic bowling set lay toppled at the far end. Even though he'd moved her to the study for her own comfort, a few of Emory's books had still spread onto the kitchen table. Miff had taken to following Clayton around all day, burning off her excess energy by chasing him up and down the length of yard that remained above the water while he giggled and cheered. Empty cups began to stack in the sink, lights were always left on accidentally, and there was no such thing as silence. Byron hadn't realised it before, but the silence in the old farmhouse had been deafening. With it gone, his head felt a little lighter and his back no longer seemed to ache—although that was probably due to the lack of physical labour.

Byron leaned back against the couch. He was happy, he realised. For the first time in a while, too. He knew why, but it was a terrifying thought.

In front of him, Clayton was drawing; three big round heads on the butcher's paper Emory had used to cover the coffee table. The biggest was grey, with hard-pressed indents for eyes and a straight line instead of a mouth. Another was a deep brown, with wispy lines that might have been hair poking around instead of ears. The third, the smallest, was in the middle. Green like the colour of Clayton's eyes, it had a big, curved smile, and its arms reached up towards the others.

It was a family portrait. Byron's chest swelled at the thought. Tears welled in his eyes.

"Papa!" Clayton tapped the grey crayon against the picture. "Look."

Byron pushed forward, resting his arms on his knees as he leant towards his grandson. "I see. Is that us?"

Clayton nodded. "Papa, Mummy, Clay." He tapped the crayon against each figure in turn, then stretched his hands above his head. Yawning, the little boy dropped the crayon.

It was about his nap time, Byron figured. They'd eaten lunch a while ago, and the kid had been going nonstop since breakfast. Miff had already succumbed to an afternoon sleep, so it made sense that Clayton needed one too.

Byron scooped the boy into his arms and started to hum. He was never a good singer, but the tune helped Clayton settle. Snuggling into Byron's arms, Clayton stuck his thumb in his mouth and closed his eyes. Byron held him close as he walked to the study and knocked on the sliding door.

Emory's voice was soft as she called for him to come in, and she was already halfway around the desk when Byron entered. She held her arms out and pulled a very sleepy Clayton into her arms.

"Did Papa wear you out?"

The boy nodded, barely, nuzzling against his mother's shoulder.

Emory gave Byron a smile and moved out of the room. Byron followed her down the hall as she headed for the tiny bed in the boy's bedroom. It was one of the easiest naps Byron had ever seen Clayton encouraged to take, but neither he nor Emory seemed about to complain. After Emory tucked Clayton into the blankets, she kissed his forehead and then stood back. It took Byron a moment to realise she was gesturing for him to kiss the boy goodnight too. It wouldn't have been the first time he tucked Clayton in for a nap, but something about this time felt wholly different. There was that feeling of something *more* again. Clayton shuffled in the blankets as Byron kissed his cheek, but quickly settled back against his pillow. Standing, Byron tapped gently on the wooden bedhead. It was an old superstitious thing, really, but he needed to be sure he hadn't jinxed himself with all these hopes of the future.

He and Emory tiptoed out of the room but paused together before stepping into the hallway. Their hands brushed together, but neither made a move to do more, or less. Clayton looked so peaceful, curled up in the tiny bed, and Byron thought of the picture still lying on the coffee table. The three of them. A family.

Could they do it?

Or, more importantly, *should* they do it?

He pulled the door closed and followed Emory down the hall. She turned back briefly before returning to the study, and Byron paused. It didn't matter to him what people might say, but it mattered how Emory and Clayton might feel. He didn't want to confuse the boy any more than he wanted to hold Emory back from her dreams. She was studying, and he still hadn't been game enough to ask her what her plans were when she finished her degree. No matter his feelings for her, he didn't want her to feel stuck here. But last night had done nothing to shake the deepening desire from his system. If anything, it had made it worse.

It had, truly, honestly, been a mistake when he walked in on her. The lights had gone out, and he'd heard her cry out, and something in him responded. He had been unable to quell the urge to run in and save her. And then there she had been.

Her body had been dripping wet, her hair clinging to her shoulders and against her bare chest. It didn't matter how fast she dropped to the floor to find her towel or how quickly he turned away. He had seen all of her, and he had known, right then, that he was done for.

Byron counted his blessings that she had let him in. That she'd let him taste her and experience her and *fuck* her. But now that he had, he wanted more.

At the end of the hallway, he should have turned left. Should have made his way to the kitchen to make a start on dinner or into the living room to tidy up a fraction of the toys. He didn't, though. He turned right and found himself facing the big barn doors that led to the study.

Just *how* important was this assignment?

Byron pictured Emory with the end of her pen propped against her lips. He imagined her eyes down, maybe a slight line between her brows as she concentrated on her work. Maybe a few strands of her hair had fallen over her face, and maybe he'd tuck them back behind her ear.

Maybe he'd press his thumb against her lips and push the pen out of the way. Maybe he'd direct her head towards his cock, and maybe, if he were lucky, she'd open her mouth and let him fuck her face.

He huffed, shaking his head to get the vision out of his mind. It didn't matter, though; he'd already pictured it now. Blood had already flowed south, and his body was already five degrees warmer. Byron rolled up the sleeves of his flannel shirt. His dick ached, pressed against his jeans.

Still, though, despite the temptation, he held back. He poked his head around the corner to see that Emory had left the study door open. Not all the way like an invitation, but enough that he presumed she'd be able to hear when Clayton woke up. Even still, he rapped his knuckles against the old wood before walking in.

Emory called out for him to enter, but instead, he leaned in. Truthfully, he didn't trust that she wouldn't be able to see the raging hard on still painful in his pants. And he didn't trust himself not to say *fuck it* and give in.

"You right to listen out? I'm heading out back to cook dinner." He gestured with his thumb toward the back yard, as though Emory wouldn't have known what he meant.

She spun on his chair until her legs were free from under the desk, then stood in a rush. "Nope. You've cooked every night and every breakfast. And most days you fix us lunch." Closing her laptop, she moved to side-step around the large desk. But her thigh collected the heavy corner. "Shit."

Byron moved on instinct, even though the rational part of his brain knew it was just a bump. "Emory," he breathed out as he neared her.

She shoved him off with a grunt. "I'm fine."

Her eyes were watering, though, and she still held both

hands over what was sure to become a bruise. Byron backed away, never wanting to overstep. Still not knowing what they were now.

"I'm still cooking dinner," Emory said as she hobbled from the room.

He followed her to the kitchen and watched as she perused the meat in the freezer.

"I took a leg of lamb out last night," he told her. "It's in the fridge. I'm going to get the coals going on the Webber and cook it outside."

Emory slammed the freezer door shut, making Clayton's drawings rustle against their magnets. "But you always cook. I feel bad."

"I like it." Byron took a chance and stepped towards Emory. Her hand was still on the fridge, so he covered it with his own. She didn't freeze at the touch or move away, so he laced their fingers together and turned her to face him. "I feel bloody useless, not being able to check the cows or fix damn fences. Cooking is how I make up for that. Please."

He didn't tell her that cooking was also how he showed he cared. Or that it was his love language.

Emory opened her mouth to rebut, but he was sure she wasn't going to admit defeat because of the way her eyebrows were still pinched together. So, he squeezed her hand and cut her off before she could begin.

"How about I cook the meat, and you can roast some spuds and carrots. It'll be a team effort."

She nodded meekly, and he let go of her hand to get the meat from the fridge. He also grabbed an array of spices from the pantry and a large baking dish. Emory sat opposite him on the bench while he prepped the meat, and followed him outside when he went to get the coals started. When Betty came over to say hello, Emory didn't shy away. She even gave the cow a good scratch under her chin to keep her from nuzzling into Byron while he lit the little pile of kindling under the flute.

"You're good at this, you know," she said as they sat down on the outdoor recliners as the coals began to heat. "Cooking. Like, I can cook a meal, and it's edible, but you have a knack for all the spices and whatever. Your meals are always a few degrees better than whatever I can whip together."

"I always liked it. Not much point when I'm on my own though." He looked out past his yard to the flooded valleys. Josie's old windmill was barely hanging on above the waterline, but for once, seeing it didn't bring a pang of grief. Instead, the feeling washing over him was hope. Like maybe, if he played his cards right, he wouldn't be lonely again. "Thank you for letting me cook for you and Clayton."

Emory nodded beside him. Her hand stretched out a little, but the recliners must have been too far apart for whatever she wanted, so she pulled it back in and hugged herself.

"It'll be strange," she said with a heavy sigh. "Leaving. I never thought I'd say it, but I might just come to miss this place."

He wanted to tell her then that she didn't have to leave. His legs twitched like he should get on his knees and beg her to stay. But he couldn't. Not until he knew for sure she'd want to.

Chapter 19

Emory

The grass was surprisingly warm under Emory's toes. Dry ·too, which surprised her considering the endless rain the past few days had brought and the mass of water that spread around the hill. But propped up on their high ground, the sun had dried all the dew from the blades. Afternoon sun glared across the water, so bright Emory had to squint, even with her sunglasses on.

Byron's so-called backyard, which was mostly just the small flat patch of grass before the drop off of the hill, had become Clayton's favourite place. He loved testing Emory's limits, inching closer to the floodwater with a cheeky grin. Each time she called him back, he stomped a foot and trudged back towards the house.

As Clayton continued to run up and down the yard, Miff chased after him, barking. She probably thought the young boy was another animal for her to herd, but he seemed to be enjoying it. And all the while, Betty mooed from her spot on the grass, displeased by her shortened leash. Emory hoped her basic knot would hold up against the cow's pulling. She'd grown accustomed to having the cow in such close quarters, but it was safer for Clayton this way.

He loved it here. It had been a slow realisation over the past few days, but Emory saw it clear as the blue sky now. She supposed he always had a giant grin on his face whenever she came to pick him up. He'd spent more time here over the past three years than he had with her at the cottage. It stung a little, but Emory was glad he was able to spend time with family while she went off to work and study.

It was all going to change when she moved to the city, though. All of it. For so long, she'd thought she was so far past ready it was inevitable, but the flood had changed her. Being here, with Byron, had changed her.

"Clayton," she warned when he stepped a little closer to the water than last time. "If you go any further, it will be time to go back inside. Come play on the slide."

He made no move towards the old play equipment, but he did turn away from the water to pet Miff. Emory called it a win.

The sun was warm, soaking through her thin hoodie and burning her legs under her black leggings. Moving backwards so she could keep an eye on Clayton, she made her way towards the porch. She wanted to stay close, though, just in case he misjudged a sneaky step and toppled into the water. Thankfully, the shade from the house reached across the lowest step. Emory sat, resting her feet on the grass and leaning her elbows on the next step higher.

She kept one eye on her son, but her mind began to wander. From that very first awkward morning, to all the little moments—and the big one—she and Byron had shared since, to what this aching feeling in her chest meant. The chemistry between her and Byron had positively sparked, and now that they had set it free, there was no containing it. She'd spent all day yearning for *more* of Byron.

A pit formed low in Emory's gut at the thought. This was meant to be fun. It was meant to be a quick release to ease the tension. It wasn't meant to be something she wanted to continue long after the flood receded. But now, that's all she could think about.

Could it continue after the bridge reopened and she was free to go back to the cottage? That was assuming she even could go back. She had no idea if it was underwater or if this whole flooded in situation was the product of an overcautious weatherman. But regardless, it couldn't continue long term, she knew that. As soon as she packed up whatever was left of the cottage and finished her course and found a job, she and Clayton would finally be on their way out of town.

She'd start her new life in the city.

With no one.

Fuck.

Emory had been waiting to leave town for three years, but one mind-blowing sexual encounter with a man, and she was having second thoughts.

There was that damned pull again. Her attraction to Byron had always been purely physical, she'd thought. But over the past couple of days, there was another layer she couldn't shed. Something deeper. Something that scared the hell out of her.

Because it was a desire that had *no* place in her current situation. She couldn't let feelings get in the way of her dreams. Not again.

Emory stretched her legs out in front of her, wriggling her toes in the grass. There was only one person she could think of who could help talk her heart out of this mess. She fished around the deep pocket of her hoodie, pulled out her phone, and dialled her best friend.

She set the phone to speaker then leaned back against her elbows. Clayton was still happily running laps, giggling every time Miff caught him.

"Is everything okay?" Mya's concerned voice echoed through the phone line. The reception had cleared a little as the storms eased, but it was always a little sketchy here at the farm. Static interrupted every line.

"What? Of course everything is fine. How are you? How's Tucker?"

Mya giggled but seemed to hold back the bulk of her laughter. "The cheek on you asking me how *Tucker* is right now?! How's *Byron*?"

At the sound of his name, Emory's heart did a little skip. It leapt into her throat and left behind an itching lump. She did her best to swallow it down.

"Your silence tells me everything," Mya teased.

The phone beeped next to Emory. "I am not Face-Timing you."

Mya huffed, and the annoying tune stopped. Only for a second, though. It didn't take much for Emory to give in. She grabbed the phone from the deck as soon as the second round of high-pitched pings started. Her arm ached as she held the phone above her, so she leant forward, propping her arms on her knees instead.

She pushed her sunglasses onto her head and took in her reflection on the screen while she waited for the video to connect. Her eyes were dark. Even in the sunlight, the chocolate brown looked deeper than usual. The rounds of her cheeks glowed with a pink blush. She could blame the sun, but she knew it was residual from the excitement of every moment she'd shared with Byron. The ones where she got to know him just as much as the ones where she got to know his body.

Mya would notice it, though, and she would make assumptions. And sure, Emory had called for her advice, but she knew how Mya would react seeing her like this. She was ... glowing. But it wasn't like she could do anything about it now. Emory's face became a tiny little square in the corner as Mya appeared on the screen. She gasped as the video connected.

"I knew it," she squealed.

Emory shook her head, cringing when the action made some of her loose hairs fly around her face. Her sunglasses toppled into her lap. "You know nothing."

"Em, honey. You *clearly* got laid. I don't see any other explanation for the colour of your cheeks."

Emory could feel them heating up already, the blush no doubt spreading, deepening, and giving away all her secrets. All she could manage was a shy nod and an audible sigh.

"I fucking knew it. I knew you would." Mya moved about, shaking the phone. The unsteady video made Emory's head spin.

"Was it good? I bet Byron would throw you around like a hay bale and it would feel fucking amazing." Mya flopped onto a bed—Tucker's bed, probably—rolled to her side, and propped her phone up. "Actually, don't answer that. It's my boyfriend's *dad*. Ew. That's kind of gross."

Emory rolled her eyes, letting them close as she pulled out her failing hair tie. Her hair dropped over her shoulder, but she looped it all to one side and tucked the front behind her ears. She looked past the phone to where Clayton was now climbing on the small wooden structure. He clapped when he reached the top, turning to her.

"Well done, Clay!" she cheered.

Turning back to Mya, Emory sucked in a deep breath. She needed her friend's opinion, but God, it was hard voicing her feelings. If they even were feelings. She thought they might be, but she wasn't sure. That was why she needed Mya's help. Ugh.

In one long exhale, she threw the words out. "We did. And it wasn't gross, it was fucking amazing Mya, but ... I think maybe I caught feelings and now I don't know what to do." With them all out in the open, Emory felt a little weight lift off her shoulders. Her neck didn't feel so tight. Unease still swirled in her stomach, though. She thought she might be sick if Mya didn't help her. Soon.

Mya hummed, scratching her cheek. Her grin peeked through her hand. "Hear me out, yeah?"

Emory nodded. She had no breath left, even if she wanted to speak.

Mya continued, "Would it be such a bad thing if you did catch feelings?"

She hadn't thought about it like that. Sure, it had crossed her mind, but Emory had been so caught up in releasing the tension and giving in to her desire and trying *not* to fall for Byron that she never really stopped to think it through. It wouldn't necessarily be a bad thing, would it?

Unless Byron didn't feel the same way.

Unless Jaxon found out, because he would surely make a scene.

Unless the town grew to hate her even more because she stole another Gardner man from all the local ladies.

Unless ...

None of it was certain, though. And all she was really thinking about were the negatives.

"What if Byron caught them, too?" Mya prompted.

Emory's thoughts began to spiral further. What if Byron did have feelings for her?

Would they handle Jaxon together?

Would she care about the ladies in town if she were in love and *happy*?

Would she still finish her degree? Would she still want to leave town when she did?

Fuck. There was a lot to think about, and Emory had none of the answers. Talking to Mya had only given her more questions. Rolling her neck, Emory considered what it would mean to stay. Clayton would be able to keep his relationship with his paternal family, and given his lack of relationship with his father, that *was* important. There weren't many marketing positions available in such a small town, but perhaps she could look for something remote. Loads of companies offered that sort of flexibility nowadays.

And, okay, Emory would still be stuck in a town where, even though everybody knew her name, nobody said hello, but it was safe. She wouldn't be starting again. Again.

And Byron would be here.

"Do you think he does?" Her voice wavered as she asked the question she so desperately needed to know the answer to.

Mya squished her cheek against a pillow but didn't answer. Emory supposed she wouldn't know anyway.

"I think the only way to find out is to ask him. You pull on your big girl panties and you say, 'Hey, about all this great sex we keep having, I really like it, and I want to keep doing it, but I also really like you,' and then you see what he says."

Pins and needles trickled along Emory's arm as she held the phone in front of her face. She shifted her position, changing hands and stretching her legs back in front of her.

"But what if he says he does?" she asked.

Truthfully, this whole situation scared the living hell out of her. She was terrified that Byron didn't feel the same way, that her stupid little heart had gotten carried away and was about to ruin everything *and* make the next week or so incredibly uncomfortable. But she was equally frightened of the thought that Byron might have the same feelings for her. Because what then? She still wanted to leave town. She'd worked too hard at her degree to throw her career away for a man. Even a man like Byron. The thought made her shoulders shake with laughter. Not the kind that comes through boundless joy, but the uncertain giggle that creeps along skin and leaves a crease between brows.

"I wish I had the answers, Emory, but you'll never know until you ask him."

Mya squeaked then. "Gotta go, bye!" she squealed as the phone disconnected.

Emory furrowed her brow, unsure what had caused her friend to hang up. There was movement behind her, heavy footsteps along the deck, until Byron sat down on the step next to her.

"Ask me what, Em?"

CHAPTER 20

BYRON

Hours after getting the dinner prepped, Byron's mind was still reeling. Once the coals were hot enough and the lamb was cooking, he and Emory had gone inside and he'd sat, awkward as anything, while Emory had chopped the potatoes. And all the while, he hadn't stopped thinking about how perfect this was. How he never wanted it to end.

The thought downright terrified him, so when Clayton had emerged from his bedroom all sleepy-eyed and rumpled hair, Byron had taken his leave. Or, more precisely, he'd run off to the den to sulk about his feelings away from the woman causing them.

He just needed a minute to figure out what he wanted, how much he should let on.

But he still hadn't cracked the code, and for the first time since his childhood, the den had bored him. The book he was trying to read didn't pull him any further from the present than watching grass grow might have. And the blues and greys of his puzzle had blurred together until it was impossible to figure out where the pieces were meant to fit. But he had stayed there all the same, not knowing if his presence was what Emory needed, or wanted.

Something had happened between them. Not the fucking, even though that was downright incredible. It was the *after* that Byron was stuck thinking about. The way Emory had melted into his arms as he kissed her last night. The little moments he caught her smiling at him. The way she was burrowing herself into his life and filling all the gaps he hadn't realised were left in his heart.

Finally, he gave up trying to kill time in the den and decided to find Emory. He had no idea what he was going to say, but he knew he needed to say something. He was just pretty darn terrified that his heart was getting carried away with him.

When he found the house empty, he crossed the kitchen and slipped through the open door. Emory was sitting on the porch steps, leaning over her knees with all her hair looped over one shoulder. To the side of the house, Betty was sulking. Looked like Emory had shortened the rope to stop the cow from interfering with Clayton's play. Byron wished he'd been around to see it happen. And Clayton played on the grass, running around as Miff chased him back and forth. She was having the time of her life with the young boy around and no work to be done. It was going to be hard on her when the flood receded and life returned to normal.

Looking out at the floodwaters that covered the vast majority of his farm, Byron contemplated whether normal was even something they could return to. This water was far higher than he remembered, although he wasn't sure if that was just his old memory being a little sketchy, or if this one really was as bad as they had forecast. As far as he knew, the cottage had been safe twenty years ago. He didn't imagine his father would have retired there if it hadn't been. But with the water *this* close to the yard, Byron supposed it just might have hit the cottage. He breathed an easy sigh, thankful that Emory had listened to all the advice and warnings—his and those from the SES— and evacuated while she still could.

He glanced down at her, still silently contemplating all the changes the flood had brought with it. She was the best of them all.

With her phone in front of her face, Emory chatted away. To a friend, presumably. Mya, most likely. As far as Byron knew, the quiet librarian was one of Emory's only friends here in Gardner Creek. He hated the town for it, but there was no point growling over things he couldn't change. Regardless, Emory had Mya, and that was something. Not wanting to eavesdrop on what he was sure was a private conversation, Byron hung back. He'd just ... wait until Emory hung up the phone. He shuffled his feet. Maybe he should go back inside.

But Emory was giggling, the sweet honey sound that warmed his heart and made him feel like everything was working out exactly how it was always meant to. He hesitated.

"I wish I had the answers, Emory, but you'll never know until you ask him." Dammit he wasn't supposed to be eavesdropping, but Mya's voice bled through the phone line, and he couldn't help it.

He wondered what Emory had been meaning to ask him. Curiosity cemented his feet in place, even though he knew he should move. It took all his willpower to take the first step to turn away, but before he had even placed his foot back on the ground, he heard Mya squeal. The phone line went silent, and Byron froze, realising Mya had hung up. No point heading back inside then.

He moved to where Emory sat on the bottom step and sank down next to her.

"Ask me what, Em?"

Her cheeks turned somehow even more red than the pleasant blush that had started to form the longer they were here. Dropping her phone into her lap, she leant forward on her knees and hid her face in her hands.

"It's silly," she mumbled, although Byron had a hard time deciphering exactly what she'd said. Her voice was all muffled against her palms.

His hand shook as he reached out to gently pry her hand back. He wrapped his fingers around hers and brought their hands down together. She pulled back from his touch, but he held firm. He gripped her hands against his leg, tracing circles on her wrists.

"Ask me what?" he repeated. His heart already thought it knew the question. The way it bounced about erratically in his chest made it hard for Byron to breathe. He wanted to tell it to calm the fuck down. To stop hoping because God, if it was wrong, this whole conversation was going to hurt like getting kicked in the chest by an angry horse.

He gulped at the dryness in his throat and closed his eyes. If she didn't say something, he was going to. The sentence started to form in his mind, but he wanted it to be perfect before he said anything. Wanted to figure out how to tell her how he felt and what he wanted without making her feel obliged to have the same desires. The very last thing he wanted was for her to get so creeped out or overwhelmed that she decided to leave after all. It had been three years of this wanting brewing inside Byron, and he'd held his emotions in check the whole time. If she didn't feel the same way, he could go back to that. Right?

"Em," he whispered as he dropped his head. His chin

hit his chest, and he sucked in the deepest breath he could muster before continuing. "Do you want me to go first?"

Emory pulled at her hands, but he held tight. He felt her body turn towards his, and shifted his gaze to watch as she rolled her neck. Her chest rose and fell with her deep breaths, but she shook her head. Byron waited for her to speak, but every second that passed was another kick to his beating heart.

Clayton's giggles and Miff's bark and Betty's disgruntled moos all faded into the background, even though Byron could still see them running around in his peripheral vision. Beside Byron, Emory sighed. She opened her mouth to talk, but no words came out, and she snapped it shut with another shake of her head.

"Em," he whispered again when he couldn't take the lingering silence any longer.

"Okay," she mumbled before straightening out her back. "I don't think getting it out of our systems was the best idea." The words came out with one quick exhale, slapping Byron across the face and delivering one final, brutal kick to his chest.

"Oh." He shrank away. That wasn't what he had been expecting. Maybe he should have, but that darned heart of his had been so caught up, he really thought, really hoped that Emory felt the same way he did.

"Wait, that's not what I meant," Emory clarified, and suddenly the sun was shining again. "I mean, it was fucking amazing, and it was the best decision I've ever made but ..." She took a deep breath, pushing her shoulders back from the rolled down position they'd fallen into. "I *thought* everything I felt for you was just physical. I thought, fuck, he is an attractive man, even if he is my ex's dad. I didn't realise it was more than that."

Again, she pulled her hands back, and this time, Byron

let her. He watched as she shied away from him, hunching over her knees and hiding her face.

"I think," she added, "I've made things really awkward, and I don't know what to do now."

Byron chuckled. He held it back as much as he could, knowing how embarrassed Emory felt and not wanting to make it worse. He moved off the step to kneel in front of her.

"Em, look at me."

She didn't, not at first. But he placed a hand on her shoulder, and she leaned into his touch. He snuck one hand under her chin and lifted her head up. Her hands pressed against her face, but he pulled them down, kissing her knuckles. She kept her eyes closed, and he wanted to pry them open so she could really *see* him, but he knew that was a step too far.

"I was selfish," he said. "I thought, finally, after almost four years, my chance with you had come. I took as much as you were willing to give, even though it wasn't even half of what I needed, because I didn't think I'd have another chance. Emory, I want another chance. I want all the chances."

His throat hurt, and his eyes filled with tears until he blinked, and they streamed down his cheeks. And his heart, well, it threatened to burst. Emory opened her eyes and gazed into his own. Chocolate brown met golden, but they were matched in tears.

"Four years?"

Byron nodded, the hand under her chin shifting so he could wipe some of the wetness off her cheek.

"Fuck," he mumbled. "I shouldn't have then, and I probably shouldn't now, but I do."

"Why shouldn't you?"

"You're too much. Too perfect. A grumpy farmer like

me has no business with someone as phenomenal as you, Em. You have your whole life ahead of you."

Emory laughed. It was nothing like the high-pitched glee when she played with Clayton. This was soft, like a summer breeze whipping around Byron and wrapping him in a hug.

"You're not as grumpy as you think." She smiled then, leaning her cheek into Byron's hands and closing her eyes. "I mean, maybe you are," she added with a wicked grin, "but I don't mind. I actually kind of like it."

Byron huffed.

"It's true," Emory continued. She opened her eyes and wrapped her arms around his neck. For a second, she glanced over his shoulder—checking on Clayton, probably —before leaning forward and placing her forehead on his. Her hands tickled in the hair at the nape of his neck. "You're this grumpy old farmer with a little extra salt in his hair, but arms of steel, eyes that see my soul, and it's like I'm the only one who gets to see your soft side. I'm the only one who gets candles and breakfast every morning. That part of you is all for me."

He couldn't resist then. Byron leant forward and closed the gap between their mouths. His heart flipped in his chest as he kissed her, but there was nothing hasty or frenzied about it. Even though he held her close and wouldn't let go, it was slow and gentle. No lust taking over, this one was all love, and Byron sank into her.

Emory shifted, never breaking the kiss, and moved into Byron's lap. He wrapped his arms around her back and traced the seam of her lips with his tongue. She opened for him, because of course she did, but Byron hesitated. He could still hear Clayton playing behind him, and it wouldn't take much for the boy to look over to his mother and see them. The reminder of the boy hit him like a shockwave and was followed by all the other things Byron knew to be true. Emory was studying for her future, and Byron couldn't bring himself to ask her to stay. He'd put two and two together. Whatever she was studying, chances were slim that she'd find a job in Gardner Creek.

As though she sensed his apprehension, Emory pulled back. Byron felt every inch between them but did nothing to bridge the gap.

"Your study," he said, still unsure exactly what he wanted to say but knowing again that it was a conversation they needed to have. "What are you going to do when you finish?"

Emory furrowed her brow, dropping her hands from his neck and clutching them together over her chest. "I don't know."

"I don't want you to leave town, Em, but I can't make you stay. I can't ask you to stay."

Emory looked over Byron's shoulder. Her eyes softened a little, but she continued to pick at her nails.

"So don't ask me," she said. "I haven't decided yet."

Byron dropped his head to her shoulder. "You can't stay for me, no matter how much I want you to."

"Byron." Emory's voice was firmer now. She shoved her shoulder, pushing him up. "For the first time since I moved to this bloody town, I finally feel like I might belong here. That doesn't mean I don't want to finish my course, but it *does* mean I might not rush off as soon as I'm done. I get to make that decision, not you, okay?"

He nodded, and a little—tiny really, minuscule—bead of hope sparked to life in his chest. Maybe she would stay. Maybe he could have her after all.

CHAPTER 21

EMORY

The days began to drag. Not in a mind-numbing, hopelessly boring kind of way, but in a softer, peaceful kind of way. Emory and Byron, and Clayton, fell into an easy rhythm. Byron cooked breakfast in the mornings while Clayton watched cartoons and Emory snoozed on the couch. After they ate, Emory would escape into the study to work on her assignments, and Byron would entertain Clayton. She heard them sometimes, running up and down the hall with Miff on their heels, or playing outside.

And every evening after Clayton had fallen asleep, Byron and Emory curled up on the couch. They'd start the evening with a movie but get distracted halfway through. The heat between them would rise, and the temptation grew too hard to ignore. The movie would end up rolling, forgotten, through to the credits while Emory and Byron got to know every inch of each other's bodies.

And, oh, how they moved in sync. Byron had Emory over just about every surface in the house, and she was still desperate for more, every time. He could be rough and raw in one moment, and tender and soft right after. Emory never knew which side of him she would get, and she loved the thrill. She felt the best kind of battered and bruised, and it was excruciatingly titillating.

Their relationship had fallen into the best kind of balanced normal, and for a while there, Emory thought maybe this was what she wanted. Maybe she didn't want to leave town if this was her new normal. The water began to creep back down the hill until four days after the rain had stopped, it started again.

This batch didn't come in rolling thunderstorms with wild winds and sheets of water that pounded on the roof. It came slow, starting as a sprinkle that never seemed to go away, even as the day pushed on. The floodwater halted its slow decline and started rising again instead. Emory watched it through the study window, running her hands through the knotted ends of her hair. This wasn't her new normal, it couldn't be. Because the water wouldn't stay this way forever. Soon enough, the rain would stop again, and eventually, the water would drain down the creek. The bridge would open.

And then what?

Would she return to the cottage? *Could* she return to the cottage? She didn't know, and she was too scared to find out. Byron's hill was the highest part in the region. The bulk of the Gardner Creek township was on the back end of the gentle hill that curved up on the other side of the river. Her cottage was on the outskirts, in the shallow valley on the other side of town. It was far from the river, but in the lowest part of town, and the water was widespread through Byron's property. She could only imagine that meant it had spread just as far on the other side of the river, too.

Oddly, she wasn't at all sad about the cottage. After all, it was never hers anyway. She was just thankful she'd taken the time to pack up all their most important belongings before they evacuated here. Besides, Jaxon was kicking her out anyway. Did an extra week or two in the cottage really make that much difference? She didn't think so.

But when the water finally came down, where would she go? For a while there, she'd thought she knew. She thought she'd run off to the city and find somewhere close to all the jobs. The university had a socioeconomic crisis team, and sure, she hadn't really looked into it, but she'd banked on their help. Even if she and Clayton ended up squashed in a tiny dorm room for a little while. She would be out of Gardner Creek and on her way to bigger things. Better things.

Only now, she wasn't sure it sounded better. The present was pretty fucking good.

It just wasn't going to last.

Emory skimmed the closing paragraph she'd just rewritten and double-checked that her reference list matched the format in the submission guidelines. Satisfied that everything was as good as it was going to get, she uploaded her final assignment to the university website. It was a bittersweet moment. Far more so than she had imagined it would be. She'd pictured champagne with Mya and the excitement of planning her trip for exams. She'd imagined she'd hit send and move right on to applying for graduate positions at all the top Sydney marketing firms.

Instead, the thick sludge of dread had settled in her stomach. She needed to make up her mind, sooner rather than later. Stay, or go. Give whatever this was with Byron a proper chance, or move on to the life she had always imagined for herself. She wasn't ready to make that decision.

With a sigh, she pushed out of the chair. Her neck

ached from the incredibly unergonomic, curled-up position she had been sitting in. Stretching out her shoulders, Emory attempted to roll off the unease that had settled. The rain hadn't stopped all day. The floodwaters weren't going anywhere. She had time.

The house was eerily quiet when she stepped out of the study. She'd been longer than usual, skipping lunch and carrying on with her work because she knew she'd been so close to finishing. Her stomach grumbled, finally realising just how empty it was. Emory made her way to the kitchen, taking the last apple from the bowl on the bench.

Byron had done so much of the cooking that Emory hadn't stopped to wonder how much food they had left, but the now-empty fruit bowl glared at her. Would they have enough? In her haste to evacuate and all the stress that had come with it, Emory hadn't brought any food with her. Even that day she went into town before the flood hit. She'd been so preoccupied, worried about keeping Clayton entertained and buying herself condoms. She hadn't thought that maybe buying some actual food instead of chocolate and snacks probably would have been a good idea.

The apple crunched as she bit into it, and her insides did a happy little dance at how perfectly crisp and juicy it was. It had been highly unlikely, considering it was the last one, but she was pleasantly surprised. Her satisfaction did nothing to quell the growing worry about their food situation, though.

Still unsure where Byron and Clayton had escaped to, Emory double-checked outside through the large kitchen window. Rain still trickled down the overflowing gutter, Betty was doing her best to avoid getting wet by standing as close to her pergola pole as possible, and both the boys' gumboots still sat upside down by the back door. The living room was empty, and she would have seen them if they had been playing bowling in the hallway. A quick check into Clayton's room told her they weren't there, either.

There was only one place left they could be. Well, two, but Byron's bedroom door was shut, and she figured it was highly unlikely that they might be there.

The den at the end of the hall was dim, the dark grey curtains blocking out what little sunlight was creeping through the clouds outside. Lit only by a glowing lamp on the small table beside the couch, the room was not at all as masculine as she would have imagined for Byron's man cave. It felt cosy and comfortable, and Byron sat on the wide sofa, nestled against a pile of navy cushions. A deep, matching blanket was wrapped around his lap. Clayton was curled under it, his head resting on a smaller pillow Byron had tucked in the crook of his elbow. He was sleeping, Emory realised.

As if sensing her presence, Byron closed the book he'd been reading and gently threw it onto the coffee table next to his feet. He smiled up at her, then down at Clayton.

Emory moved to sit next to Byron, lifting Clayton's legs and placing them over her own. She kicked off her slippers and propped her feet up beside Byron's. There was a thin gap between them, running the whole length of their bodies. From her shoulders, right down to her feet, Emory had left a little space, making sure they wouldn't touch. Byron was having none of it, apparently.

He didn't let her get settled, reaching his free arm across her and pulling her in by the waist. He didn't speak of it, just made sure she was close, then carried on. Emory's heart skipped against her chest.

"He didn't want to sleep," Byron whispered. "But he

was wrecked. I was reading to him in the living room, but he kept trying to find the remote and turn the TV on. He didn't want a bar of his room either, so I brought him here. He didn't last long; I'd barely read a page before he drifted off."

Emory leant forward, stretching her arms over her legs to pick up the book Byron had been reading. "I don't blame him. I doubt Stephen King is very entertaining for a toddler."

"We were reading The Hungry Caterpillar, actually." Byron kept his chuckle to a whisper as he gestured to the other book on the coffee table. "I picked up *my* book after I realised Clayton was no longer listening."

She leant back, letting the corner of her mouth curl up into a huffed smile. "I can see why you like it down here. I'm sorry if I'm intruding."

She looked around the room. Behind her, the floor-to-ceiling bookshelf lined the whole wall, filled with books arranged in a faded rainbow. She needed to borrow a new book, but had been too unsure about coming into the space. It seemed to hold too much history for Byron, so she'd done her best to keep it as his own private sanctuary when the craziness of sharing his house with a toddler became a little too much.

"You are always welcome down here, Emory. I should have made that clear sooner."

Byron's hand found her thigh, the weight of his touch spreading through her. She noticed for the first time just how at peace she felt when she was with Byron. Her heart seemed a little lighter, and her shoulders more relaxed. The usual constant pit in her stomach, the feeling like every decision she made was the wrong one, the constant worry over literally everything. It was all gone, replaced with an easy kind of comfort.

She dropped her head to the side, resting on Byron's shoulder. This was what she wanted. She just didn't know how it would work.

"Hey, Byron," she said after a grumbling in her stomach broke the silence between them. "Are we going to run out of food?"

CHAPTER 22

BYRON

Tucker looked fucking ridiculous, paddling his little boat across the flooded valley. Even in the mostly overcast light, the sun reflected off his golden hair and made Byron squint. And from a hundred metres back, Byron could see the wide smirk on his son's face. Byron would never admit it to Tucker, but buying the dinghy was a good call.

Even with all Byron's careful planning, he'd still miscalculated just how much food they would need while they waited out the flood. Clayton snacked like a teenager, and Emory and Byron were burning off more energy than he'd thought they would. They still had pantry staples that could have tied them over a little longer if he needed, but they'd eaten through all the fresh produce, and frozen fruit and veg just wasn't the same. So, Byron had called Tucker for help. It wasn't worth bothering the emergency services, and the floodwater had settled into a relatively still lake that Tucker could easily paddle over.

Byron tapped out his gumboots and slipped them on before stepping ankle deep in the water that spread up the hill towards his humble backyard. Clayton dropped the block he was about to place on his skinny, teetering tower and moved to follow Byron down the hill. He held his hand out to stop the boy.

"Let me help Tuck, then we'll all play. You stay dry."

He expected the young boy to protest, but Miff licked Clayton's hand, stealing his attention. Clayton ran off back up the hill, and Byron watched him go. He heard Emory call out right as she stepped into his line of sight, scooping up Clayton and spinning around. Their laughter floated down the hill and did what it always did. It made Byron smile and made his life feel whole.

"You gonna help me, or you gonna stare off at the forbidden fruit?"

Byron choked. As he turned to face his son, he was sure his cheeks must have been a bright shade of red, for how they burned. He did his best to ignore the comment, stepping further into the water and helping Tucker pull the rowboat onto dry ground.

"I wasn't staring."

Even as he mumbled the words, Byron felt the tips of his ears turn hot. He could blame it on the sun peeking out through the clouds all he wanted, but there was no fooling anyone. Byron was head over bloody heels for Emory because being with her was everything he imagined it might have been and then a million times more.

"How's town?" he asked in a desperately vain attempt to change the subject.

Tucker just scoffed, hoisting a large crate from between the two small bench-style seats in the boat. Fine, if Tucker could ignore Byron's question, then Byron could ignore Tucker's. It was childish, Byron knew it even as he stormed past his son and grabbed the smaller bags from either end of the small boat. They were heavier than he imagined they would be. A lot of weight for a tiny boat, Byron thought. But he supposed Tucker had made it across the water alright, so he'd be fine to make it back once they'd cleared out all the food.

He marched up the hill, carrying the bags and chasing down his adult son. Scoffing and changing the subject aside, there was something he needed to chat about. Byron hadn't *really* given much thought about when he would hand the farm over to his son. It had always felt like some far-off moment that he didn't need to worry about yet. But with each day he was stuck here in the house, Byron felt his love for the farm wear a little thinner.

Truth was, he knew his time was nearly up. This flood had just made that all the more clear, and he finally understood why his old man had called it quits when he did. There was something about *not* having to work on the farm while isolated in the farmhouse that felt almost freeing. His mornings were more relaxed, his afternoons peaceful—even with Clayton's noise—and his evenings were calm. Gone were the aching muscles that left him collapsed on the couch as the night wore on. Instead, his days felt rich and full of life. Not at all the strenuous monotony he'd grown accustomed to.

Now, he was realising that passing the farm to Tucker was no longer some distant future event. It was a reality that was far closer than he had imagined. And surprisingly, he wasn't at all sad about it. He felt a little bad, sure, lumping so much responsibility onto his son. Tucker was no older than Byron had been when he took over, and look how that had ended up. Maybe this whole tradition of keeping the farm in the family was finding its slow end with this generation.

Most of the land had been sold off as the years wore on anyway. The farm Byron had inherited was barely a quarter of the size it used to be. Back when the town was established, you could stand up on the high paddock to look out over the horizon, and all you'd see was Gardner land. But as the years wore on, each generation sold off a little more. Byron's farm was relatively small in comparison to so many others, but he wasn't complaining. It was more than enough for him, and he was willing to bet it would be more than enough for Tucker.

As he passed Clayton and Emory playing with the blocks on the grass, Byron did his best to hold back the wide grin that crept across his face every time he looked at her. He was kidding himself if he thought she wasn't part of the reason his days felt so easy now. That's what scared him the most. The what-ifs that he would never be able to answer.

Like, what if she left town and he was stuck without her, back to his lonely old self, running the farm? Or what if she decided to stay? He wasn't sure which one scared him more. Not having her, or her giving up a part of herself, her dreams, just for him.

He trudged into the house, not realising how far down his shoulders had rolled. It had nothing to do with the weight of the bags he carried and everything to do with the weight of the future. He knew he should talk to her, but every time he tried, his throat jammed up and he just couldn't. Something screamed at him to just enjoy the now and not worry about the future. Because whatever she wanted to do when she finished her degree, it felt as though one of them was going to end up hurt. Or both of them.

In the kitchen, Tucker had already started unloading the crate of fruit and vegetables into the fridge and pantry. The fruit bowl was once again filled, and the crisper was beginning to overflow. Byron rifled through the bags he'd brought in and started making room for everything in the pantry. It was a lot. Far more than he'd told Tucker they would need.

He gruffed, clearing his throat, and was about to tell Tucker to take some of the food back with him, but Tucker cut him off.

"Apparently, Emory told Mya that Clayton is going through a growth spurt; that's why he is eating so much." He closed the fridge and handed Byron a beer. "And the SES said the bridge should be open in a few days, but I don't trust it."

Byron didn't either. The water was still far above the bridge.

"I didn't realise you and Mya were close?"

Tucker took a long sip from his bottle. He drank slowly before looking up at Byron. "She's staying with me. We've already checked, and her house is clear, but only just. The road is still closed."

"She's staying with you?"

"And Emory is staying with you."

Byron scoffed. He moved past Tucker to sit at the table but gave his son a swift kick to the ankle as he passed. "That's different."

"Fuck," Tucker yelped. Reaching down to rub one hand along his ankle, he shifted his grip on the beer bottle to give Byron the finger. "It's not that different. You like Emory, I like Mya. We're all just seeing what a few weeks stuck in a house together does for our relationships."

"Who says Emory and I have a relationship?" Byron did his best to keep his tone light and his demeanour cool. Didn't stop his fingers from picking away the label on his beer, though.

"You just fucking then?"

Byron choked on the sip he'd taken. Frothy bubbles

reached his nose as he did his best not to spit out the mouthful of beer. Tucker dropped his hands to his knees, shaking his head as he cackled.

"Fuck, you are," he spat out between gasping laughs.

"Watch your tone, Tucker," Byron warned, even though he knew he'd never get away with it. He could dad-voice Tucker all he wanted, but ever since he'd left the farm, Tucker had always seemed a little more like a friend than his son. Sure, Byron was still there anytime Tucker needed some fatherly help or advice, but they got along better when Byron let go of his parental persona a little.

"Actually," Tucker added when he finally had his breathing under control. "I really don't want to know."

"So, stop asking."

Tucker pushed off the bench and sat opposite Byron. His elbows propped onto the table, and he swung the near-empty beer between his fingers.

"You know," he started, his eyebrow cocked as he smirked up at Byron, "the thing about living with a chick is that they talk. A lot. And they get emotional."

Byron had a feeling he knew where this was going. He'd been under no illusion that Emory wouldn't have told her best friend about ... well, everything. Her degree, definitely. The fact they'd finally given in to the temptation they'd both apparently been holding back for a while now? Probably. At least it seemed that way after the conversation he'd overheard the end of.

He didn't respond to Tucker's jest. Figured he'd call on his right to remain silent.

"You want to know what has her so worked up, she ends up crying most days?"

Well, that was unexpected. Byron downed the last dregs of his beer and got up to pull a second from the fridge. He grabbed one for Tucker without asking, dropping it onto the table before sitting back down.

"Emory's thinking of leaving."

Ouch. Byron knew that was on the cards for her, but he also knew that what they had was *something*.

"According to Mya, Jaxon is kicking Emory out of the cottage. She said there's no point finding a new rental when she might move to the city in a few months anyway. As soon as the flood's down, Emory is going to start looking at somewhere to go."

Byron rolled his shoulders forward and slouched into his chair. He dropped his head against the table, no longer caring if Tucker saw just how deeply this cut him. All this time, he'd been wondering if she would stay here once Jaxon kicked her out, and she'd been planning her exit. He should have done something sooner, made sure she knew just how much he cared for her long before she even thought about leaving.

"She can't leave." He meant to say more, he wanted to say more, but the grating sound of the back door sliding open cut him off.

Emory carried Clayton inside, kicking her shoes into the bucket before pulling Clayton's off. Byron jolted upright in his seat and took a long swig of his beer. The frothy liquid did nothing to ease the lump in his throat, but he was starting to suspect it was becoming permanent.

Clayton ran for Tucker as soon as Emory let him on the ground and climbed into his uncle's open arms. When he reached for Tucker's beer, Emory moved it to the centre of the table and dropped a red water bottle in its place.

"There's a bag of stuff for you on the counter," Tucker told her. "Smells fruity and fresh. Mya said you'd appreciate them?"

"My candles," Emory squealed. She dropped her nose

into the bag sitting on the bench, inhaling deeply with her eyes closed. "Ever since I finished the one Byron bought, I've been dying to try the other scents. Please tell her thank you."

Tucker's eyes widened, and he kicked Byron under the table. Byron gave his head a sharp shake and kicked him back.

"So ..." Oblivious to their silent berating, Emory moved back to the table with a grin. She shoved her hip against Tucker's arm when he didn't respond. Byron watched as she tried to get Tucker's attention, poking his arm and humming loudly.

"Ugh." She gave up, dropping into the seat next to him. "How's Mya?"

Tucker ignored the inflection in her question. "She's fine. Didn't you just talk to her last night?"

"Yes, but I want to know what *you* think."

This, Byron realised, was one of the many things he loved about Emory. The friendly banter she could get in with just about anybody. He loved it most when it was directed at him, but Tucker was a close second. There was nothing romantic or lustful about how Emory and Tucker got along. They were family, that was all. He watched her jab at his arm, waiting for him to give in. His chest pulled toward her, but the reality of what Tucker had said began to sink into his bones.

He loved her, but she was thinking about leaving town.

There was no time to dwell, though, not while Tucker was still here at least. Because his own troubles aside, Byron was curious how things were going with Mya and Tucker. He hadn't even known Tucker liked the reserved librarian, let alone that they were close enough for her to move in during the flood.

"Okay, okay. Fuck, stop. I mean, fudge." Tucker cowered behind Clayton, hiding from Emory's persistent poking. He covered Clayton's ears, as though that could stop the boy from hearing what he'd said a minute ago.

Byron felt the weight in his shoulders easing a fraction. "Clayton, why don't you go build a racetrack for the trucks? We'll play once Tuck heads home?"

Wriggling in Tucker's lap, Clayton refused. His mop of sandy hair fell to his face, but he blew it away with a sloppy exhale.

"I go on the boat?" he asked.

Tucker and Byron looked to Emory, who glared between them. "I should have known he would ask that." She sighed as she settled her gaze on Tucker. "I have his swim vest packed somewhere. Do you think it would be safe enough?"

"If you're comfortable with it, sure. We can stay close."

Emory nodded and reached out to tuck Clayton's hair back off his face. He looked up at his mother with soft eyes, and his lower lip poked out.

"Go play while Tuck finishes his drink. Then you can go on the boat, okay?"

A grin as bright as the summer sun spread across Clayton's face as he clapped. Tucker shifted the boy off his lap, and Clayton toddled off toward the toys spread around the living room.

Byron watched the whole interaction with a wide grin of his own. He couldn't shake the feeling of how right this was. Emory's presence had done more than just soften Byron's heart. She'd embedded herself into their family and engraved her name on his chest. It was going to hurt if she left. When she left. Because the more he sat there in his feelings, the more he realised she would. She'd have to, and he didn't blame her in the slightest.

Tucker's deep sigh caught his attention, and Byron shook his shoulders out. Tension was building again.

"Mya is good," Tucker said. "We just ... it's been tough. My house is as isolated as here right now, and for a while, there was no point even heading out on the boat because everything in town was closed anyway. Being stuck together probably wasn't what we needed right away."

He downed the last of his drink and dropped his head between his hands on the table. Byron leant forward in his seat, too far to provide any real comfort, but Emory placed a hand on Tucker's shoulder.

"You really like her?" she asked.

Tucker's whole upper body moved with his nod.

"She likes you, too. Okay, it's been rough. But she'll go home soon, and everything will be back to normal. You can go about starting a relationship the right way."

"What if she doesn't want that?"

"She will."

Tucker looked up at Emory then, and even from across the table, Byron could see the glisten in his eyes. Byron had no idea Tucker was so invested in his relationship with Mya, but it made him proud.

Emory nodded at Tucker, and he did the same. A short, quick movement before sitting up straight in his chair. He slapped away the moisture on his cheeks and crossed his arms over his chest. Damn boys and their emotions, Byron thought, even though he was exactly the same.

CHAPTER 23

EMORY

In the days that followed Tucker's emergency food supply trip, the water slowly began to recede. First, Emory noticed the mud on the ground by the second chicken coop became less sludgy. Then the trunks of the fruit trees that lined the back of Byron's backyard space came into view.

A few days later, the smell hit. Wet grass, soggy mud, and the dank scent of moss filled the air. Emory started lighting the candles Tucker had brought as soon as she woke each morning, but the subtle aroma did nothing to clean the air. Byron didn't seem fazed by it, and Clayton probably hadn't even noticed. But Emory held her breath as often as she could.

The bridge was still closed, but by the fourth day of receding water and no more rain on the forecast, it became clear that their period of isolation was, finally, coming to a close. It caused a pang in Emory's chest she hadn't been expecting. As it turned out, being trapped in a house with Byron had been so much better than she had imagined. She didn't spend her days hopelessly trying not to feel her raging attraction to Byron, and she didn't spend her nights lying in bed, on edge and unable to sleep due to the pulsing tension in her core that ached for release. No. Instead, she spent her days and nights in some kind of lust-filled bliss. She could gaze longingly at Byron as often as she wanted and not fear being caught out. Because all the times he did see her staring, he went right on and stared back. They shared affectionate touches and passion-filled glances, and every chance they got, they shared more too.

They'd fallen into the perfect rhythm, and Emory didn't want it to end.

She sat, staring out the study window, willing herself to focus on her revision. With the receding water came the notice of her final exams. She still hadn't brought it up with Byron, even though she knew she had to. But the truth was, she was scared. Her heart wanted her to stay, but her brain wanted to go, and she felt like no matter what decision she finally came to, she was going to get hurt.

Looking down at the giant tome in front of her, the words swam. Something about marketing and target audiences, but nothing that stood out as crucial anyway. She slammed the book shut, giving up for the day. Maybe she needed some fresh air, even if it would smell like a grotty swamp out there.

Blowing out the candle she'd lit earlier, Emory tugged her zip-up hoodie back over her shoulders. Clayton's gentle lullaby rang out down the hall, so she tiptoed in the other direction with her fingers crossed. Byron had done so much for her while they'd been stuck here. He kept Clayton entertained every morning while she studied, putting him down for a nap whenever he needed one. Emory would emerge from the study once Clayton was asleep, thankful she wasn't the one to fight the battle that day.

Today was no different, only Byron wasn't fixing them both a warm drink in the kitchen when Emory walked in. He wasn't there at all. She supposed maybe he'd gone to the den. Maybe he wanted a moment alone? He hadn't before, and the thought was like a nail chipping into Emory's temple. She hesitated, turning back and forth in the kitchen, trying to decide if she should go down there and see. If Byron *did* want to be alone, she couldn't take that from him. And she shouldn't really blame him for it either. They'd spent so much time together over the past two weeks, and maybe he just really wanted to get to the end of that book he'd been reading.

It would probably do Emory some good to spend a bit of time alone, too. Although she'd spent plenty of it, every morning, in the study, none of her time had been really hers. She'd been too focused on studying—mostly—to let her mind wander. And she did have some big decisions to make after all.

Fresh air, she finally decided. Well, stinky air, but outside all the same.

She grabbed her earphones from the little tray on the bench, stepped out onto the porch, and pulled her gumboots from the crate. Dropping the lid down, she used it as a stool while she tapped them out and pulled them on. All the little things that had become habit since she'd moved to Gardner Creek. Keeping lids closed so snakes couldn't get in, tapping out your shoes to check for spiders. If she moved back to the city, she wouldn't have to worry about any of it.

But she wouldn't be with Byron.

Fuck, that's what she always came back to, every time

she tried to imagine herself finally moving on from this tiny outback town. She wouldn't be with Byron.

With a huff, Emory stood and marched past Betty, still tied to the pergola, and down the yard towards the chicken coops. She wasn't sure what drove her, but she had a need for physical labour she couldn't explain. On her way past the shed, she grabbed a shovel and a wheelbarrow. Hens clucked from the largest coop. They were squished in there, but it had been necessary to keep them all safe and dry. Now that the lower coop was clear of water, she might as well start cleaning it out for them. Sticking her earbuds into her ears, she played the best noughties playlist she could find and got to work.

The ground inside the coop was caked in mud. Emory wasn't sure if there was supposed to be grass underneath it, but when she cleared the top layer, all she found was more sludge. She kept working, though, until the muddy ground was level and the wheelbarrow was full. Her back strained as she hefted the wheelbarrow back out of the coop. She hadn't thought this through.

What exactly was one to do with a wheelbarrow of swampy dirt?

Emory tipped her head up to the sky and huffed out a deep sigh. She wouldn't be able to steer the heavy barrow very far, even if she did know what to do with its contents. Resigned, she tipped it out into a small pile between the coops. That would do, for now at least.

Back inside the coop, she had to crouch to enter the henhouse. Mud lined the wooden floor, and Emory got to work scraping it away and reloading the wheelbarrow. It was harder work than outside, but she welcomed the way her arms burned with each scrape of the shovel.

The physical labour helped to clear her head, and even though she was in a dim, smelly henhouse, she found the clarity that she had been hoping for. She could do this kind of work for a moment. Clear out the henhouse as a small token of her thanks to Byron for letting them stay. But it was not at all how she imagined herself spending the rest of her life.

She'd come to this town on Jaxon's arm, hoping she would finally find her place in the world here in Gardner Creek. But she didn't. Because, she knew now, it wasn't where she belonged. All her life, she'd followed people around. Her parents as they hopped from major city to major city, then Jaxon here to this rural community. She couldn't follow Byron to the farm any more than she could expect Byron to follow her to the city. Sometimes people's lives just took different trajectories. They belonged in different places.

It was a hard fucking pill to swallow and left her gasping for breath. But it was the truth. She had to pursue her dreams in the city. It wasn't fair to herself if she didn't.

Something a little like hope still flickered in the back of her mind, though, no matter how hard she tried to snuff it out. It still pondered on the what-ifs.

Like, what if she didn't get a job? Was she really *meant* to be in the city if she spent her time there struggling to make ends meet or back working in some little café just to pay the bills?

She didn't know the answers, but she knew there was only one way to find out. She had to try, at least.

Pulling out her phone, she paused her music and logged in to her university email. With a few taps, she opened the first of many draft emails she'd written the day after she submitted her final assignment. One by one, she sent each one off. Emails to all of Sydney's biggest marketing firms, complete with her CV and whatever graduate application form she could find on the website.

With each little *whoosh* from her phone, she grew more confident in her decision. Putting herself out there, and the thought of moving to the city, still scared the hell out of her, but it felt right to be taking another step towards her dream. Once they were all sent, she stared down at her phone as though waiting for a response. That was silly, she knew. Most firms would take a few weeks to get back to her, at least.

She shook her head, laughing a little at herself. The ringing of her phone shocked her, so much so that she nearly dropped it onto the grubby floor. She fumbled for it, swiping to answer without looking at who was calling.

"Hello, Emory speaking," she chirped, *just* in case it was one of the marketing firms.

Mya's laugh boomed through the phone. "What the fuck," she cackled. "I've never heard you sound so ... prissy."

Groaning at her friend, Emory connected the call to her wireless earbuds and shoved her phone into her pocket. There was only a small section of floor left to clear, then she supposed she should look for some hay.

"I thought maybe you were a marketing firm."

Mya snorted, but Emory's silence must have told her it wasn't a joke, because she corrected herself. "Oh, you're serious? I didn't realise you'd started applying."

"Yep, today though, so the chances were slim it actually was one of them." Her breath heaved as she shovelled another heap of mud into the wheelbarrow. "What's up?"

"Wait, what are you doing? Why are you all breathy? Are you ... Oh, fuck, don't tell me."

"Mya, chill, I'm cleaning out the chicken coop. There's mud everywhere."

She could almost hear the way Mya froze. "You? Doing hard labour?"

With the old wooden floor now clear, Emory dropped the shovel and hoisted up the back of the wheelbarrow. Mya was right, Emory and hard labour didn't normally mesh well. This had been therapeutic, though, and Emory wondered if that's why so many people enjoyed physical work as much as they did. Endorphins or something, maybe. She waited until she had steered her load out of the coop and tipped it out onto her little pile of dirt before answering Mya.

"I felt like I needed to help, that's all. But it's shit. I'm not doing it again." The women shared a little giggle before Emory added, "I was made to sit at a desk, clearly."

"You'll be great at it," Mya mused, her voice trailing off at the thought. They both knew what Emory's career ambitions meant for her living situation, and neither was ready to voice how much they would miss each other. Emory supposed she could come visit. It would be good for Clayton to still have a relationship with Byron and Tucker—they were his family, after all—and Emory could stock up on her best friend's book recommendations and comforting hugs.

"Anyways," she remembered, "what did you call for?"

"Oh, ha. You spoke to Tucker."

Emory gulped. Was she not meant to? She stammered, trying to find a response.

"It's okay. It's good, actually. The roads opened today, so I'll go back to my place, and we agreed to start from scratch. Being so isolated was ... not great, but I think we both realised it doesn't mean we won't work long term. Tucker just needs to learn not to leave the toilet seat up or use all the hot water."

"So, the two of you are ...?" Emory felt herself smiling. Tucker was like family to her. Mya, too. Knowing the two of them were becoming something filled Emory with a special kind of proud joy.

"I think we are, Emory." A moment of silence passed as Emory made her way to the shed in search of hay for the coop.

"Hey, Emory." Mya's voice was soft and crackled through the patchy reception around the far side of the house. "What about Byron?"

Emory closed her eyes. "That's what I'm trying to figure out."

CHAPTER 24

BYRON

Sneaking out of Clayton's room after the boy was finally asleep, Byron had expected to find Emory curled up on the couch. Or still in the study, getting ready for her exams. But the house had been empty when he made his way down the hall. He'd even risked tiptoeing back down the hallway to check the den.

Byron felt worry creep along his spine when he couldn't find her. It shouldn't have been this hard, considering they were still surrounded by water in all directions. The bridge was still closed. She couldn't have left, but she wasn't *here*. He froze in the kitchen, unsure of what to do next. His pulse throbbed at his temple as he got a glass of water to try to quell the growing dryness on his tongue. The window above the kitchen sink looked out over the far side of his yard, past the chicken coops and into the fields below. The water was barely halfway up the side of the hill now and was draining more and more every day. It looked still, but Byron knew floodwater could be unpredictable. If Emory had fallen in, there was every chance an undercurrent had swept her away. The thought clawed at Byron until he couldn't breathe.

He'd call her. He didn't need to panic until he knew he needed to panic. If she didn't answer, then he could let the fear wash over him. But his pockets were empty, and his phone wasn't in the little dish on the side of the bench. He couldn't remember where he'd left it.

Movement out the back window caught his eye, and he spun back around to see Emory emerge from the smaller henhouse with a wheelbarrow full of mud. It swayed under her grip, but she directed it around the fence and tipped it over in the wide gap between the two coops.

His heart stopped pounding, and his ears began to ring as the adrenaline began to wear down. She was … cleaning the chicken coop. It was the very last place he ever would have imagined finding her. Emory was so far from being a country girl, he doubted she'd ever pushed a wheelbarrow around, let alone cleaned up after a flood. But there she was in gumboots and leggings that hugged her curves so perfectly. She'd rolled the sleeves of her grey zip-up hoodie up above her elbows and left the zip undone, revealing that same pink lace tank that had been engraved in Byron's brain. Out of everything she wore, that was his favourite. The way the lace revealed her cleavage both tugged at his heart and had his balls drawing tight.

Emory stormed away with the now-empty wheelbar-row, off past the chicken coops. The only thing down that way was the hay shed. Byron watched her go, an unusual desire rolling through his bones. Emory looked good working on the farm. Nah, more than that. She looked downright fucking stunning with mud on her boots and her sweaty hair clinging to the back of her neck. He wanted to race after her and show her just how perfectly she fit in here, but something held him back.

He reached for the baby monitor on the bench and turned it on. Clayton was still sound asleep in his bed, and he'd probably stay that way for another hour. Byron swallowed down the hesitation and grabbed his boots from by the door.

It wasn't Clayton that had held him back, it was the thought that no matter how much Emory could look the part here on the farm, it wasn't what she'd ever wanted for herself. Tucker's warning rang in his ears, but he ignored it. He wanted Emory, and she needed to know exactly how much.

She was trying to haul a bale of hay into the wheelbarrow when he caught up to her in the shed. To her credit, she'd grabbed the smallest bale of them all, but it still toppled over the wheelbarrow, too big to fit in the tub. From his spot by the door, Byron could see the small white headphones in her ears, and he hung back, appreciating the way she swung her hips to whatever boppy tune was playing.

He glanced down at the monitor in his hands, still in range and still showing a peacefully sleeping toddler. A little sigh of relief and anticipation escaped him as he dropped the small display screen onto the shelving unit.

Emory continued wrestling the hay bale, not noticing as he moved in behind her. When he slipped his arms around her waist, she gasped but sank into his touch. Byron removed her earbuds, tucking them into his jacket pocket. He nibbled the soft pad of skin below her ear.

"You look good," he whispered.

She turned around, wrapping her arms around his neck and pulling up onto her toes. "You always look good."

Byron kissed Emory all slow and tender at first. A peck to her nose, another to the corner of her mouth, one up on her forehead. He wanted to take his time because for all he knew, this could be the last. The water was going down, and even though the burning attraction they shared was ever increasing, no flood meant life would go back to normal. Emory would leave. She'd find somewhere else to live. In town, maybe, or further away, most likely. He didn't want to think about it, not yet. For now, he just wanted to experience her. All of her.

Crashing his lips against hers, he let temptation and desire take over. He gripped her cheek, tilting her head and coaxing her mouth open with his tongue. She obliged, moaning into his mouth and stepping into his embrace.

He guided them backwards, pulling her jacket off her shoulders first, then his own. Emory's legs hit the low stack of hay bales against the wall of the shed, but Byron held her steady while he placed his jacket over the straw. Still holding her mouth with his own, Byron lifted Emory under her legs and dropped her onto his jacket. He leant over her as he lay her down, still giving everything in his kiss. Emory took it all, holding him close and pulling his lower lip into her mouth.

Byron's bones ached with arousal. Heat spread between them until he couldn't handle the suspense. He pressed into Emory, grinding his erection against her. There was too much between them, and it hurt. Byron kissed his way down her body, pulling one breast—lace tank and all—into his mouth. Reaching between them, he unbuttoned his jeans and then tugged at her leggings. Emory lifted her hips, and Byron dropped to his knees in front of her. He took his time pulling her pants to her ankles. She wriggled to kick them off, but he held her still.

"Keep them there," he drawled. His voice had never been so deep and guttural, but the sound made Emory whimper, and that was enough for Byron.

He ducked under her legs, spreading her knees and wrapping her ankles around his head. If he had thought she was a sight earlier … he had no fucking idea what this was. Her pussy glistened, begging him closer. So much for taking his time.

Emory moaned when his mouth made contact with her clit. There was nothing gentle about the way he devoured her. He ran his tongue along her seam, then swirled it around the bundle of nerves. It made her squirm, and he enjoyed every fucking second of it. With her clit between his teeth, Byron pushed two fingers inside her. She stretched for him easily, already so wet and ready for more.

Pumping his fingers in and out of her, he curled them up to stroke her inner wall. Emory's mouth dropped open with a breathy gasp. Her legs began to shudder around Byron's shoulders, just the way he liked it. As her pleasure grew, Emory began to move her hips into Byron's face. Her ankles held him close, even though he had no intention of going anywhere.

"Take what you need, Em," he growled against her, never fully taking his mouth off her cunt.

And she did. She ground her hips against Byron's face, forcing his fingers deeper. His teeth grazed against her clit as Emory's release came hard. Her legs constricted around him, and her inner walls began to flutter around his fingers. He slowed his pace, pumping slowly and lapping her up until she finally stilled.

Byron reached below his waist, freeing his aching dick from his jeans. He stood, still trapped between her legs, and leant over Emory to run his length through her wetness. Fuck, it felt good. Fuck, it would be so easy to just slip right in and feel her, properly. He wanted to. Every bone in his body begged him to.

Pulling her up, Byron held Emory close as she caught her breath. He kissed her, moaning as she bit his lip and reached between them. Her fingers on his dick were like heaven. Almost. He could think of something even better, but he hadn't thought this far ahead when he chased her out here.

Emory pumped his cock in her hand, directing him towards her cunt. One little thrust, that's all it would take …

"I didn't bring a—"

"I don't care."

"Em, that's—"

"Silly, I know. But you can pull out. And Clayton was an … anomaly … I have polycystic ovaries, the chance of me getting pregnant is really low. Please."

Well, fuck, if she was asking nicely.

Byron thrust into her, and just as he suspected, he slid right in. Emory gasped, but her body adjusted to Byron's length. He paused, part waiting until she was ready and part making sure he wasn't going to blow his load too soon. Fucking Emory was always incredible. But fucking Emory raw, it was something else. Byron couldn't remember anything ever feeling this amazing.

"You're fucking perfect, you know that?"

She didn't answer. Wrapping her arms around his neck, Emory slammed their mouths together. This time, their kiss was wild and frenzied. A tangle of lips and teeth and tongues. Emory rocked her hips into Byron.

"Move, please," she moaned into his mouth.

Something rumbled from Byron's chest. "Perfect. Fucking. Manners." He slammed into her with every word.

They moved in sync, using each other as they headed

towards a fierce peak. Byron reached between them, pressing his thumb against her clit. Emory's head dropped back as her release tore through her. The fluttering of her walls on his dick tipped Byron over the edge. He felt his balls draw up and yanked out of her, spilling his seed into his hand.

Emory had dropped back onto her shoulders. Her chest heaved, and her mouth hung open, but there was a glint to her face.

"Maybe I should work on the farm more often," she said with a smirk.

Byron closed his eyes. Fuck.

"You can't," he grumbled, turning towards the old tap in the corner.

The water was icy cold, and there was barely any pressure left in the pipes, but it was enough to wash his hands. He splashed a little water over his face for good measure, then adjusted himself and pulled up his pants.

He turned back to Emory with what he hoped was a sorrowful expression. Her face was down, chin practically on her chest as she pulled her leggings back over her waist. She didn't look up when he stepped in front of her.

"Emory, look at me, please."

For a moment, he thought she wouldn't. She searched the ground for her hoodie, wrapping her arms around her middle. When she looked up, there were tears in her eyes.

"What are we going to do, Byron?"

He bit his lip. He had been meaning to ask her the exact same thing. "I don't want you to go," he admitted. "But you can't stay. You've worked too damn hard to throw away your degree just to work on an old farm with me."

"But I don't want to be without you."

Byron wrapped his arms around her and kissed the top of her head. Her hair was loose in its ponytail, and he sank into it. Coconut, he realised. And lime. It must have been her shampoo, but the smell was comforting. He soaked it in.

"I don't want to be without you either, Em."

Chapter 25

Emory

Emory was still reeling over, well, everything when Byron woke her up for breakfast the following morning. She'd barely been able to sleep, worried about the potential implications of what they'd done in the hay shed. It had been, to be frank, unbelievably fucking mind-blowing. Something extra had charged through them, and she'd been so swept up in the moment, she'd done something she didn't want to regret.

She hadn't lied to Byron, but there was always going to be a slim chance. Her overconfidence in her diagnosis had failed her once before—even though she considered Clayton her best mistake. With everything between her and Byron as fresh as it was, the last thing she wanted was to end up forced into a decision. Again.

She'd said as much to Byron last night. He'd reached across the bed and pulled her into his chest, kissing the top of her head and running his fingers along the length of her arm. Without telling her they didn't matter, he'd held her fears and promised they'd figure something out. That no matter what happened, it would be okay. For the most part, she'd believed him, but the fear gnawed at her from deep inside her chest.

In any other situation, it was an easy fix. Not an ideal one by any means, but only a quick trip to the pharmacy and an embarrassing form to fill out. But last Emory checked, unless they called Tucker to bring his boat back, they still couldn't leave Gardner Farm.

At least that's what she'd thought.

She yawned as she shuffled into the kitchen. Her arms spread wide over her head as she stretched out the kink that lying on the couch for an hour or more always gave her. The feasts of previous mornings were, apparently, no longer. Toast replaced hashbrowns, the eggs were scrambled instead of perfectly poached. But the bacon was just as crispy and delicious, so Emory wasn't about to complain. She'd gotten used to being woken up with a five-star breakfast feast, but she couldn't expect Byron to cook every morning. Especially now that more of the farm was clearing. Her work in the chicken coop yesterday had barely scratched the surface of the clean-up required, now the flood was receding.

"So ..." Byron took a long pause, as if mustering up the courage to talk. "I figured out the solution to our ... ah ... potential issue."

Emory choked on her coffee. She did her best to swallow down the hot drink instead of letting it dribble onto her plate. Beside her, Clayton snorted with laughter at her. His bacon was gone, gobbled up the moment he had sat in the chair. "Eat your eggs," Emory told him.

Turning back to Byron, her eyes were wide as she raised her eyebrows. "Go on."

"The bridge is clear. The SES bollard is still there, but they probably have a million other things to do and know I can move it myself. We can go to town." Byron took a bite of his toast. Under the table, Emory felt his foot move against hers. "To the pharmacy," he added.

She should have been more excited about it, but all Emory could think about was the implications of the road being clear. They were free. And, okay, the timing was some kind of perfect hug from the universe, but it meant everything was about to change.

"I'll head down after breakfast," she said once the reality had sunk in. "I'll return all the toys and books from the library, and I should probably check the cottage ..." She let her thoughts trail off, wanting to see Byron's reaction at the mention of her old house.

A deep line formed between his brows, and a distinct grunt escaped him. "The cottage will be fine. I'll send Tucker to check it out first. We'll go get what we need and be back before Clayton needs a nap."

We?

Emory shook her head. He didn't need to come. This whole thing was her doing and she could think of a hundred things she'd rather do than buy the morning after pill from the pharmacy, where everyone knew her name and her business. Most likely, they'd all figure out why she needed it and who the other party was, anyway. Byron being there wasn't going to change that outcome, but it was going to make things a hell of a lot more awkward.

"You don't need to come," she said with a shrug. Her eggs, despite being cooked to perfection, began to churn in her stomach. She pushed them around the plate. "Everyone will know, I mean, they probably will anyway, but if we rock up in town together, it will just confirm all the rumours and people will talk. They always talk. I can get whatever you need while I'm there."

"Let them talk." Byron had pushed his chair back to stand over the table. He frowned down at Emory, but there was something unusually soft behind his harsh demeanour. "This was my mistake, too, Emory. Let me help fix it."

Emory started to protest, but Byron cut her off, rapping his knuckles against the hardwood of the table. Clayton copied him, standing in his chair. Emory tugged him back down and turned to Byron. Her mouth dropped open as she began to protest, but Byron held up a hand.

"Let. Them. Talk." He drawled out each word, deep golden-brown eyes staring directly into Emory's soul. "I don't care if every gossiping woman in town is dragging on and on about it. I *want* people to know about us, Emory. I want there to be an us worth talking about."

His tone dropped with his final sentence, along with his body. He sank back into his chair and let his head fall forward. "But if you don't want that, I'll stay here."

"Byron, *is* there an us worth talking about?"

"If there's not, I'm really damn hung up on something that I shouldn't want." He looked up again, leaning his elbows on the table and supporting his head with his hands. Something like sorrow filled his expression.

"Let's go to town," Emory said. She was certain her cheeks would glow red the whole way there, but she was pretty hung up, too. Who cared what other people thought? Sure, she did, but she cared more about Byron than the opinions of nasty gossips anyway.

The pharmacy, thankfully, was all but empty when they arrived, manned only by the old pharmacist who owned the small store and his wife. They'd been perfectly respectful, hardly blinking twice when Emory asked for what she needed. Byron held Clayton on his hip, wandering the aisles and pointing out random colours, while Emory filled out the form. After they paid and returned to the car, she swallowed the little pill dry.

Relief washed over her as she felt it sink down her throat. One dilemma over. The bigger one remained, though, the actual one, not the almost one. By the time Byron pulled into the near-deserted parking lot in front of the community library, dread had filled Emory back to the brim. She still had no idea what she was going to do, but she hoped Mya would be able to talk some sense into her. She hadn't been sure the library would be open and had texted Mya before they packed all the borrowed toys and books into the car. The voice message she had received almost instantly practically begged Emory to come down.

Clayton ran towards Mya as soon as Emory let go of his hand inside the library. For a long time, Mya had been the only good thing left in Gardner Creek. She was the closest thing Clayton had to an aunty. It was always going to be hard leaving her behind when Emory moved to the city, but the thought of it, on top of everything else, was just another weight over Emory's already hurting shoulders.

With a deep sigh, she swung her tote full of books onto Mya's little desk and began dropping each one under the returns scanner. It took Byron two trips to bring in all the toys. Mya had taken Clayton over to the kids' corner and was reading him a story, but she watched Byron intently. Emory could feel her piercing gaze darting between the unlikely couple.

Once everything—right down to the very last purple truck—had been scanned back into the library catalogue, Byron let his hand drop onto the small of Emory's back. He brushed his thumb along her spine, leaving a tingling feeling. Without a word, he moved over to the bean bag beside Mya and dropped into it. Clayton climbed onto his lap.

"Papa read," he said, his tiny, grabby hands reaching for the book Mya still held.

She gave Byron the book and stood. The whole interaction could have been from a silent movie, but there was so much unsaid in the room that all three adults seemed to understand. Mya had picked up on it as soon as she realised Byron had come into town with Emory, and she seemed itching to discuss it.

Emory protested her shoves, but eventually gave in and allowed Mya to steer her towards one of the small study nooks in the far corner.

"Did you hear from any of those jobs?" Mya asked as soon as they were seated at opposite sides of the desk.

Emory dropped her head to the table. The laminate coating was cool on her forehead. "No, but it's still early. They might not even look at applications until after Christmas."

"Did you decide what you're going to do if you get one of them?"

"Also no."

"Because you're too busy playing happy family?"

Emory shifted her head, lifting up and dropping her chin onto the table so she could glare at her friend. There was a glimmer in Mya's eyes, a twinkle in her smile that evaporated all of Emory's resolve. She sat up, pulling at the sleeves of her cardigan.

"I'm not pretending to be happy, Mya. I am the happiest I've felt in a very long time. And it scares the shit out of me because I don't think there is any way this can go that doesn't end up in some kind of heartbreak." Pressing her palms into her yes, Emory took a long breath. "What do I do?"

"Do you want comfort or advice right now?"

"Can I have both?"

Mya placed a hand on Emory's elbow. "Not really, but I'll try?"

A tear Emory hadn't noticed forming escaped down her cheek.

"The comfort is that you're choosing between two really wonderful situations, you just need to look at them separately, right? You've been working on your degree for more than three years, and you've been planning on getting a city marketing job for most of that time. When you get an offer, if you take it, you'll be achieving that dream."

Emory released a shaky sigh.

"And if you decide to stay here, with Byron? It'll be because you found love. Real love, not the bullshit Jaxon had you believing in. And that's not something everybody gets to experience."

Mya sounded like a well-lived old lady, even though she was only a few years older than Emory. Maybe acting as pseudo-therapist to half the town who needed a judge-ment-free space and found it in the library was rubbing off on her.

"But I want both those things. I want a job that I love in a place that I love, but I also want the man that I love, and I wish I could have it all, but I can't. I have to make a choice, and I'll never know what the right one is." Emory's voice was barely a whisper. She was so cautious of the silent, echoey library, and the last thing she needed was for Byron to overhear. When she finally told him she loved him, she didn't want it to be because he overheard her mention it during her debriefing session with Mya. She also didn't want him overhearing just how far away she was thinking of moving. It was hard enough with him thinking she would move out once the cottage was clear, she couldn't handle the heartbreak she was sure to see behind his eyes if he found out her dreams were set in the city.

"You do love him?"

"Of course I love him, Mya. He is ... everything. Gentle and kind and generous and protective and probably the most quietly caring person I've ever met. He cooks me breakfast and does everything he can to support my dreams, even though I'm sure he knows if I follow them, it might break both our hearts. The past two weeks, he has done nothing but put me first. So, fuck, I feel selfish for even thinking about leaving him. It eats at me, knowing that I've fallen in love with him when my dreams are going to tear us apart."

She was sobbing, big, ugly tears pooling onto the table. Every bone in her body ached, and there was nothing she could do to stop the pain.

Laughter echoed through the room. Clayton's squealing giggles matched with a deep timber from Byron. Their joy only served to hurt her more.

"I have to try, though," she admitted through sobs. "I can't give away my hopes and dreams for another man. Byron is different, I know that with every fibre of my being, but it wouldn't be fair to *me* if I dropped everything for him. I'd always wonder if I was meant for more than this town." As she drew in deep, shaky breaths, Mya moved to sit next to her on the small bench seat. Emory leaned her head down onto Mya's shoulder, finding a little comfort in her friend's embrace.

"I think you won't really know what you want until you've tried all your options."

Mya was right, trying was the very least Emory needed

to do. If she *did* manage to find the perfect job in the city, she'd work it out then. She wiped her cheeks with the rough sleeve of her knitted jumper, and on the inside, she built a tiny, cushioned wall around her heart. She deserved to give herself a proper chance at her dreams, and if she was going to do that, she needed to make sure her heart stopped falling.

Never mind the fact that it had already fallen all the way into Byron's arms.

CHAPTER 26

BYRON

The lack of gossiping busybodies in town had surprised Byron. He couldn't say he wasn't thankful for it, though. The way he felt about Emory hadn't changed since the morning, and he still wanted the world to know about it, but there was something painful in her eyes as they had left the library. She'd gone off to chat with her best friend and come back sad.

Byron had felt a sudden urge to kiss all her pain away, but over Emory's shoulder, he'd seen Mya, arms folded, shake her head.

"Give her time," she'd said as Byron followed Emory and Clayton out towards the car.

He had no idea what that meant, but he kept both hands on the steering wheel the whole way home. No matter how much he wanted to drop his hand onto Emory's leg or wrap his fingers around hers.

As far as he could tell, he had two options here, and neither of them sounded overly appealing. He could back off, give Emory space as she figured out what she wanted. Or he could sit her down and demand she talk to him. The last thing he wanted to do was anything that might make her decision harder, but he didn't know which was the lesser of two evils.

In the driveway, Emory unbuckled Clayton from his car seat and carried the sleeping boy into the house. Byron hoped Clayton wouldn't protest when Emory tried to settle him into bed.

He stacked the two crates of toys and books and carried them to the house. Most of the books were for Clayton, so he lined them up on the shelf underneath the coffee table and left the handful of novels on the kitchen bench. The covers were all bright with floral accents and matching fonts. It was a series, he figured, but he couldn't work out which was meant to be first. He flipped the blue one over in his hands, skimming the blurb. A grumpy farmer and a much younger city girl ... This story was starting to sound a little familiar, and he wondered if that's why Emory wanted to read it.

It didn't matter, though; Emory could read whatever she wanted. Byron hadn't read many romance books, but from the few he had, he was certain the farmer and the city girl would go on to live happily ever after in the end. Maybe it would help convince Emory that they could, too.

Still lost in his thoughts, Byron didn't hear the crunching of gravel on the driveway or Emory's rushed footsteps as she raced down the hall. He didn't notice anything was happening until the front door slammed open and a voice he hadn't heard in a long while bellowed through the house.

"Dad!"

Emory hushed him, but her pleas to keep the noise down went ignored. Dropping the book on the counter, Byron stormed through the house towards his eldest son.

"Jaxon," he warned. "You need to lower your voice."

He moved forward, placing himself between Jaxon and Emory. She stepped around him until they stood side by side. Together, they formed something of a blockade, preventing Jaxon from moving into the house. The door still hung open behind him. He shuffled his feet, head dropping for a second before he puffed out his chest and looked between them.

"What are you doing here?" he snapped, settling his gaze on Emory.

That deep protectiveness stirred in Byron. He curled his fingers into a fist by his sides. He would not punch his son. *He would not punch his son.*

He wanted to, though. How dare Jaxon turn on Emory with such a judgemental tone as though he wasn't the one kicking her out of her home? A deep growl rolled through his chest. Emory's fingers wrapped around his wrist, sending a warmth through Byron. The beast didn't retreat, it was still ready to roar if Jaxon so much as *looked* at Emory in the wrong way, but her touch had tamed it somehow.

"It's not your business," Emory stated coolly.

She'd taken off the green knitted jumper she'd worn to town, revealing another of her tight, lacy tanks. Byron took her in, hating that Jaxon got to see her like this.

Jaxon's eyes dropped between them to where Emory still held Byron's hand in her own. Her small fingers wrapped around his fist so tightly her knuckles were turning white. Byron began to suspect the hold was just as much to calm herself as it was for him.

Jaxon's face turned a deep red. His nostrils flared as he lifted his gaze back to Emory. With a deep crease between his brows, he spoke slowly, through bared teeth.

"I want to see my son."

Over his hand, Byron felt Emory's fingers twitch. He

felt the way she shuddered beside him and instinctively stepped closer to her. Their shoulders pressed together, and he wanted more than anything to wrap an arm around her, but he had a feeling it would make the whole thing worse.

Emory blew out a puff of air, then sucked in a deep lungful. Composed, she spoke firmly. Byron could hear the tiniest shake in her voice, but she hid it well.

"He is asleep. If you'd like to see him, we can arrange a supervised visitation." Her resolve crumbled a little, but Byron shifted his hand to wrap his fingers around hers now. "As per the custody agreement you signed," she added in one quick breath.

"He's my son."

Shaking her head, Emory let out a short laugh.

"You all but gave up the right to call him that when you walked out before he was even born. You haven't ever met him, and *now* you decide you're ready to play dad? After you kicked him out of the only home he has ever known? No."

Her laugh morphed into something that resembled a cackle. Emory doubled over, dropping her hands to her knees. The movement pulled Byron forward. He tried to pry his fingers free from her hand, but she'd twisted their fingers together and held them tighter as she caught her breath. Standing, Emory tucked her hair behind her ears and over one shoulder. She shifted, moving in front of Byron. She dropped his arm but grabbed it again quickly with her other arm to wrap it around her front. He hesitated, hovering his hand away from her, but she covered it with her own and held his close.

"Byron has been more like a father to Clayton than you."

Jaxon snorted. "Apparently, he's been more than that

to you, though. I should have known the damage you would cause. First, you played your stupid little tricks and tried to trap me, then you stole my son away when you realised I didn't love you. And now that conniving little brain of yours is trying to steal my dad? Back the fuck down and go get me my son."

Emory crumbled in Byron's arms. He felt every last little piece of her courage melt to the floor at Jaxon's words. They were wrong, all of them. Byron knew it, but he could see the way they hurt Emory all the same. And he was having none of it.

"Watch your tone." Blood boiled in Byron's ears. The only thing stopping him from yelling at the pathetic excuse of a man in front of him was the young boy sleeping down the hall. His hands balled into fists, resting only when Emory rubbed against them with her fingertips.

With a sarcastic smirk, Jaxon darted his eyes to Byron. "Or what?" he snarled. "I'm your son, you're supposed to be on my side, remember?"

Oh, Byron remembered alright. He remembered the first few months after Jaxon left. All the unanswered phone calls and unreturned messages. Byron had tried to reach out, over and over again. He had tried to make things right between Emory and Clayton and Jaxon, sure, but when those pleas were ignored, his focus had shifted. All he had wanted to know was that his son was okay. That Tucker would see his brother again. Jaxon leaving Emory, leaving town, shouldn't have meant that Byron and Tucker never got to speak to him. But apparently, to Jaxon, it did. Byron had spent too many sleepless nights worrying over Jaxon. He'd ended up calling on an aunt he had in the city. She'd tracked Jaxon down and assured Byron he was okay. It had been a small comfort, but did nothing to ease the sting.

"You do not get to lecture me on what it means to be family. Not when you wouldn't even be able to tell me the colour of your son's hair. Emory did not try to 'trap' you and it's insulting to your son for you to even think that way, but I don't think you give two shits about that little boy. If you did, you wouldn't have gone running off, and you certainly wouldn't have failed to make any effort to get to know him. You made your fucking bed when you ran out of town to get away from your responsibilities, now it's time for you to lie in it." It hurt, talking to his son like that. Driving the wedge between them a little further. In the depths of the crack in his chest, he wondered if they'd ever make it back from this. But then again, maybe they were never going to make it back anyway. Byron would always be ready to let Jaxon back into his life, but not like this. Not at Emory's expense.

Emory shifted in front of him, but Byron held her close. Jaxon opened his mouth to speak. Not wanting to hear a word of what he had to say, Byron cut him off.

"I don't need to hear your shitty excuses, Jaxon. You need to leave now."

"I'm your son. If you kick me out, you're no better than me."

A laugh rumbled through Byron. It was laced with irony that seemed to fuel Byron's rage. "The difference between you and me," he drawled, stepping out from behind Emory and right into Jaxon's space. Byron towered over his son and almost cracked a smile when he saw Jaxon tremble. "Is that Emory and Clayton belong with me. And I love them both with every single tiny little piece of my heart. But she *never* belonged with you. I should thank you, really, because every shitty thing you did only served to bring her closer to me. You're a worthless piece of shit and I am *ashamed* to call you my son. But that's what you are, so there will always be room for you in my life, but only when you're ready to start making things right."

Jaxon took a step back, stumbling over the threshold.

"But ... you ... my ..."

Byron was done. Adrenaline raged through him. His hands were tight fists again, and each breath burned his lungs. Stepping forward, Emory reached past Byron and swung the door shut in Jaxon's face.

They stood, staring at the door until they heard Jaxon's old car revving off down the driveway.

Emory stepped in front of Byron and leant her shoulder against the wall. "I should have told you he was in town. I forgot, I'm sorry."

"You knew?"

Nodding, Emory ran her hand along her arm. "I saw him before the flood. The day I bought the condoms."

That explained why she had been so off guard that afternoon. Fuck, Byron felt terrible. Not because she hadn't told him, but because *Jaxon* hadn't. As far as Byron was concerned, it was just another big X against his adult son.

"I should have told you," Emory added. "I meant to tell you, but then you saw the condoms and I was so embarrassed again and I just ... I forgot."

Byron shifted his shoulder and winked. "I distracted you."

Dropping her head to the side, Emory leant more of her weight on the wall. "He was right, you know, I ..."

"No." Byron stepped forward, turning Emory so her back was on the wall, caging her in with his arms. "You did none of those things, Em. Don't let him get inside your head."

"Clayton deserves to know who his father is."

"He deserves a man who loves him to death and would

do anything for him. Not some spineless excuse of a father who only wants to see him as a way of getting under your skin."

Emory placed her hand on Byron's chest. His heart calmed under her touch.

"He has that, Byron. He has you."

"Then he has everyone he needs."

Chapter 27

Emory

Emory knew what she wanted, and the finality of her decision sparked through her until all her hairs stood on end. There was still the question of how it would work: her job and the town and the farm. But those things seemed inconsequential compared to the love that was racing through her. All that mattered was that she loved Byron, and he loved her. He'd said so.

The rest they could figure out, but she *knew* they had to be together. Somehow.

Byron's arms dropped a little from the wall on either side of her head. His hands fell onto her shoulders, and she tilted her head to run her cheek along his wrist.

"You know," she said, looking up at Byron through her damp lashes, "Clayton will probably be sleeping for a while longer."

He didn't seem to take the hint. Falling forward, he rested his forehead against the wall next to her ear. "Emory," he whispered. Her name caught in his throat, and she thought for a moment he was crying. "It's going to fucking kill me when you go back to the cottage."

Leaving was going to kill her, too. If telling Byron where she planned to go didn't do that first. More and more, she was wondering how she would cope, if she would cope, or if she'd hate her whole adventure to the city and come running back to Byron. She turned her head, nudging Byron's face with her own. "I know," she whispered, still too afraid to have the conversation she knew they needed. "But I don't want to think about that right now."

"What do you want to think about?"

"You."

Emory kissed his cheek. Her lips lingered on the rough stubble from his grown-out beard, the tingle sending a shiver straight to her core. Her body remembered how fucking good that stubble felt on other parts of her. Byron groaned, but turned into the kiss and claimed her mouth with his own. His hand slipped up her shoulder to the back of her neck, and he sank his fingers into her hair.

Tilting her head into his hand, Emory deepened the kiss. She ran her tongue along his lip and opened her mouth for him. Byron's tongue flattened against hers. Their chests rose and fell in sync, Byron pressing himself into her and slipping his leg between hers. Emory felt his erection against her waist and rolled her hips towards him. Friction hit right where she needed it to, sending electricity and lust through her veins until it settled in her core.

She whimpered when Byron broke their kiss, but gasped when he dropped his arms to her waist and lifted her up. He held her against the wall as she wrapped her legs around him. Lowering her down to grind his cock against her, Byron kissed down her neck.

Heat raced through Emory, her pussy throbbing with need and her heart pounding with love. She tilted her head back as Byron kissed towards the neckline of her top.

Rolling her hips into Byron, Emory cursed the fabric between them. One of his hands dipped between her legs from behind and he pressed the seam of her pants against her clit.

"Too many fucking clothes," he groaned.

Stepping back from the wall, Byron turned and carried Emory through the house to his bedroom. Dropping her on the bed, he ripped his flannel shirt off his shoulders, tearing the buttons free. Emory reached for him and let her fingers dance across his chest and down along his abs. She pulled her lower lip between her teeth and kept her eyes on his as she unbuttoned his jeans. Byron pulled her hair into his fist while she shifted his pants lower until his cock sprang free. With a smirk, Emory looked up at Byron. She kept her eyes locked on his as she leant forward and flattened her tongue against his shaft. Starting with slow, almost lazy licks, Emory wet Byron's cock before grabbing it in both hands and sucking the tip into her mouth. She watched as his eyes rolled back. His fingers pulled tight in her hair as a shudder ran through his body.

She loved it, seeing him come undone like this and knowing it was her causing it. With his dick in her mouth she moaned, sucking him deeper until he hit the back of her throat. She held him there, waiting until his stuttering breaths turned into a deep, low growl. Pumping her hands around his cock, she sucked at the tip, working him until the muscles in his legs grew tense.

"Fuck, Em," he growled as he pulled himself away from her lips.

She wanted more. Needed more. Her own arousal had grown until it was almost painful, but still she wanted to taste him again. Byron looked down at her, his face caught somewhere between a decadent smirk and an all-consuming smile. He nodded, and she thought he was going to slide between her lips again, so she nodded back with a smile and opened her mouth. But instead, Byron spun her around and pushed her onto all fours on the bed. He wasted no time pulling her pants around her knees. The sudden cool air against her pussy shocked Emory and she gasped at the unexpected sensation. It was replaced in an instant with Byron's hot breath. He ran his tongue along her pussy, dipping it into her opening and circling her clit. His fingers dug into the globes of her ass.

"Fuck," Byron said as he drew back. His voice was husky and low, and Emory turned her head back to watch him. He pulled his lower lip into his mouth, gazing down at her. There was a twinkle in his eye and a hunger painted across his face. Emory watched as he rolled a condom over his length. She wriggled her butt at him, wanting him to touch her.

He did. His fingers spread her ass cheeks wide, and his thumb dipped between them. He spat down onto her and rubbed the moisture around the tight, puckered hole.

Emory had never been touched there. It had always seemed so ... forbidden. But then, everything about her and Byron was forbidden, and so with him, it felt exhilarating.

"Do you like that, Em?"

Mmhmm. She did. She liked that very much. "Yes."

Byron held his thumb against her tight hole, rubbing his cock along her pussy as he did. Emory held her breath, waiting for the pain, but it didn't come. Instead, he pushed his cock into her at the same time he pressed in with his thumb. She could hardly breathe. Pleasure hit her with force. She felt full and whole, and *fuck*, she needed him to move. Rolling her hips into Byron, Emory moaned.

"Always so impatient," Byron chuckled.

Then he was pounding into her, thrusting over and over, hitting her deepest, most sensitive spot in the most incredible way.

Each thrust sent Emory closer and closer to an edge higher than she'd ever been.

"Oh, God."

Byron reached around her, pulling her up so her back was against his chest.

"He's not here, Em. Only me. Always me."

He palmed her breast over her tank, and she dropped her head back onto his shoulder.

"I don't care if you live in the cottage or on the other side of the goddamn world," Byron growled into her ear. He traced her lips with his fingers. "You're made for me, no one else. These lips are mine. These tits are mine." His hand dropped back to her breast, pinching her nipple through the thin lace fabric of her top before moving lower still to pinch her clit. "This pussy is mine. And this ass is mine."

He thrust into her again, his thumb still deep inside her. Emory felt every inch of him as he pounded into her. Pleasure burned her from within until all she could think about was Byron and how she needed him every day for the rest of her life. Fuck the city.

Byron held her tight as he pumped into her, and she came apart in his arms. Emory's orgasm raced through her, sending her flying off the cliff with no hope of landing on safe ground. Under the sheer intensity of her orgasm, every muscle in her body drew tight. She didn't just see stars; she saw the whole galaxy in the edges of her vision. Byron's release came with hers, and he grunted as he filled the condom, still buried inside her.

They collapsed on the bed together, panting. Byron pressed his forehead against Emory's and closed his eyes. "You're mine, Em. And I'm never letting you go."

"Nah," she whispered. She kissed him before continuing, "You're mine. And I'm never letting *you* go."

CHAPTER 28

BYRON

Mud caked the ground, but Byron still lowered himself to a squat and eventually seated himself on what was once a field of wildflowers. They'd been beautiful only a few weeks ago. But the change the flood had brought with it was more visibly apparent here than anywhere else.

Stretching his neck, Byron looked up at his late wife's old windmill. Thanks mostly to the work Byron and Tucker had done to reinforce the supports, it had survived. The posts needed to be double-checked as the ground started to dry more, but for now, it was good. Byron could focus his clean-up efforts elsewhere. The mooing from the cows up in the high paddock could be heard even from down here. What had been a small space for them two weeks ago likely felt overly crowded by now, especially after he returned Betty, the wildest cow of them all, to the herd earlier. Byron would have to get to work fixing up one of the larger paddocks.

A few moments of peace wouldn't hurt, though.

Byron had come out to the windmill as soon as he

could. He always found a kind of serenity when he sat in the grass in the shade of Josie's favourite glorified lawn ornament, but when he saw it standing today, something else had washed over him. It was cool despite the warm sun on his neck, and made his pulse race even as he sat calmly on the grass. An intense readiness had smothered all the worry out of him.

After Josie had passed, Byron had come to accept the fact that he would likely die alone. He had figured that he'd had his great love story. It was someone else's turn now. He never expected to find love again, let alone a love as wholly consuming as the one he had with Emory. They shared something that ran far deeper than the lust-filled attraction he had assumed was all she felt. It was as though their souls had been tied together all along, every moment in their lives leading them to this point, to be together.

They'd make it work. They'd have to.

Byron was still hopeful she'd finish her degree and find a remote job so she could stay in town. Even though he knew the chances were slim. Regardless, it was beyond time they had a proper chat about the future he hoped they could share.

He looked up at the windmill one last time, muttering a thanks to his late wife for giving him the last bit of courage he needed.

"Mum's windmill survived, then."

Byron jolted from his near meditative state at Tucker's voice. He'd been so lost in his own head, he hadn't heard the quad bike approaching. Pushing to stand, he swatted away the biggest chunks of mud on his old jeans. They were made to get dirty anyway.

"She'd be thankful," he said as he turned to his son.

Tucker's blond hair was getting long. He pushed it off his face and tucked a little behind his ear. His hand lingered on his cheek, scratching at the grown-out stubble. He looked … Byron wasn't sure what the most appropriate word was. Rough, maybe? Unkempt.

Byron wondered how things were with Mya, now that the flood had cleared. If the uneasy way she and Tucker had fallen into living together had settled now that they could spend some time apart. They were both still young. They had time to sort their shit out and Byron hoped that they would. It would do Tucker good, not to be alone.

They'd all been alone far too long, and Byron was ready for that to change for all of them.

The gnawing in his gut returned as Tucker moved to stand on Byron's left. They looked up at the windmill, and a collective sigh rolled through their bodies. Byron contemplated it all. There was a distinct emptiness on his right side, one he suspected might never feel filled again. The previous day with Jaxon near proved it.

Byron hated the way his eldest son made his blood boil, and he'd always be around when Jaxon finally decided he was ready to live up to the Gardner name again, but Byron suspected that wouldn't be for a long while yet. He wasn't sure what went wrong with Jaxon, to lead him to skipping town on his partner and kid and family. But he was done trying to blame himself. Jaxon made his own choices.

In the corner of his eye, Byron saw Tucker cross his arms over his chest. With his eyes closed, Tucker looked peaceful. His loose, unbuttoned flannel flapped against his back, fighting the wind.

Did he know his brother was back in town? After all, Tucker had been into town a few times and hadn't been restricted to his own property. Byron would have to ask. After Emory, Tucker had taken Jaxon's swift departure the hardest. Still living with Byron at the time, Tucker had not been able to comprehend how his brother could just ... leave. Without saying goodbye or letting them know what his plan was. Byron and Tucker had found out from Emory when she'd called, asking if they knew where Jaxon was. If it wasn't for the scribbled note he left on the counter at the cottage, they'd probably still be wondering, fearing he was dead.

Tucker had been a wreck. Despite all the evidence it had been Jaxon's incompetence as a father that led to his leaving, Tucker blamed himself somehow. He'd looked up to his brother, and without that role model, he was lost. He'd holed up in his room, trying over and over to reach out to Jaxon—all to no avail. Byron could still remember the way his voice cracked as Tucker had pondered if he could have helped more, done more, to make Jaxon want to stay.

It took a long time, and a lot of convincing, for the teenager to accept that there was nothing he could have done. Still, Byron wasn't sure how Tucker would handle his brother suddenly showing up in town.

Even more so, he wasn't sure how exactly Jaxon would react to Byron's decision to hand the farm solely over to Tucker. It didn't matter though; Jaxon could act as piss poorly about it as he wanted for all Byron cared. The decision was made. Truthfully, he'd made it a while back. He just hadn't acknowledged it yet. He probably needed to check it all over with the lawyer, though.

Now that he had, he had to figure out how best to tell his sons.

"Suppose we should go let your cows out?" Tucker asked, nudging his shoulder against Byron's.

"Need to fix all the fences first. And the gates. Probably clear some mud first and see if we can find grass for the beauties to stand on."

It was a long list of cleanup. No wonder his dad had called it quits.

He'd loaded everything they needed into the trailer of his tractor before leaving the shed earlier. A few fresh rolls of barbed wire, a lot of new posts, bags of cement, shovels and all the rest. It was going to be a long day, and he was glad Tucker had shown up to help. As the flood cleared further, he'd be able to call his farm hands back to work, but for now, Tucker was all he had.

They'd barely made it around the length of one paddock before the afternoon chill began to hit the air. Almost every post needed fixing in some way. The good ones needed a nudge in the right direction and a little more cement around the base. The bad ones needed to be torn out completely with brand new posts erected and barbed wire wrapped around. The flood had wiped out almost everything.

It was good, in a way, because the strenuous labour had stopped Byron's mind from spiralling the way it had been all morning. Didn't take away from the fact that he still had a lot of conversations to have, but it was nice not to think about them all for a while.

The stench from the muddy paddocks followed them back to the big shed. It was like the putrid smell of manure turned all the way up, with a dash of mould. Byron had been able to ignore it at first, but it still lingered. Thankfully, the hay stacked at the back of the big shed had managed to stay dry. It still had a sweet, grassy scent that was a welcome relief as Byron got to work unloading the trailer.

Tucker followed him into the shed after parking his quad bike under the carport.

"Did you know," he called out as he stepped into the

wide space. His voice echoed from the high ceiling. "Jaxon's back in town?"

Byron stilled. So Tucker did know. He turned to face his son, trying to read the expression on his face. His cheeks were a little red from the sun and wind, but nothing about him expressed anything other than indifference. Byron grunted an acknowledgement that sounded a little like "I know," and shrugged his shoulders.

"I saw him at the supermarket, but he took one look at me and turned the other way."

Sounds like Jaxon, running off instead of facing his problems. Byron was surprised he'd managed to make it to the farmhouse at all.

"When was this?"

"Yesterday, late afternoon."

Hm, made sense.

Byron squared his shoulders, dropping the end of a shovel to the ground to lean on the handle. "He came here. Don't think he was happy with what he saw."

"Oh, God, Dad, what did he see?"

"Nothing bad. But he didn't like that Emory was here. With me. Apparently, when he kicked her out of the cottage, he failed to consider that there wouldn't be many other places in town for her to go."

Tucker got to work unhooking the trailer from the tractor, thick metal chains clattering to the ground as he unscrewed the pins. For a second, Byron thought Tucker had moved on from the conversation, but as the last chain fell, he stood up. One foot hitched up on the A-frame of the trailer, he leant forward to rest his forearm on his knee.

"You know Jaxon best out of all of us. Do you really think he thought about where Emory would go?"

"Of course not. He was only thinking about himself. It's all he ever does."

"Did you stop to think about *why* he might be kicking her out of the cottage?"

Byron rocked one shoulder up in a shrug. "Em said he mentioned his money had run dry. I suspect he had nowhere else to go."

Tucker ran his fingers through his hair, pushing it off his face before he continued. "He needed somewhere to fall back to. The last thing on his mind was where his ex was going to go, but I doubt it ever would have crossed his mind that she'd come here. You and Emory are adults, and I'm just happy to see you smiling again, Dad. But she's his ex, and you're his dad. It was never going to be an easy conversation."

Tucker was right, and Byron's shoulders sank forward. Jaxon might have done some shitty things but then again, lately, so had Byron. He should have known that his relationship with Emory would drive a bigger wedge between himself and his son. Hell, he *had* known. He'd been fighting this attraction with Emory from the moment he met her, and Byron knew deep in his bones that Jaxon's disapproval wasn't going to change how he felt. But it was still going to sting a little. There was probably a better way for Jaxon to find out, though.

With a sigh, he grabbed the last of the tools from the trailer and set them against the wall of the large shed. His back and knees ached after the day's labour, but now his heart felt heavy too. His whole plan counted on Jaxon still choosing to be completely out of the picture. He'd been naïve, or maybe hopeful, to think Jaxon wouldn't come back. That thought did more than sting; it was a knife to the throat and made Byron choke on his sharp inhale. Had he really wanted Jaxon to stay out of the picture forever?

No, he hadn't wanted it, he was sure of that. He'd just expected it, and as a result, he'd come to count on it.

"Thanks for your help today." He turned to face Tucker, trying to change the subject. To forget about his impossible decision and the worry of the future, for a moment at least. He knew that one look at Emory would make everything feel right again. He just needed to get to her.

Tucker shoved his hands into the pockets of his jeans, brow furrowed as he glared at Byron. "You really think you can just kick me out when you realise how fucked you are?"

"Sometimes I think you forget I'm your father."

"Ha. So do you, apparently." He took a few steps towards Byron, stopping short a few feet away to run a hand along his face. "Look, Jaxon is Jaxon. But Emory is Emory. I can see what she's done for you, and that's not worth giving up. Jaxon is either going to get over it and stick around, or he'll fuck off again, and the only thing that will change is you being happy instead of being a grumpy old fucker all the time."

"There might be more that changes, though. She handed in her last assignment."

"I figured." Tucker stepped forward and wrapped an arm over Bryon's shoulders. He pulled Byron into the closest thing to resemble a hug the two had shared in a long time. He patted his fist against Byron's back a few times before pulling back.

"You have a lot more cleaning up to do before I agree to anything, though."

CHAPTER 29

EMORY

E mory's phone buzzed on the corner of the bench as she poured two mugs of tea. In a third—plastic—cup, she added a dash of hot water to Clayton's milk. After her own tea had brewed, she dropped the bag into his drink for a short second before pulling it out and dropping it into the sink.

"Do you have biscuits too?" Mya called out from the living room.

Emory held back her smile as she picked up the packet she'd already pulled from the pantry. There was nothing Mya loved more than dipping a crumbling biscuit into her tea, and even though Emory found the thought gag-worthy, she wasn't about to deny her friend.

With the lid snapped onto Clayton's sippy cup, she tucked it and the biscuits under her arm and balanced a mug in each hand. Her phone still vibrated along the counter, but she was ignoring it for a reason.

It was, more than likely, Jaxon. Or his property manager. There were only two more weeks left on her lease, and since she was yet to formally acknowledge that she'd be moving out, she imagined someone was calling to confirm she would, in fact, have the property vacated on time. She still hadn't been back since evacuating to Byron's for the flood, and the more time passed, the less she cared. There wasn't anything of worth left there anyway. Jaxon could deal with all their old furniture.

The number flashing on the screen caught her eye, though. It was, as it turned out, neither Jaxon nor the number she had saved for the property manager. It wasn't even the café, calling to ask her if she could come back to work. She rushed the hot drinks to the coffee table, nearly spilling half the liquid over the side.

There was only one other person she could think of. Well, a few people really, but all with the same intent. A warm drop of hope spread behind her eyes, and the cool sludge of dread bubbled in her stomach.

"You okay?" Mya called as she raced back to the kitchen.

Emory didn't answer. She lunged for the phone, connecting the call and bringing it to her ear with a deep breath. Her heart raced, but she stood as tall as she could and forced a fraction of composure through her voice.

"Hello, Emory speaking."

Shit, so much for composure. Instead of the professional flair she had been hoping for, her voice had come out all high-pitched and breathy.

"Hi, Emory, my name is Ashleigh. I'm calling from Sydscape Media. Is now a good time?"

Holy even more shit.

Sydscape Media was Emory's number one preference for a marketing position. Applying for their highly exclusive graduate program had been Emory's stretch goal. The application she sent was purely so she wouldn't spend the rest of her career wondering 'what if'. She never expected to hear from them, let alone so soon.

She nearly dropped the phone, fumbling it between her fingers. There was no time to falter, though, so she pushed her shoulders as far back as she could and turned away from Mya's prying eyes.

"Hi, Ashleigh, yes, of course. How are you?"

The conversation was brief. Ashleigh mentioned being impressed with Emory's determination and persistence with her course, given her circumstances, and gave her a breakdown of how the graduate program ran. Emory managed to talk herself up without being at all cocky or condescending. All traces of her imposter syndrome were kept firmly at bay. There was a natural rapport between the women that helped the conversation flow well.

Overall, Emory was excited, and hopeful.

"It would be great to chat with you more about the position and your skills," Ashleigh said as the conversation hit a natural pause. "Can we set up a formal interview later in the week? Maybe a video call while you're still out in Gardner Creek?"

"That would be great. Thursday?" Emory held her breath. This felt too good to be true.

"Thursday is perfect. Does mid-morning suit? I'll email you with an invite and some extra details."

Shit, she'd only said Thursday because it was the first weekday that came to mind and all the research Emory had done on interview skills said that it was better to offer a date for the next step than leave it too open. But Thursday was only two days away. She had a lot of work to do if she wanted to impress Ashleigh in a formal interview.

Emory fumbled her way through a pleasant goodbye, suddenly flustered and increasingly overwhelmed at the gravity of what having secured an interview with Sydscape meant. Hanging up the phone a moment later, Emory sank the back of her legs against the bench and dropped her hands to her knees. She should be happy, right? Ecstatic even.

So, what was this squeezing feeling inside her chest? It made it hurt to breathe, and she couldn't stand up straight. She sank to the floor, sucking in short gasps of air through the pain.

A hand dropped to her shoulder. The ends of Mya's green sundress tickled Emory's cheek, and she crouched down. Emory instantly fell into her, curling into Mya's open arms.

"What happened?" Mya whispered.

"Sydscape wants an interview with me," Emory choked out through sobs.

God, it wasn't even a job offer, and she was like this. The pain of even trying hurt so deeply, she wasn't sure she could continue.

"Oh, thank fuck," Mya swore under her breath. "I thought someone had died."

"It feels like someone died. And it's just an interview."

"Like someone good died, or someone bad?"

Emory swiped her cheeks with the back of her hands and shifted out of her friend's arms. "What kind of question is that?"

"The kind that makes you stop crying?" Mya stood from her squat and grabbed the two mugs of tea she'd brought over but left on the bench. She slid her back down the kitchen cabinet and passed one drink to Emory. Cradling the cup in both hands, she took a sip and stretched her legs in front of her.

Emory tracked each movement, wondering if she really

was acting that intensely. This wasn't the kind of issue that warranted a kitchen floor conversation. Was it?

She supposed maybe it was. It felt like her life was beginning and ending all at once, right when it was just starting to get *good* again.

"I should have known that falling into bed with Byron was going to end like this."

"Who said it's ending?"

"Ah, the interview? The fact that I need to move to the city to get the job of my dreams? The fact that I can't stay here, even though it breaks my heart to acknowledge that."

All her resolve from the day before had crumbled. Yes, she loved Byron and didn't want to leave him. But she couldn't see any way in which the two of them could be together. He loved the farm, he loved the town, and she didn't. They were too different, no matter how perfectly their bodies fit together. Whatever it was that floated between them was always going to be finite. She knew that going in, she'd just let herself get too swept away by it to care.

Her heart had fallen, utterly and completely, into the deepest murky waters of the flood. And now she was left, crying on the kitchen floor because achieving her dreams was going to break it.

She had to, though. She had to break her heart, and Byron's. He'd be okay, eventually. He had Tucker here, and now Jaxon was back in town, Byron had a chance to make things right between them again. She wasn't going to be the thing that kept them apart any more than she already had been.

"Can I ask you something?" Mya's voice was tender, and she nudged her toe against Emory's leg.

Emory didn't think she had the stamina for words.

Not when everything was falling to pieces around her. She looked up, placing her mug of cooling tea on the floor. Her cheeks were wet again, but this time she let the tears spread. Everything else was a mess, her face might as well join the crowd.

"Does Byron feel this way, too?"

Of course he did. Emory hugged herself, wanting to believe it. He'd said as much, hadn't he? Sure, it had been in a fit of protective rage, and he'd said it to Jaxon, not to her, but it still meant the same. Didn't it?

Oh, God, she wasn't sure. What if his words had been a lot more general than she had interpreted them? What if he simply meant that he cared for her, the same way he cared for Clayton? Not that he *love* loved her. She had to believe all the times he said he didn't want her to go, but the more she thought about it, the more she realised that all of those things had always been said in the heat of a very lust-filled moment.

Neither of them had said as much when they were fully clothed. Emory wondered why that was. Why Byron was hiding his true feelings behind their wild sexual encounters. Why she was.

"I think," Mya answered when Emory didn't, "that if you don't know the answer to that question easily, you need to give this interview everything you've got. Get all your options clear and on the table, and maybe then, the right choice will become more obvious."

Yeah, Emory could hope so. But with her back-and-forth emotions over the past week, she just wasn't sure. It was as though every time Byron was near, desire flooded her body faster than the water had flooded the fields. It took over every part of her until there was no room for anything else. She couldn't think straight in this house.

It didn't matter how far Clayton's toys had spread, or that his television shows were constantly streaming nursery rhymes through the house. It didn't matter that she'd taken over the study or that she had her own bedroom, even though she hadn't slept in that bed for a week now. It was still Byron's house, and he was every-where even when he wasn't.

Picking up her tea, she gulped down the now luke-warm drink. It did little to ease the scratching in her throat, and nothing to reduce the pressure on her chest.

"I don't think there is a right choice," she admitted when her mug was empty. "At least not one that can be made while I'm staying here. Any time I come even close to realising that I should still work on my dreams, Byron swoops in and makes us breakfast or stands up for me or fucks me senseless. All the rational thoughts leave my brain until all that's left is this never-ending need for him."

Clayton's clapping at the end of a song echoed through to the kitchen. Maybe she should take him back to the cottage. Take the couple of weeks left on the lease to properly pack away all the furniture and try to return to something that resembled normal life. Although she had no idea what normal looked like anymore.

Her phone pinged in her lap. The email from Ashleigh, already. The firm's eagerness was exhilarating, and surely a good sign.

The tips of Emory's fingers tingled as she opened the email and read through the invite. The first two paragraphs outlined the position, and that Ashleigh was the hiring manager and graduate coordinator. Most of the informa-tion was exactly what Emory had expected. The job was, on paper, made for her and her dreams. She wouldn't just be some lackey of a graduate, making coffee and taking minutes. Sydscape gave their newest employees a small portfolio of clients, and they were mentored through the year as they managed everything in the account. It was the proper chance at utilising her marketing degree that she'd been hoping for all along.

It just really sucked that it would cost Emory her heart.

CHAPTER 30

BYRON

An odd silence ran through the house when Byron slid open the back door. He froze, half inside, waiting.

"Get in, it stinks out here." Tucker shoved him from behind.

Still, Byron hesitated. Something was missing. Stepping in, he moved to the side, trying to catalogue what had changed since he left to work on the farm that morning. Nursery rhymes still chimed from the TV, granted, they were far more upbeat at this time of the afternoon. But even so, the space was too quiet. Clayton wasn't singing along or banging toys together like makeshift cymbals. Emory wasn't shuffling about, tidying after her son, or tapping away on her keyboard and humming from the study. And neither of them had greeted him at the door.

He hadn't realised just how used to their presence he had gotten. It worried him, but not as much as their absence did. A sour taste lined his tongue that had nothing to do with the stench of the flood outside. He tried to swallow it away, but it came back ten times stronger with each dry gulp.

Where were they? Wasn't Mya supposed to be here too?

He didn't dare call out in case Clayton was sleeping. That would explain the young boy's absence, at least.

Tucker stood in the kitchen, one eye on Byron as he pulled two beers from the fridge and popped open both bottles.

"Jesus fucking Christ," he swore under his breath. "How fucking gone are you?"

Byron forced himself to stand a little taller. He raised an eyebrow, silently daring his son to make another remark.

As expected, Tucker took the bait. Although as he spoke, Byron realised he wasn't winning this bet.

"Seriously," Tucker said, "that's why you look like Miff when she sniffs out a rabbit. You're trying to figure out where they are."

Ignoring the truth in Tucker's words, Byron stormed over and grabbed his beer. He'd had enough of Tucker's wisdom for the day. For a while yet, actually. On light feet, he paced through the house, towards the hall. The gentle hum of Clayton's lullaby floated through the front of the house, and a little of the weight that had been sitting on Byron's shoulders began to ease. Emory was still missing, though. And Mya, he supposed, which gave him a little comfort. Emory was just entertaining her friend, surely, but Byron didn't understand *where* they were.

Well, the further into the house he got, the more he realised where they must have been. The den. Emory had never gone into the room without Byron there, at least not that he knew. But they weren't anywhere else, and he knew her enough to know she wouldn't have left the house while Clayton was asleep. Not when the monitor had still been on its charger in the kitchen.

He inched past Clayton's room, pausing at the door to peek in at his grandson. Something warm filled Byron's chest at the sight of the little boy all curled in his bed. Yeah, Byron had gotten used to them being around. And Tucker was right; Byron was so far gone that any memory of his life before Emory and Clayton came to stay was a mere speck on the once dusty horizon.

Clayton shifted in his sleep, his tiny mouth falling open with a sigh as he curled around his teddy. The kid deserved so much more than what he had. He deserved a loving father, and sure, Byron knew he'd never be exactly that, but he was determined to be the next possible thing. Years ago, he'd worried he was overstepping, but as time went on and Jaxon remained out of the picture, Byron found comfort in becoming the fatherly figure in Clayton's life. Those same fears of overstepping washed over him now. If, and it was a big if, Byron and Emory settled into something more than what they already had, what would that mean for Clayton?

Byron doubted the boy knew who Jaxon was, but as time went on, he was surely going to ask questions. It wouldn't be fair to try to hide the truth from him. Byron had to believe that there would come a time when Jaxon would come to his senses and want to be a part of his son's life. If Byron were also in the picture, it would only make things more difficult. But that did nothing to stop the longing behind Byron's eyes.

He was going to be there for Clayton, always and in every way possible. He had to trust the universe on this one, even though he'd never been one for that sort of thing. Life had worked out the way it did because he and Emory were destined to be together. Maybe, after all, love did conquer everything else. Maybe, when you found a love like he shared with Emory, it was worth all the crap.

Sneaking back out of the room, Byron pulled the door shut but didn't let the handle click. He turned back up the hall, but Tucker hadn't followed him. The bottle in his hand grew wet, condensation beading along the glass. He took a swig and let the neck of the beer dangle between his fingers before creeping further along the hall.

The women's hushed voices caught him as he approached the den. He found it odd that Emory would take Mya into this room, of all of them. His brow furrowed, and he ran his tongue along his teeth, but the clattering of pool balls chipped away his suspicions.

Emory had expressed her complete disinterest in pool, and Byron hadn't really cared. It wasn't like he played much anymore. The table was a mere leftover from his younger, more social years. One that, like most of the other things in the den, he hadn't bothered to get rid of. It got a little use when Tucker came to visit, usually, but otherwise it was used more for puzzles than pool. Byron had always figured that one day Tucker would come take over the farmhouse, and find use for it again. Mya must enjoy playing. He heard her voice from deep in the room.

"You sure you don't want a turn?"

Emory laughed her off. "Even if I liked pool, I don't think I could concentrate."

Byron heard the clicking of laptop keys and another *clack* as the pool cue hit a ball. Emory took a loud, very satisfied-sounding intake of breath. "Sydscape works with the *Hemsworths*. Like, okay, his parents, but oh my *God*."

Sydscape?

The very last thing Byron expected to find himself doing in his own home was eavesdropping. And he hated that he was, even if it had started by accident. But now that he had started, he wanted to find out exactly why Emory was looking into whatever this Sydscape was and why they were connected to the Hemsworth family.

He held his breath. A sip of his beer would have been nice, but he didn't dare in case they heard. The only thing worse than the eavesdropping would be if he got caught.

"You know you have to do it, right?" Mya said before taking another shot on the pool table. It sounded like whatever ball she hit found the pocket, and her soft *whoop* confirmed Byron's thoughts. "Like, you said you were going to research and make a decision about the interview, but all you've done is tell me wonderful things about the position and the company. I think you knew all along that you would give it your best shot."

"I did," Emory admitted. Byron hated the hint of sadness in her voice. The way the words dragged and the subtle rustle as she sank back against the couch. "There was just a tiny piece of me that hoped I'd find something terrible about them so I would have an excuse to cancel the interview. If the company reviews were shit or the position didn't pay enough to cover rent on an apartment for me and Clayton or they donated money to some shitty cause. Because I know that I have to do this, no matter how much leaving is going to hurt."

Hold the fuck on. *Leaving?*

It didn't matter how glaring the signs had been or how often he'd tried to come to terms with it. None of those moments had felt as final as this. Emory had an interview. With Sydscape, which he now realised must be a big marketing firm in the city. She was actively trying to find her way out.

Every hair on Byron's neck stood on end. His temple throbbed, pain spreading across his forehead. He rolled the beer bottle over his face, the condensation cooling a little of the heat he felt rising through him. Closing his eyes, he tilted his head back to stretch his neck, bringing the bottle back down. But it was wet, and the glue on the paper label had been thinned by the condensation so much that it wasn't sticky anymore. It slid through his fingers. Byron fumbled with the bottle, but it fell to the ground, shattering on the hard slate floor.

"Shit," he muttered, doing his best to keep his voice down. It was useless, though.

Both girls appeared in the doorway to the den. Emory's eyes were wide, her mouth dropped open a little. Mya probably looked the same, but Byron couldn't see her. Not really. Emory was, as always, the sun that filled the dim hallway with the brightest light.

"You're leaving?" The words choked him. He cleared his throat, determined to hold back against the stinging in his eyes.

Mya shoved past Byron, tiptoeing over the broken glass and splashed beer. Her hands pressed against Byron's back as she pushed him into Emory. He wrapped his arms around her, holding her steady as Mya continued to shove him from behind.

"I'm going to clean this up," she grunted as she forced Byron and Emory into the den. As soon as they were down the small step that led into the room, Mya reached past Byron's shoulder to grab the door and swing it shut.

He didn't let go. Even when Emory planted her feet firmly on the floor. She stepped away from him, but he held her close, nuzzling into her. He backed her right into the pool table and sank his lips against the softest part of her neck, right below her ear. Right where he knew she loved it.

She didn't tilt her head to make room for him, though. Or turn towards his kiss or whimper into his ear. She held her ground. Her hands were flat against his chest, holding him back as much as she could.

"You knew, Byron. You knew I was studying, and you knew I wanted to get a job in the city."

"Not the city. I didn't think you would go that far," he admitted. He retreated from her neck, dropping his hands to rest on the pool table on either side of her legs.

Her hands still planted on his chest, Emory let her fingers curl against him a little. "I *have* to, Byron, even though I don't want to. Because all of this between us ... it's just us. I still hate this town as much as most of the folks who live here hate me." She sighed, a fraction of her composure dropping as she sank her weight against the table and dropped her hands from Byron's front. "All my life, I've followed other people around. My parents when they first came to Australia when I was young. Then to every major city as I grew up, as they hopped about, trying to find their place. I thought *not* following them back to New Zealand was me finally finding some power of where I ended up, but I just followed Jaxon here. I *need* to get a job in the city because, for the first time in my life, it's my chance to lead, not follow. I hate, *hate*, that it's costing me my heart, Byron. But I can't stay."

Her voice began to shake, but Emory held her breath and forced her lips together. Byron could see the glisten in her eyes as tears began to swell. His own vision started to blur, but he made no effort to hold back his tears. He let them trickle down his cheek until he could taste the saltiness in the corner of his mouth.

"I'm sorry," he choked out. This was all his fault. Giving in to temptation had been his idea. If he hadn't encouraged her, neither of them would be in this mess. Their hearts would still be fine.

Emory shook her head, dropping her hand beside her

to grab Byron's. She squeezed his fingers and traced her thumb along his knuckles.

"This is as much my fault as it is yours. I'm sorry, too."

Reaching up, Byron wiped her cheeks with his thumb and cupped her face. He leant in, pressing their foreheads together first, then kissing her. His lips lingered over hers, waiting to see what she would do. Emory kissed him back, but kept her mouth closed. She gulped, turning her face away from him.

"Please don't make this harder," she said.

He didn't plan to. He planned on making it easier, he just thought he'd have more time to figure it all out. And until everything was settled, he didn't want to get either of their hopes up.

Chapter 31

Emory

Emory tugged at the collar of her shirt. The buttons strained against her chest, not so much that it looked bad—especially through a computer screen—but enough for her to feel uncomfortable in Byron's grand desk chair.

Don't fidget, she told herself. Don't stretch your arms forward. It'll be fine. Look at the camera, not yourself. Smile, but not too much. Pause if you need to, don't say um.

She still had twenty minutes before the interview was meant to start. Byron had promised to keep Clayton entertained outside, so she'd hauled herself into the study earlier than needed. She didn't want to be late, but even she could admit that twenty minutes was probably a little too early. Maybe she could go and get changed. Surely the interview would go better if she were comfortable.

Running through the clean clothes she still had packed before the flood, Emory compiled outfits in her head. The blue sundress might work—it looked a bit like a shirt on top, she supposed. And only her shoulders would be on the screen anyway. But she'd worn it a few days ago. Was it washed? Was it dry? It probably needed an iron. Nothing else was even close to suitable. All tight tanks or oversized sweaters. A few daggy T-shirts she wore to work. This too-small, off-white button-down was her only option. She'd have to make do.

Leaning against the tall back of Byron's chair, she tugged her legs under her knees and twisted her hips. The movement forced the chair to spin back and forth underneath her, and she closed her eyes. She let her body feel the gentle movement and tried to ground her racing emotions. Anxiety was beginning to fill her up, and no matter how hard she tried, she couldn't ease the way her heart hammered in her chest or settle the churning in her gut. At least, she told herself, it was only a video interview, not the real thing. At least, if she utterly failed to impress them, she'd have a reason to stay.

Dropping her head back, Emory let out a long, determined breath. She shouldn't think like that. It was doing nothing except sending a message to the universe that she didn't really want this job. And she did, she wanted it so badly, even with the cost. She had to try.

With five minutes to spare, she stood from the chair and did a few star jumps, making sure not to stretch her arms too far or exert herself to the point of sweating. Just enough to throw out some of the adrenaline that was starting to take over her body. She sat down, pulling a small twisty fidget into her lap.

Time to shine.

She was only logged into the meeting for a minute or so before Ashleigh joined the call. After a quick internet sleuth, she had been expecting the woman's eccentric style, but seeing it still brought a smile to Emory's face. Ashleigh was wearing a bright yellow, frilly top, and her mop of tight brown curls was tied high on her head. Bright red glasses framed her face, complemented by a matching necklace. On Emory, the whole ensemble might have appeared gaudy, but on Ashleigh, it just worked.

Something about seeing the woman helped to calm Emory. Maybe it was her sense of fashion or the larger-than-life smile, or maybe it was just because once they started chatting, Emory felt instantly at home. If she got this job, she had a feeling she would fall right into place within the Sydscape team.

She'd need that, to find friendships with her coworkers. Otherwise, she would have no one when she moved to Sydney. No one to catch up for coffee with, no one to call when she needed a hand with Clayton. It didn't matter how far she moved, she knew she would always be able to call Mya when she needed a chat, but it wasn't the same as having a support network close by.

Emory couldn't have finished her degree without Mya's help. And Byron's. Was she crazy to think she'd be able to cope without them when she moved?

She bit back the thought. Ashleigh was giving her another brief rundown of the graduate program and some of the clients they expected to hand over to their next cohort of employees. Emory needed to pay attention. Under the table, she twisted the fidget toy between her fingers. It helped her focus on Ashleigh, but she still tracked each word carefully to make sure she didn't miss any important details.

"Since you'll be coming in from a rural community, we thought you'd be the perfect fit for one of our newest clients. It's a small Sydney business that works directly with farms to buy all the produce the supermarkets don't want, so it doesn't go to waste. They're still in start-up mode, and I think your tie to the farming industry, even if it is a bit roundabout, would really give you a leg up on their marketing."

Ashleigh's enthusiasm seeped through the screen as she spoke. Every sentence was as though Emory already had the position, and this interview was a mere formality. Emory hoped that was the case, but thought through every response all the same. She shouldn't get too far ahead of herself, she still needed to prove her worth.

The conversation continued to flow, and Emory became more and more confident in her chances with every pleased smile Ashleigh sent through the screen. Professionally, at least, Emory was convinced. Talking with Ashleigh, she'd almost forgotten all the so-called cons of this job. The thought of moving to the city was back to being the exciting adventure she had always thought it would be. This job was everything. She couldn't wait to get started, and she didn't even have the job yet.

"I just have one more question for today," Ashleigh said with another of her enthusiastic smiles. "Moving from Gardner Creek is a big step, and I know we've spoken about the job potential and how excited you are to start your career, but are you ready for such a big location change?"

Emory froze. Maybe if she sat still, didn't blink, for long enough, she could fool Ashleigh into thinking the connection had dropped out.

"It's not my place to say whether you are or not, but your son is still young, and it will be a big adjustment. If you're confident you're ready, I won't question your judgement," Ashleigh continued when Emory remained silent. "But it's something I want you to think about before we go through the next steps."

Emory's breath shook. She should have said something, anything, to squash Ashleigh's concerns, but she had nothing. For the first time through the whole interview, she didn't have the answer. In one short enough sentence, Ashleigh had broken all Emory's resolve. Of course, she was still excited about the job, but Ashleigh was right. Moving to the city would be a big—no, huge—adjustment.

Three weeks ago, Emory would have brushed off the question with a laugh. She'd had nothing keeping her tied to Gardner Creek. But now?

Now, she knew that leaving town also meant leaving Byron. And the thought of that had enveloped her with worry. It wasn't just not being with Byron that had her concerned. It was not being around anyone who supported her. She didn't have much in Gardner Creek, but Mya was here, and Tucker. They were as good as family to her and Clayton. Byron was the closest thing Clayton had to a father figure, and the past few weeks aside, he had been nothing but helpful and supportive.

So maybe she had been hasty in thinking it was going to be an easy exit on her eventual way out of town. Her new—and incredibly overpowering—emotions for Byron aside, she wasn't sure how she ever thought she could cope. Her ribs tightened, but she couldn't find the right words.

Ashleigh's brow furrowed at her lack of response. She looked away from the screen for a moment.

"Sorry," Emory gasped, firmly aware that she was creating doubt not just in herself but in Ashleigh's mind, too. "It would be a big change, but I've been working towards this through my whole course. I always knew that leaving Gardner Creek was in my future. Even if it is scary, I'm ready."

She nodded then, pushing herself to sit a little taller. She was ready, and it was okay to be scared when faced with such a big change. It wasn't okay to let her fear carry her away. Or hold her still.

Ashleigh looked pleased. She nodded, an overexaggerated movement that might have seemed over the top in person but through a video screen felt genuine and enthusiastic.

"We would be willing to support you in whatever way we can. Our relocation team typically works with higher-end management, but I'm sure we could convince them to help you with securing a house or apartment, as well as childcare for Clayton." She paused, leaning forward into the screen a little. Emory matched her posture. The shirt strained along her back, but Emory no longer cared. This was going well. She was sure of it.

"That would be really helpful, thank you. What are the next steps in the interview process?"

"I'll be really honest, Emory, I like you. I think you're a wonderful fit for our graduate program, and I'm excited to move forward with you. After this round of interviews, we have successful applicants come into the office for a team-building exercise. It's mostly a formality, but we do use the opportunity to see how the new graduates will work with each other, and within the whole Sydscape team. Would you be able to come to Sydney for that?"

Emory felt a shudder run through her spine. The fidget hung loose on her lap. If she'd understood correctly, Ashleigh was as good as offering her a position. Sure, it was all formality, and she still needed to impress them on this group interview day, but Emory could practically taste her ticket out of town.

"Yes, of course. It'll take a little planning, but I can make it work."

She'd have to. She'd do anything to make sure it

worked, even if it meant covering Mya's ticket to Sydney so she could watch Clayton for the day.

"Fantastic, you've got a while to figure it out. We don't have a set day yet, but it's typically later in November, after university exams have all finished. I'll send you a tentative offer later this week, and we can confirm the details once the date is finalised."

That was it? Emory grabbed the fidget from her lap, twisting it around her fingers in some feeble attempt to hide her eagerness.

"That would be great. Thank you so much." She grinned so wide her cheeks hurt. There was no hiding how excited she was now.

"Take your time," Ashleigh cautioned her. "Big changes are always equal parts scary and exciting. Make sure you give yourself time to feel both. Please reach out if you need anything."

"I will, thank you."

After a pleasant goodbye, Ashleigh discontinued the call, leaving Emory staring at her own shocked face. Her eyes were wide, her chin dropped low, but her open mouth was covered by her hands.

She'd done it.

She'd more than done it.

Three years of insane juggling and multitasking, of long nights studying and spending her work shifts reciting marketing techniques in her head in the lead up to exams. Three years of feeling utterly *stuck* in a small town that seemed to hate her. Three years of working for this moment, to finally have the road out of town cleared for her.

Ashleigh had offered her a position *and* the support she would need to find her feet in the city. It was everything she had been wanting and then some.

Tears began to fill her eyes as the overwhelming rush of emotion bled through her. She was proud and excited and determined. And, okay, she was also terrified of the change, but she was ready. Wiping her face, Emory pushed away from the desk and unbuttoned the top of her shirt. For the first time since she put it on, she felt like she could breathe again.

Her hand was on the door, ready to slide it open and share her big news, when she heard Byron's voice from behind it.

"Not yet," he hushed.

Emory heard the pattering of footsteps near the door.

"Mummy will be out soon," Byron continued. His voice faded away as he guided Clayton back down the hall.

Something new joined Emory's bubbling cauldron of emotion. It turned thick in her stomach and pulled at her shoulders. No matter how excited she was to leave Gardner Creek, it was really going to suck leaving Byron. If she stayed here any longer, she was going to chicken out of leaving the town altogether.

She knew what she had to do.

Reaching above her head, she pulled her hair out of the respectable bun and scratched at her scalp.

How on earth was she going to tell Byron it was time for her to move out?

CHAPTER 32

BYRON

Byron tipped back onto the ground, swinging his legs up and lifting Clayton above his chest. Clayton giggled in the air, rocking side to side on Byron's feet as he hummed exaggerated aeroplane noises. It was a silly game, but Clayton loved 'flying' through the air almost as much as he loved pretending to drive the quad bike.

He was such a playful kid, and Byron could get lost in his imagination with the boy. It didn't matter where they were, the two always seemed to find fun.

It didn't matter where they were.

Byron reminded himself, even though his decision had already been made. Looking back, Byron had known for a while now that his days on the farm were numbered. He'd known it long before the flood came through, and recent events had only solidified his decision. It was time for him to move on to his next big chapter.

When his legs began to ache, he lowered Clayton to the ground. "Papa needs a drink. Can you get the trucks out?"

"Race track?" Clayton asked, pulling the tub of trucks from the shelving unit under the TV.

"Yeah, start building the biggest one we've ever made, okay?"

Clayton didn't answer. He tipped the tub on its side and started pulling out all the bits of road from the bottom. Hopefully, building such a big track would take him a while.

Now that Emory was secluded in the study for her interview, Byron had a call to make. One that he didn't want her knowing about. Not yet. Not until it was all final and she couldn't try to talk him out of it.

It had been a long time since Byron had called his lawyer. Back when Jaxon had arrived in town with Emory by his side and the two needed somewhere to stay. He'd transferred the cottage into Jaxon's name and adjusted his will, and he'd thought that would be the end of it. But he needed legal advice now. Needed to make sure he could do what he wanted. Standing from the floor, he grabbed his phone and moved towards the kitchen. Close enough he could still keep an eye on Clayton, but far enough from the study that there was absolutely no chance Emory would hear if her interview finished early.

The old lawyer's secretary picked up after a few rings, and upon hearing Byron's name, she transferred the call. It helped, coming from the family who founded the small town. A small pang fluttered through Byron's chest, but he ignored it.

"Byron, I've been waiting for your call," the lawyer said through the phone.

"Really, why?"

"People always tend to call when an estranged child comes back. What do you need?"

Straight to the point, no pleasantries. I guess that's

how life goes when you bill by the minute. Byron didn't care, he would give up everything in his bank for his plan to work.

"Actually, I want to transfer the title of the farm now. Instead of waiting until I cark it."

"To who?"

"Tucker." He had to swallow down the itching at his throat.

The old lawyer sighed through the phone. Byron imagined him leaning back against his chair, maybe crossing one leg over the other. "That's … not what I was expecting."

"You thought I would give part of it to Jaxon?"

"I thought with Jaxon back in town, you'd consider your options and make him consider his. You wouldn't be the first rich man to put caveats on an inheritance."

Could you do that? Leave conditions on your will to ensure your benefactors acted the way you wanted? Byron supposed you must be able to, if his lawyer was suggesting it. It wouldn't matter, though; Jaxon was Jaxon, and Byron doubted any amount of money would change that. With a huff, he told the lawyer as much. "I don't even think the promise of an inheritance would turn Jaxon into a good father."

The lawyer sighed again, and a small tinge of doubt began to creep into the corners of Byron's vision.

"Could he contest it, if I transfer the farm to Tucker?"

"Not really, no. There's always a chance he could try, but given the strained relationship and the cottage already being in his name, it would be unlikely to progress even if he tried."

"Good."

The old man was silent. Byron could make out the creak of his chair and the sound of gentle tapping.

"So, can we do that? Start the process to move the farm into Tucker's name? All the other investments will stay with me." Now that he knew it was possible, Byron was eager for it to be sorted as soon as possible. His foot tapped underneath him.

"If you're sure, it's easy enough. There'll be taxes involved that one of you will need to cover, but otherwise there's no issue with transferring the title as a form of early inheritance."

"How soon can you draw up the paperwork?"

"A day or two, I'll get one of the contract writers started on it tomorrow." He clicked his tongue before continuing. "Byron, have you thought this through?"

Byron thought for a while, wondering if he should tell the old man his plans. It wouldn't hurt, he supposed, to let someone in on his secrets, but it wouldn't be fair on Emory. "I have."

His lawyer didn't say anything. Byron could hear heavy breaths through the phone and held his own as he waited for the old man's response.

"Fair enough," was all he said. There was no questioning in his dry tone. Byron supposed the lawyer was probably just indifferent. He wasn't paid for his opinions on the legal choices of the people he wrote contracts and wills for.

Byron thanked him and hung up the phone. One step down, and only a few more before he could tell Emory.

Spotting Clayton rushing toward the study, Byron clambered after him. He scooped the boy up before he reached the door, hushing him and moving back towards the toy trucks. He glanced back, expecting to see the old sliding doors still shut, but Emory pushed them open as he looked over his shoulder.

Her hair hung around her face in messy strands, and

the top few buttons of her shirt were undone, revealing the beige lacy tank she wore underneath. Byron swore she had one in every colour, and he would not be satisfied until he had seen her in all of them. And torn each one from her body so he could enjoy what was underneath. The glistening of Emory's cheeks drew Byron's attention away from her breasts. She'd been crying. Mascara had smudged under her eyes, but the corners of her mouth pushed her cheeks into the widest smile Byron had seen on her.

She moved towards him, and, still carrying Clayton on his hip, Byron closed the gap between them.

"I got it," Emory whispered when they were close. Her hands lingered on Clayton's back, and she kept her body a half step away from Byron. "I mean, there's a group interview after exams, but she said it was just a formality and she will send me an offer tomorrow."

She tipped back on her heels and tilted her chin up to look at Byron. Despite the wide smile, there was a hint of sadness in her eyes. The way they still glistened from tears he knew weren't of the happy kind. Byron shifted Clayton on his hip, adjusting the boy's weight so he could free a hand. He used his thumb to wipe away Emory's tears, but she flinched at his touch.

"Don't," she whispered.

"We still have time." Byron hoped, at least. She'd mentioned exams before, but they weren't for another couple of weeks. Emory had mentioned how she wouldn't need to go all the way to the city for them, because the university held rural exams only a few towns over. She and Mya had organised to spend the week there. It would be close to a month before she had to go to the city and even more before the graduate position would start after Christmas. They had time.

He had time to finish getting everything sorted and surprise her with his big plan.

Emory didn't respond. She looked away from Byron and grabbed Clayton under his arms. Byron let her pull the little boy against her chest. Clayton hugged her, splattering kisses all over her wet face.

"We have time," Byron repeated. He could feel her slipping through his fingers even as she stood firm in front of him.

"We don't," Emory said. "I don't. If I stay here, I'll convince myself not to go. And I have to go."

"Of course you have to go, Em. There's not a single piece of me that thinks you should stay in this town. But that doesn't mean we don't have time. That doesn't mean we can't enjoy the time we have left."

"Byron, please, don't." Emory took another step back and steered herself towards the hallway. "Please don't make this any harder."

She disappeared into Clayton's room, but Byron followed her in. Emory dropped Clayton playfully on the bed, then moved about the room, packing away toys and folding laundry. It was busy work; Byron could see she was tidying what was around her because she couldn't tidy her thoughts.

"Em, the other day, I promised I would never let you go. I meant it. And I don't mean I'm trying to stop you from taking this job and leaving town because I know how important that is to you. I know you need to do it, and I would never hold you back from your dreams. But I need you like I need air. I need you to understand that you leaving town will not be the end of us."

Pain clawed through his skin, in his chest, in his head, in his bones.

"We have time, Em," he pleaded. *Give me time.*

"Stop." Emory stood in the middle of the room. Clayton jumped on the bed, shocked by his mother's harsh tone. Her voice wavered, but Emory crossed her arms and planted her legs. She squeezed her eyes shut, turning to face Byron, then forcing them open. "Stop. Mya's parents are still up with her aunt. Clayton and I will go stay with her while I figure something out. I can't be here, okay?"

She pulled Clayton's suitcase from the wardrobe. A handful of sleep suits and jumpers were still stuffed in the bottom of it. She'd always been ready to leave, Byron realised. She always knew she was going to go.

He couldn't try to stop her. It wouldn't be fair on her. What had she said? All her life, she'd followed people around. This was her chance to lead.

And maybe it was Byron's time to follow.

"If I go somewhere, will you still be here when I get back?"

Emory looked up at him and shrugged.

"Please, be here when I get back. I promise I won't try to make you stay."

Throwing a handful of clothes from a drawer into the suitcase, Emory nodded.

EMORY

"This whole thing feels oddly familiar," Mya huffed as she dragged the full suitcases up the hallway.

As soon as Byron had left the farmhouse to go ... wherever it was he needed to run off to, Emory had called on her best friend to help her pack. Again.

It was crazy to think that it was only a few weeks ago they'd been doing exactly what they were doing now, loading Emory's car with everything she and Clayton had. So much had changed in those few weeks, and Emory knew she'd hold this month close to her heart for the rest of her life.

Moving in with Byron had been her only choice, and in a way, Emory was glad she'd been forced to play this hand. She didn't regret the time they shared together; she only wished the circumstances were different. She wished she'd fallen in love with the town and the farm long before she fell in love with Byron. That she wanted to stay instead of feeling this overwhelming need to leave.

She wished she'd done a better job at protecting her

heart. Because fuck, it hurt now. The odd thing was that her soul didn't. Her soul was singing with possibility.

Mya dumped the suitcases by the door and joined Emory on the floor of the living room. Clayton scribbled on the paper-covered coffee table beside them. A small wave of guilt scattered along Emory's skin. She had to do this for herself. But she'd never stopped to consider if it was fair for Clayton. The poor kid had been moved around more in the past month than he had in his whole life, and when they moved to the city, it would be an even bigger change for him.

No more fun days with his Papa; he'd be off to daycare while Emory worked for the future they both deserved. It was okay, daycare would be good for him, and Emory didn't feel sad or bad about it in the slightest. But it was going to be a massive change that he wouldn't fully understand.

It felt like everywhere she looked, Emory was reminded of all the things that were going to make moving to the city hard. That was why she needed to get out of this house. Not just because every moment she spent with Byron was a step further down a cliff that felt too much like a love she couldn't walk away from. Not just because everything in this house reminded her of him and them and just how perfect the past few weeks had been. But because it was a very blinding reminder of how different life in the city would be for Clayton as well as herself.

It was going to be hard leaving Mya's, too. There was no doubt in Emory's mind that no matter where she was, it was never going to be easy. At least at Mya's house, she wouldn't feel hopelessly in love as well.

Fuck.

She was, wasn't she? Hopelessly and endlessly and utterly in love with Byron. And she was about to leave.

Maybe Mya had been right all along. Maybe coming here in the first place was not such a good idea.

It was done now, though, and the whole thing had cost Emory her heart. All she could do was hope it would start to heal in the city.

"You okay?" Mya asked. She'd settled on the floor next to Emory and pushed the plastic tub away from their laps. Emory didn't try to fight her for it. She'd stopped filling it a while ago. The truth was, she had no idea how many of the toys and books came with them from the cottage and how many were here all along.

"No," she admitted. The truth was always easier with Mya. "I thought I had everything figured out. I was so close to finishing my course, and I had all these grand plans to move to the city and finally do what was right for me. Don't get me wrong, I still want that. I still need that. But every time I see Byron, I wonder a little more what the cost of my dreams will be."

"I don't want to stay," she continued after swallowing back her sobs. "I hate this town and everyone in it. I hate how everything is a reminder of the life I thought I would have with Jaxon. And that's okay, really, I'm not sad about him leaving anymore. I don't miss him, but it really sucks seeing that reminder all the time. I hate the way everyone in town still somehow blames me for his leaving, as though he's not the one who showered me with promises then skipped town on his kid and never looked back. I hate that being here isn't *me*. I don't belong here, and I never will. Byron can't change that, no matter how much I love him. I'll always hate it here."

She sank to the floor, lying back until she was staring up at the ceiling. Clayton, seeing his mother flat on the ground, toddled over to climb on top of her. He nestled his head into her neck and settled his weight on her front.

His tiny body pressed against her lungs. It forced her to breathe in slower, more focused inhales, sending a tiny sliver of calm through her.

Mya remained silent, as though she knew her best friend had a lot to get out. Wrapping her arms around Clayton, Emory continued.

"I hate it here, but I love Byron. And every time he is close, I forget a little how far from *home* this town is for me. I can't get swept up in that. I need to not be around him, even if it's only for a little while. So that I can think straight. So that I can remember *me* and my dreams and my future."

Lying beside Emory, Mya twisted to her side. She propped an arm under her head and placed her free hand over Emory's on Clayton's back. "Can I tell you something?"

Emory hummed. Her eyes were filled with tears that threatened to spill over her cheeks if she turned her head.

"Byron and Tucker talk a lot. Like, a lot. More than I thought a dad and his adult son would talk. But I think because Byron is technically kind of young to have fully grown kids, it's different. I think Byron filled a bit of the void that Jaxon left behind in Tucker's life, and they've had a different kind of relationship since then."

"Why are you telling me this?" Giving up on holding back her tears, Emory turned her head towards Mya. Her hair followed her, falling over her face and clumping together on her wet cheeks.

Mya stretched forward to tuck the stray pieces behind Emory's ear.

"Because I overhear a lot of conversations," she said, so hushed she might as well have been whispering. "And what I don't overhear, I weasel out of Tucker. He tells me everything."

"Mya," Emory warned. She furrowed her brow and huffed. Mya needed to get to the point. There was only so much wallowing Emory would allow herself, and she was nearly done with her quota.

"Honestly, you'd think they were brothers, not father and son. It's kind of weird, really." Mya pushed onto her elbow and tucked her hand into Clayton's armpit. He squirmed under her tickling fingers. "Hey, Clayton, buddy," she chimed. "Reckon you could go get a bottle of water from the fridge. Actually, two, one for me and one for Mummy?"

He leapt from Emory's chest, crawling free and hustling to the kitchen. The little kid loved nothing more than being helpful, and this was about as helpful as it could get.

"I don't know if he can even open the fridge, Mya."

"Ah, well, it got him out of the room." Sitting up, Mya pulled Emory off the rug.

God, Emory was braced for whatever inappropriate comment Mya was about to make. She didn't need to hear it, any more than she needed to be told that Byron told Tucker everything. Surely he didn't tell his adult son *everything*? Like, maybe he let Tucker in on their little fling, that wasn't a secret. But not all the details? She hoped not. She chewed at the inside of her cheek, her eyes darting around, looking anywhere but at her best friend. Mya must have seen the terror lining Emory's face because she dropped her hands onto Emory's lap.

"Oh gosh, Em. How dirty did the two of you get?" Mya cackled with laughter but quickly quietened her laugh when Emory scowled in response. "Sorry, not important. I clearly don't know those details, and I don't really want to know either. But I *do* know that Byron has been increasingly torn over the past few weeks. He loves you. Tucker kept trying to tell him about how you wanted to leave town, but he either didn't listen or had already fallen too far."

It wasn't a surprise, hearing that Byron loved her. Because, sure, he hadn't said those exact words to Emory, but the intent was always clear with every little action he took. But if he was telling other people, that had to mean something. "Why didn't you tell me sooner?"

"Because one, I thought he deserved the chance to tell you himself. If he didn't, he's a bigger dummy than I thought he was. And two, I didn't want how Byron feels to change how *you* felt. I wanted you to give the interview absolutely everything you had. You have a hard choice to make, and even though it's hard, you deserve the chance to make it. If you knew how Byron felt you wouldn't have tried so hard, just so that you could turn around and say, 'Oh well, I didn't get it' and stay here with Byron."

Of course, Mya would play the hand that left Emory with as much choice as possible. She was right, if Emory had known, she would have deliberately flunked the interview and used it as an excuse to stop trying. She would have fallen onto the easy path.

"You always would have wondered what if, and that didn't seem fair."

Emory fell forward, dropping her head onto Mya's shoulder. Her sobs were soft, but she still left a wet patch on her friend's oversized shirt. Mya was right, Emory always would have wondered what if. Now, she would always wonder what if she had never gotten the job.

With impeccable timing, Clayton scurried back around the couch.

"Mummy! My! Water!" he cheered.

Emory had to force herself off Mya. She wiped her cheeks with the back of her sleeve before pasting on something that resembled a smile and turned to the three-year-old.

A small, brown glass bottle hung in each hand. He clapped them together and Emory cringed at the loud *clink*. Thankfully, they didn't break.

"Woah, you got the fridge open, hey?" Mya said. She hid her wicked grin behind her hand.

Emory gave her a look that was part annoyance, part amusement. Her eyes rolled a little, and her mouth forcibly closed, but dimples appeared in her cheeks to give away her hidden laughter. She steadied herself with a slow exhale and turned back to Clayton.

"Thank you so much, buddy!"

He placed the beers in her lap, clapped to himself, then grabbed the remote from the coffee table. Emory watched in surprise as he turned the TV on. It loaded directly onto the kid's channel that had been playing last. Clayton bounced on the spot, a smug little grin covering his face. Emory dropped her mouth open. Byron had taught him that, for sure. She certainly hadn't.

It didn't matter, though. Sure, she'd have to keep the remote hidden so Clayton couldn't keep the TV on twenty-four seven, but him knowing how to turn it on wasn't necessarily a bad thing. A little hint of independence was good, and the TV had really been their saviour during the flood.

Emory pulled herself up onto the couch and twisted one bottle open. She passed the beer to Mya and opened her own. Water schmwater. She needed something stronger to help process the hundred and fifty emotions that had been flooding her faster than the actual flood had covered the farm. It was a lot, and she wasn't sure she'd ever fully recover.

Not here at least.

She took a long sip of her beer. The bitterness left a tang on her tongue. She clicked it away, standing up.

"Let's take all this to the car," she said, gesturing to the tub of toys.

"You still want to leave?"

"I have to. For the same reason you couldn't tell me about Byron until after the interview. If I stay, I'll sabotage myself. I need to think straight, and I can't do that here."

Mya seemed to understand, or at least accept, Emory's reasoning. She placed the lid onto the large plastic tub, hauled it into her arms, and stood up. The beer bottle hung loose between two fingers, but Emory reached out to grab it before it fell.

She followed Mya down the short hall and placed the bottles on the entry table.

"Hey, Mya, why did you tell me about Byron?" she asked as she grabbed the two suitcases.

Looking over her shoulder, one foot across the threshold, Mya shifted the weight of the large tub against her hip. "Because I think you might need to brace yourself for what comes next."

CHAPTER 34

BYRON

Byron didn't waste any time after leaving Emory at the farmhouse to finalise his plans. He'd planned to go to Tucker's first, but he was barely across the bridge when he passed Mya's bright red Toyota on the road. That couldn't have been a good sign, and Byron knew then that he would need to get shit done as quickly as possible.

He called Tucker instead.

"What did you do?" Tucker said as he answered the phone. The line was echoey and full of static through the Bluetooth. It always was through this part of the road into town.

"Huh?" He'd heard, he just didn't understand. "No, 'Hey, Dad, what's up?'"

"Nup. Emory called Mya. Sounded like she was crying, and Mya rushed off to the farmhouse. Told me not to expect her back because she was helping Emory move back into town. I think she is going to stay with Mya. I thought you were making it right?"

Fuck. He had less time than he thought. "What does Mya know?"

Tucker groaned. "I told her you liked Emory, and you didn't want her to leave. That was it ..."

His voice faded off, and the back of Byron's neck tingled. He knew when his son was telling lies, or half-truths. One hand on the steering wheel, Byron reached behind his head to scratch at the clawing sensation under his hairline. "Tucker?"

"Fine, I probably got ahead of myself and told her I thought you were going to give me the farm."

Byron huffed, but Tucker continued talking in one quick breath. "I'm sorry, okay? I know you're not yet, but the other day it sounded like you were thinking more about it. I didn't mean anything by it, just wishful thinking of a young bloke trying to impress his new girlfriend."

"Tucker, I did mean something by it. I do. I just hadn't got all my shit sorted yet and now I'm running out of time."

"Dad? I don't understand."

Byron dropped his head back against the seat. He stretched out the tense muscles quickly, keeping an eye on the road. Gripping the steering wheel ten times tighter than necessary, Byron steered the car along the winding road and sighed.

"Emory wants to leave town. She has long before I convinced her to fall into bed with me, and I refuse to be the thing that keeps her here. But I can't go back to how I was. I was grumpy and miserable. Emory brought light into my life, and if she's gone, I don't want to be back to that lonely old farmer I used to be." He took a deep breath and waited for Tucker's response.

None came, nothing except the hissing feedback through the phone line and something that sounded a little like an exaggerated hum.

"I'm giving you the farm," he continued when it became clear Tucker was waiting for him to elaborate, "now."

There was a distinct *ha* that came through the phone before the sound of muffled laughter and the clattering of Tucker dropping his phone. Byron cleared his throat. His brow dropped low, squinting his eyes as close to shut as was safe while driving.

Tucker's laughter began to ease, but his voice remained wheezy as he attempted to talk. "I don't ... I can't ... you ... wait."

Byron heard the phone knock against a hard surface. Tucker's rapid breaths were barely audible through the line.

"It's not a joke," Byron called out, hoping Tucker would hear him.

This was ... not quite the reaction Byron had expected. He'd known Tucker would be surprised and a little taken aback. But he was laughing like he'd just been roasted by his favourite comedian, and this wasn't meant to be funny. Reaching town, Byron pulled into the parking lot of the small shopping strip. He threw the car into park and got out, leaving the engine running. It was terrible for the environment, but the sun was blasting down, and Byron didn't want the car heating up too much. He'd be quick.

"Tucker," Byron warned. He shielded his eyes from the sun with his hand and ducked across the street.

There was another fumbling sound through the phone before Tucker finally spoke. It seemed he got most of his amusement out, but he spoke in a flat voice like it might slip to the surface if he let it.

"You want me to run the farm?"

Byron hovered outside the boutique homewares store. He'd always wondered how a shop like this managed to stay open in such a small town. Everything felt overpriced, from the organic wool rugs to the hand-poured candles Emory loved. It wasn't Byron's kind of place, but with every day Emory spent adding her little feminine touches to the farmhouse, Byron had started to see the appeal.

And Emory really did love those candles. She burnt through the first before the bridge had reopened, and had a new scent melting on the counter every day since Tucker brought her more. It was the only time Byron had ever seen Emory truly care for something that came out of this town. He had to make sure she wouldn't go without them in the city.

"Yes," he said with a smile. He leant his back against the red brick wall to the side of the shop and propped one foot back.

"Have you thought this through? You'd be giving up a lot."

"I know, but the truth is, I barely wanted the land in the first place. I've spent a lot of time building up other investments, so I'm not relying on it, and now it's time for me to let it go." Byron let his head tip back. The sun was warm on his face, but not as warm as his heart. It had been practically singing ever since he'd come up with this outlandish plan.

Tucker hummed in contemplation. "And you're doing all this because Emory is moving to the city?"

"Because," Byron started. He pushed off the wall and began pacing the sidewalk. He needed to get off the phone with Tucker so he could get to the cottage and then back to Emory. She'd said she would still be at the farmhouse when he got back, but Byron didn't want to test that any more than he needed to. "I've lived my whole life here. I met your mother, we had Jaxon and then you here, I took over the farm when my father retired. Everything I wanted to achieve here is done. Emory has her whole life ahead of her. It's selfish to want her to spend it with someone like me, but there's something between us that neither of us were expecting. Something worth more to me than the history I have in this town."

If his son figured it out, so be it. Byron would be home to tell Emory himself soon enough.

"Woah. You really like her, huh?"

That warm feeling continued to spread until Byron was sure his giddiness was written all over his face. "I more than like her Tuck, I fucking love her. And it's about time I show her."

Byron's car was filled with the bursting aroma of a few dozen candles when he finally pulled into the driveway of the cottage. The poor woman at the store had nearly had a heart attack when he told her he was going to buy all her stock. She'd clutched at her chest and tried to argue through bated breaths.

"It's too much, you don't have to do that," she had said, even when Byron insisted.

Eventually, she had packed each little jar into a few large boxes and helped Byron carry them to his still-running car.

He'd thrown his credit card over the reader before she'd had a chance to tell him the price, and he still didn't want to know. But at least now Emory would have no shortage of her new favourite candles in the city.

Byron knew he was counting on her going along with his plan. They'd shared a lot over the past few weeks, and he was sure she felt the same way that he did. If not, he was going to end up heartbroken *and* homeless.

Even though there were still a few days left on Emory's lease, he'd taken a gamble that Jaxon would be here. And he was right. Jaxon stepped out onto the porch of the cottage before Byron had made it up the small path.

The ground was damp, but not covered in mud and gunk like the farm. Turned out the cottage had been fine all along. Emory could have stayed here. Byron was glad for the overcautious predictions of the SES and his own overprotective side. Without them, Emory never would have come to stay, and they'd probably still be lonely and pining without knowing they both felt the same way.

He needed to not think about Emory for a moment, though.

"What do you want?" Jaxon called. His arms were folded across his chest, and a deep scowl was painted on his face. His stance was exaggerated to the point it was comical, and Byron knew his son was forcing out an anger he didn't really feel.

"To talk. Can we go inside?"

"Nope."

Right. Maybe a little of the anger was genuine.

"Well, I came to remind you that I transferred the cottage into your name when Emory first fell pregnant. It was meant to be my retirement home, but I thought it was better for you and your family to have somewhere to live than for me to hold onto it."

"You can't have it back, if that's what you're getting at."

A deep throbbing started in Byron's temples. For fuck's sake, all Jaxon could think about was himself and Byron had been stupid to think this conversation would go any other way than this. Might as well cut to the chase then.

"I don't want it back. I'm reminding you because I'm giving Tucker the farm."

"But the farm is worth more, that's not fair."

Byron's hands curled into fists by his sides as Jaxon trailed off. A few days ago, he'd had to plead with himself not to punch his son, but now he was starting to forget why that was.

"What's not fair," he growled, striding forward, "is you skipping town on your son and never looking back. What's not fair is you weaseling out of paying Emory child support by letting her stay in the cottage for free, even though I gave it to you *for* Emory and Clayton. You should be grateful I'm letting you keep it."

"It's in my name, you can't take it back."

Byron took the last step onto the porch and towered over his son. Jaxon was right, he couldn't rescind the title, at least he didn't think he could. But he didn't want to anyway. Although he felt little empathy for Jaxon, and nothing but anger and disinterest swirled through Byron's veins, Jaxon *was* his son, after all. He might not deserve the farm, but Byron wasn't going to cut him off completely. That choice was Jaxon's.

"No, but letting you keep it does make it easier to give the whole farm to Tucker."

"You always said the farm would be mine," Jaxon spat out, glaring up at Byron.

The anger flooding Byron's veins threatened to bubble to the surface. "That was when you were acting like you cared about it. I don't care if you don't think it's fair. You get the cottage; Tucker gets the farm. The decision has been made, and the paperwork as good as signed. If I hear you're causing him grief, so help me, I will come back to this town and take this house back. Understood?"

Jaxon nodded meekly.

Turning on his heel, Byron didn't look back as he stalked to the car and slid into the driver's seat.

The odd blend of perfumes should have been overpowering, but instead, it calmed him. The not-so-subtle reminder of Emory smothered all the anger left in him. It was time to go home and finally tell her that they could always be together.

As he crossed the bridge towards his farm, there wasn't a single angry cell left in his body. A calm sort of joy washed over him instead. Byron had always expected the flood would bring change, he just hadn't expected the change to be this wonderful.

CHAPTER 35

EMORY

A bead of sweat trickled its way down Emory's back, tucking into the lace trim of her tank. She shoved the last plastic tub into the back of her car and dropped her hands onto the faded fabric of the boot. These tubs weren't this heavy last time she had loaded them, even though the contents were exactly the same.

She'd triple-checked that everything she was packing away had come to the farmhouse with her. All the toys Byron kept here for his days with Clayton had been catalogued and packed away in their baskets before she'd gotten to work loading the tubs. There was no reason for their luggage to be heavier now. Nothing except the added emotional baggage she now carried.

After helping her carry everything out to the car, Mya pulled out her phone and gasped at whatever message she'd received. She hadn't bothered to squeeze her oversized phone back into the pocket of her jeans before mumbling something about checking on Clayton and running back inside. Emory had rolled her eyes, but was thankful that her friend was here to help. It was easier than having to keep an eye on Clayton while she played Tetris with their belongings.

Emory had taken her oversized sweater off under the heat from the outback sun, but it now burned at her shoulders. Sweat beaded on her forehead and back, and all the little wispy strands that had escaped her messy bun were stuck to her neck. She would not miss this. Sydney was sure to have its own weather annoyances, but the extremes here in Gardner Creek were surely worse than whatever the city could throw at her.

With both large tubs squashed into the boot, Emory hauled a suitcase up. Mya had done this part for her, all those days ago, when they were packing up the cottage. Now, Emory wasn't quite sure how she was supposed to manage lifting the oversized suitcase into the high boot of her small SUV. She propped it against the opening, shifting her grip so she could squat underneath it and use her shoulders to push the suitcase up to the height she needed. If she could just ...

The suitcase toppled from her grip, falling from her shoulder and hitting the gravel of the driveway with a *thud*. She could have called out for Mya's help. All those mornings her friend spent helping haul groceries for her parents meant she would always be stronger. Emory had lost count of all the times she'd relied on Mya's upper body strength over the past few years. Building Clayton's cot when he outgrew the tiny bassinet, bringing in the new TV when Jaxon had taken the old one with him, loading her car when she had to evacuate for the flood.

That flood had changed almost everything, but it didn't change how much Emory needed her best friend. It was time for Emory to depend solely on herself. She could do that. Right?

Besides, if she got Mya to load and unload the car now,

how could Emory expect to be able to do it herself when the time came to move to the city? She was going to be alone, she might as well get used to it.

Her eyes began to burn. Emory bit her lip, catching her breath, determined not to let something like a silly old overfull suitcase upset her. She reached down for it, positioning it against the car. The black fabric looked rusty from the red dust of the driveway. Everything had dried off so quickly under the spring sun that came out after the flood. The rapid change would never make sense to Emory.

She rolled her shoulders and reached down to pull the suitcase into her arms again. Bending her knees, she wriggled her shoulder underneath the weight, then rose slowly, keeping the suitcase balanced between her hands and the tubs in the boot. The wheels dug into her arm, but with a final heave, she felt the top of the bag tip onto the tub. Emory released all the breath she was holding and slid the suitcase into place.

All her emotions came out with that breath. Every ounce of sadness she felt about leaving the people she loved in this town finally released. All the tears she thought she had gotten out while packing reemerged tenfold, streaming down her face. She was not going to miss this town, but she would miss some of the people.

Tucker, and the way they had fallen into an almost sibling style friendship. She remembered the time he fixed her car when the engine light came on and how he mowed the lawn every week when Clayton was still a baby.

Mya. Of course, Mya. Emory was going to be so lost without her best friend. Phone calls and video chats would simply not be the same as all the late-night confessions or hushed chats in the library. She was going to miss knowing her best friend was always only a few minutes away.

And Byron. Her chest panged and her knees went weak as Emory thought of how much she was going to miss Byron. Not just because of the past few weeks, though. Emory was going to miss the way he always saved her fresh produce from the farm and eggs from the chickens. She was going to miss seeing Clayton's face light up every time he saw Byron's farmhouse through the car window. After Jaxon left, Byron was the first person to show Emory any ounce of kindness, and his generous nature hadn't waned since. He gave her everything he could to help her, comfort her, to make her feel welcome in a town that felt so far from home. And after living with him through the flood, Emory saw something else in him, too. Something she would miss just as much. Byron was still the broody, almost grumpy guy everyone in town knew him to be, but Emory had gotten to know the gentler, almost cheerful side of him. She loved how he had opened up to her, and she loved the man she got to know.

It didn't matter anymore that he was a little bit older or that he was Jaxon's dad. It only mattered that he was hers. And she was his.

And fuck, she was going to miss him.

Leaving Byron was the hardest part of all. It made her dreams feel inconsequential next to her love for him. She wasn't even leaving town yet, only leaving the farmhouse, and she felt like this. How was she going to cope when it really was time to move to the city?

That was why she had to move out.

Dropping to the ground, Emory pulled her knees to her chest and hugged herself as she let her tears fall.

She was so lost in her sobs that she didn't hear the crunch of the gravel driveway under Byron's large ute. She didn't notice the shadow that moved over her as he parked next to her car, or the way the air shifted when Byron got out and stood over her.

She didn't notice anything until he dropped to his knees in front of her and gently tugged her hands away from her face. Emory tried to fight against it, pressing the palms of her hands into her eyes and doing her best to lock her elbows in place, but Byron's persistent yet soft force coaxed them down.

"Please don't cry," he said, dropping his head down to rest their foreheads together. "This will be so much harder if you're crying."

Emory sobbed. If her eyes had been a little drier, she might have noticed the tears beginning to well in the corner of Byron's, but her vision was a blur. "It already is hard. Please don't make it worse."

"Fuck, Em, I'm trying to make it better."

"I'm sorry, okay? I'm sorry I got carried away, and what was meant to be a little fun became so much more. It sucks, I know, I'm feeling it. But it *was* fun, Byron, and I'll never be sorry for that. I'm only sorry that it can't be anything more."

"What if it could be?" Byron let go of her hands then, wiping her tears with his thumbs. Emory opened her mouth to explain for what felt like the hundredth time why she *had* to leave, but Byron held his thumbs over her lips. "And I don't mean you staying in Gardner Creek. But if there was a way for us to be together, would you want it?"

Of course she wanted that, but there was no use dreaming and imagining. She had to face reality. Emory's nod was feeble, barely there before she decided against it and turned her head to the side. "But we can't."

"Emory, listen to me. If we could, would you want that?"

"How!?"

He wasn't listening to her, and it was only making the hurt worse, even though he said he wanted to do the opposite. Emory flinched free from his tender hold and stood. She slammed the boot of the car closed and dragged the second suitcase to the back seat. If she turned it on its side, propped it up against Clayton's car seat, maybe she could make it fit. Okay, she'd have to push her seat forward, but that didn't matter. She needed to leave before she fell back into Byron's arms again.

She was still wrestling the suitcase into the too-small gap between the seats when Byron's hand covered hers. He spun her around, out of the way, so he could close the car door. Moving back, Emory pressed herself against the cool metal as he caged her in.

"You need to move to Sydney," he said. His voice was low, and he leant close to her. So close she could feel the warmth of his breath on her ear, but even so, he kept his body off hers. "And I need to be with you, Em. There's only one path here that doesn't lead to either of us with our hearts broken or our dreams crushed."

Emory's brow furrowed. This whole messy fling was going to end in heartbreak no matter what. She'd known it long before she was even close to falling, and she knew it innately now. Byron was talking nonsense.

"Please stop," she pleaded. "Please."

Byron groaned in her ear before pushing back. The golden amber of his eyes was dark yet glistening with moisture. "No, let me explain. Fuck, I'm no good at this Em and maybe I should let you go off to the city and live your life and find someone who knows all the right things to say, but I can't. I can't let you do that without me. I've been lonely for a long fucking time. Longer than I ever really knew. But you brought life back into me. You melt away the cold façade I've kept up for so many years, and you make me feel like myself again. You make me feel like everything is right, and I can't let that go. Without you, this town means nothing to me. This farm means nothing to me."

Emory watched his Adam's apple bob as he gulped back the sobs that threatened to take over his speech. She closed her eyes, waiting for him to finish and trying, really trying, not to get carried away on the hope that was starting to bloom in her heart. She said nothing, instead letting her head fall back against the window of the car. Byron followed her, staying close but still not pressing his body against hers in the way she always seemed to crave.

"If you go," he whispered, "there's nothing left for me in this town. So let me come with you."

He moved a little closer, standing with his feet on either side of Emory's, so close she could feel her chest brushing against his with every rise and fall of her bated breaths. Leaning in, Byron kissed her salty cheeks.

"Please," he added. "Let me come with you."

"What about the farm?"

Byron cupped her cheeks with his hands and dropped his forehead against hers. She could smell the woodsy body wash he always used and the subtle smell of petrol that seemed to linger on his clothes after he came in from riding the quad bike around the farm.

"This old place? I was getting sick of mending fences anyway."

A slight, almost laugh escaped between Emory's sobs. "But you love it here."

"Only because I had nothing else to love. Then you came and looked at me the way that you did. God, I thought how fucking inappropriate of me to want all the things I want with you. How selfish of me to hope you'd want someone as worn down as me. But then we both started to fall—don't look at me like that, I know you did."

She'd raised an eyebrow, but he was right. She fell right alongside him, and it was the best kind of freefall she'd ever experienced. "Okay," she admitted, tilting her head towards him so their noses pressed together. She could feel the ghost of his breath along her lips. "I fell too."

"And then we were falling, and I don't feel like I have to love it here anymore, Em. I love you instead. I don't want to be here on the farm, lonely again. I want to be with you, living life, chasing dreams."

Emory let her lips press against Byron's. The air between them was hot and heavy, and her chest pounded. "But moving to the city is *my* dream, not yours."

"Right, but you are my dream."

He spoke the words directly into her mouth, then sealed them with a kiss unlike any they had shared before. The lust and passion was still there, it always would be, but this kiss was softer, slower. It was laced with the love that poured between them. Byron ran his tongue along Emory's lips, and she opened her mouth for him, tilting her head to deepen the connection. She swirled her tongue around his and nibbled gently on his lower lip.

"I love you," Byron whispered when they broke the kiss.

Emory felt a warmth that had nothing to do with the sun spreading through her. It wrapped around her heart like a comforting hug. "I love you, too."

Vaguely, she registered the sound of the screen door clanging, of footsteps along the gravel, and of Mya's sharp gasp.

"Clayton, buddy, let's ... um ... go back inside. We'll show Mummy the picture later."

"Papa!"

Underneath Byron's mouth, Emory smiled. She'd always loved the relationship Byron and Clayton shared, even if he let her son watch too much TV and taught him how to climb over the back of the couch. He'd adjust, she knew. And they would deal with the questions as he grew. Nothing would be too hard, not when the love between all three of them was so strong.

Still, there were certain things a three-year-old didn't need to see. She moved to the side, trying to wriggle herself free from Byron's hold, but he pulled her back in place.

"He should see how in love his mum and Papa are," he whispered.

CHAPTER 36

BYRON

Later that evening, whilst Emory settled Clayton into bed, Byron found himself in the den, staring up at the wall of books. This dim room had seen more light in the past few weeks than it had in the previous decade. What started as Byron's small escape from the temptation he'd been determined to resist soon became a lively room. Clayton loved exploring the bookshelves almost as much as Byron and Emory, and Byron was a little annoyed at himself for not thinking to bring him down here sooner. All this time, he'd brought books out for Clayton instead.

It didn't matter, though. Because they'd be moving soon.

The thought pinched at something near Byron's heart. It was the right call, but knowing that didn't make the reality of saying goodbye to the farm any easier. He'd grown up here, he'd fallen in love here—twice now—and he'd had the boys here. Tucker and Jaxon, sure, but Clayton too.

Saying goodbye was going to be hard. He was glad he could pass it on to Tucker, though. The Gardner legacy over the farm would live on for at least one more generation.

With a sigh, Byron leant his weight against the pool table and started calculating how exactly they were going to move that many books. If they'd even have space for them in the city. There was a lot to figure out, but it didn't faze Byron. Not really.

Although maybe Tucker would want to keep all the books here, then they wouldn't have to pack them all up. Byron was fit from his years working on the farm, but even he knew how heavy books could get.

"You know," Emory's voice cut through his thoughts as she stepped into the room. Byron shifted his gaze to take her in. Perfect, she was always perfect.

Falling into place next to him, Emory nudged his arm with her shoulder before continuing her sentence, "Weeks ago, I really thought you were down here hiding because you couldn't stand the thought of me being in your space."

A chuckle rolled through Byron's throat. "I was hiding," he admitted. "But I was hiding because I thought if I saw you making yourself at home in my house, I'd never let you leave."

"Thank you for letting me leave." Emory's voice dropped, and she wrung her hands in front of her stomach. "But are you sure you want to move to the city? You've never even *been*. This farm has been your whole world."

Byron shifted his weight off the table and stood in front of her. His hands rested next to her thighs, caging her in against the table, and he towered over her so she had to lift her head to look at him. A tiny crease sat between her brows, and her lips pressed together.

"It was my whole world, Em. But that's not always a good thing. And besides, it's not anymore."

She furrowed her brow further, and Byron kissed the wrinkles from her forehead.

"You're my world now, Emory, and I would move to the other side of the Earth if it meant I could spend my days with you."

A tiny tear escaped his eyes, trailing down his cheek until it pooled in the corner of his mouth. Byron poked his tongue through his lips to lick the salty liquid. Emory's eyes tracked the movement, her worrisome look melting away as her mouth dropped open ever so slightly.

"Thank you," she whispered. Her eyes never left his lips, and her voice began to shake as Byron closed himself into her.

"You know," he said as he shifted his hands to graze up her arms. "I never showed you how to play pool. It would be a shame if we left and you never learned."

Emory tilted her head. "You better show me then."

He stepped back, hating the chill the gap between them sent through his bones. He racked the balls and grabbed a cue from the wall, never quite taking his gaze off Emory. She watched him with her arms folded across her chest. The line was back between her brows, and she bit her lip as she tracked how he set up for the game.

Byron took the first shot, breaking the triangle and sending the balls flying across the felt. Satisfied at the spread, and ignoring the balls that dropped into pockets, Byron turned to Emory and held out the cue.

"Didn't you get some in?" she questioned.

Maybe she did know a little pool after all. Byron held back his smirk, shrugging away the question and tapping the cue on the floor in front of her. Emory shook head with a laugh as she took it from him.

Emory's long hair hung down her back as she circled the table, checking the white ball and looking for a good play. When she chose her target and stepped forward, Byron moved in behind her. His legs on either side of hers, he pressed against her and wrapped his hands over her arms. The little gasp she let out at his closeness stirred inside him, as though this hadn't been his plan all along.

With their bodies together, Byron moved her arms into the right position and leant her torso down with his own. They took the shot together, sinking the ball. Emory squealed, jumping in excitement. Byron took the cue from her, swiping it across the table to push all the balls up one end.

"Ah, look at that," he growled, "you're a natural."

Spinning her around, Byron held her close and kissed her. Their mouths crashed together, charged with an explosive energy that Byron had never felt before. He ran his tongue along her lips, and she tilted her head for him. The kiss was flirty and frenzied, but nothing about it was rushed. They explored in sync, breathing each other in. When, finally, Byron pulled back, it wasn't to stop the kiss. He pulled her tank over her head as they panted for air, then fell back against her mouth.

Hastily and clumsily, they shed their clothing. In nothing but their underwear, Byron lifted Emory onto the table. Leaning on her hands, she arched her back as Byron made his way down her body. He licked along her bra line, nipped at her sensitive nipples through the thin padded fabric, and left a line of wet kisses down her torso.

At the apex of her thighs, he dropped to his knees between her legs. Emory was his favourite meal, and he'd never tire of showing her just how much he enjoyed devouring her.

There was a wet patch on her panties. Byron pressed

against it with his thumb and teased along the seam with his mouth. She whimpered, flinching at the way the delicate touch of his tongue tickled her sensitive skin. Moving the fabric barrier to the side, Byron flattened his tongue and licked her pussy. The taste sent a pulsing to his groin and a heat straight to his core. Emory was going to be the death of him, but he'd live for every moment they could spend together.

With his tongue on her clit, Byron pushed two fingers into her, curling them up to stroke her anterior walls. Emory squirmed beneath him, but he held her still and pumped his fingers into her over and over. Sucking her sensitive bud, Byron coaxed her orgasm out of her until she was panting and writhing. Her hands pulled at the ends of his hair as he licked her clean.

As the muscles in her legs began to relax, Byron stood, shifting out of his briefs. His firm cock sprang to life. He fisted it, remembering how fucking incredible it felt when he sank into Emory bare.

It was tempting to give in to desire. After all, giving in was exactly how they ended up here, in love. But they couldn't. He knew it worried her too much.

He gave himself a small taste, running his dick through her slick folds and pressing the tip toward her entrance. Emory held her breath as he did, and maybe that meant she would be okay with it, but he didn't want her to get caught in the moment.

With a groan, Byron wrapped Emory's legs around his waist and lifted her from the pool table. He took long strides down the hall and into his room. Dropping her on his bed, he fished a condom from the bedside drawer and rolled it over his cock.

Emory had positioned herself in the centre of the bed with her knees up and her legs spread wide. She looked fucking incredible like this. Wet and ready for him. Byron crawled forward, pausing to lick along her again before positioning himself between her legs.

He pushed in slowly, giving her time to adjust to his size and giving himself time to soak in the feeling. Having his cock buried deep inside Emory was his favourite state of being.

Wrapping her arms around his neck, Emory pulled Byron close and kissed him.

"I love you," she moaned into his mouth as he rocked his hips into her.

"I fucking love you too, Em."

They moved in sync, rocking together as their pleasure grew and grew into a cliff they could dive off. Kissing as they rode out their orgasm, Byron and Emory fell into oblivion together.

"And you're sure the books can stay?" Byron asked Tucker for what felt like the fifteenth time.

Everything else was packed into the large moving truck and on its way to the city, and Byron had loaded his and Emory's cars with anything they might need before the truck arrived. It should only be half a day behind them, but it was going to have to go slow through the winding backcountry roads.

"Are you kidding?" Tucker stood beside him and slapped his hand across Byron's back. "I'm trying to get a librarian to fall for me, I need all the books I can get my hands on."

Byron turned to his son. "Don't do anything stupid with the farm."

"What exactly do you think I'm going to do, grow poppies?"

With a laugh, Byron and Tucker hugged goodbye. Across the driveway, Emory stood with Clayton on her hip. Even from here, Byron could see the way her cheeks glistened with tears as she said goodbye to Mya.

"You gonna be okay in the city, Dad?"

Byron took a deep breath. It had been two months since Emory first got the job offer at Sydscape, and they'd been preparing for this day ever since. Virtual house viewings, packing everything they owned into boxes, and tidying up the farm, ready for Tucker to take over. She didn't start until the new year, and logistically, making such a big move the weekend before Christmas probably wasn't the best idea, but they'd decided to move early so they *both* had time to settle into city life.

The house they'd found—and Byron had bought—was nestled in the inner suburbs on a distinct green wedge of large enough blocks. There was enough of a yard for Miff to enjoy, although Byron had plans to build her some kind of obstacle course to help burn off her energy. That, and lots of walks.

Byron was going to be a stay-at-home Papa, and even though it was new and yeah, okay, it was scary, he was looking forward to it. Maybe change wasn't always such a bad thing.

They had a long drive ahead of them, though, and while it was still relatively early in the morning, they needed to get going soon. Tucker and Mya were joining them for the trip, to share the driving and make sure no one was tackling winding roads and exhaustion on their own. Tucker and Mya would fly back from the city after Christmas. Byron wasn't sure if Jaxon would be joining them on the twenty-fifth. He was invited, but other than a few quick thumbs up in response to his texts, Byron hadn't heard from his eldest son since that day at the cottage. He was used to it by now, but the invitation was always going to be there for when Jaxon was ready to make amends.

"You ready?" Emory called out.

Byron shook off the unsettled feeling that always seemed to wash over him when he thought about Jaxon. There wasn't much else Byron could do, really, other than hope that one day, Jaxon would want to be part of their lives again. He was welcome as soon as he made that call.

Moving to meet Emory in the drive, Byron swept her into his arms between the loaded cars. On the other side of Emory's car, Mya leaned into the back seat to strap Clayton into his chair.

"I'm ready if you are," Byron said, wrapping his arms around her.

He was, truly, ready.

As it turned out, all that change he'd been so worried about the flood bringing had been exactly what he needed after all.

EMORY

5 Years Later

Pushing her keyboard back, Emory rolled her shoulders forward and let her forehead rest on the desk. How she was supposed to help the public image of a cattle farmer who publicly outed himself as a vegan was beyond her.

Social media comments were flooding in faster than she could keep up. At least she had notifications from social media apps turned off on her phone. Five years of working in marketing had taught her that, even if she was at a loss on how to handle this.

Byron was fuming, the meat markets were wary, and what she had considered to be a very successful social media presence was beginning to crumble. She'd kill Tucker for this. And Mya, too. Knowing her best friend, it was probably her idea to stop eating meat in the first place. Emory would bet she'd fallen in love with one of the cows and swiftly decided never to eat beef again. And even after all this time, Tucker was still doing his damn best to impress the librarian who had stolen his heart.

Gardner Farm was the sole social media account

Emory had kept on her books after she finished her graduate program with Sydscape and was promoted to marketing account manager. She had a small team of graduates who all turned to her for guidance, as well as two wonderful social media managers who, in every other situation, handled the notifications and social feeds of the accounts under her management. Something had always held her back from handing over Gardner Farm, though. There was too much legacy there to leave it all to someone else's probably very capable hands.

This, though, made her want to rip her hair out.

Stretching her neck out, she glimpsed the large metal clock on the wall of her small home office. The desk from Byron's farmhouse had made the trip to the city with them and sat in the centre of the room. Emory still got a little giddy every time she thought about the first time she sat behind it. So much had changed since then.

Technically, Emory had five minutes left of her workday. But her stomach was growling. The delicious scent of rosemary and lamb wafted under the closed door from the roast Byron was cooking, and she could resist it no longer. Besides, there was nothing she could realistically do to save the face of Tucker's farm until tomorrow. She'd called him to the city for an emergency meeting, and it took everything she had not to let Byron into the boardroom when they met. He'd be far more than a fly on the wall of *that* meeting, and she did not envy Tucker right now. He was going to get an earful.

With another heaved sigh, Emory shut down her computer and adjusted the new top to the desk back to a seated height. Reaching down, she hauled the walking pad out from under it, replacing it with the chair she was definitely going to want to slouch in when morning came. Her afternoons were always spent standing on the pad, although she very rarely had it turned on. It was the thought that counted.

She poked her head into Clayton's room on the way past. At eight years old, he barely resembled the tiny toddler she remembered from their days in Gardner Creek. His mop of blond hair had darkened, and he kept it trimmed short now. Plus, all the baby fat he'd held around his cheeks had thinned out as his jaw shifted to accommodate his growing adult teeth. His smile was gappy as they grew, but Emory loved it all the same.

"Dinner's nearly ready."

Clayton looked up from the handheld gaming console, acknowledging her presence briefly before quickly looking down and jabbing at the buttons. "I can't pause, just let me kill this guy." He grunted with the words, twisting the console between his hands as he fought off whichever animated monster boss he was up to.

Closing her eyes so he didn't see her roll them, Emory took a second to compose herself. No matter how tight it made her jaw, she couldn't blame Clayton for wanting to finish the level. She'd have been the same at his age. Hell, she still was the same, in a way. She could never stop reading mid-page, or even mid-chapter. And she hated pausing a show midway through a scene. Just because he was a kid didn't mean the expectations should have been any different.

"Thanks, Clayton," she managed after a long breath, before turning back into the hall.

She found Byron sitting on the living room floor, surrounded by piles of clothes. A near-empty laundry basket sat next to him. Emory watched as he rifled through the clothes to find a pair of socks. He bundled them into the neatest little parcel, a trick Emory had no patience for most days. When she did the socks, one was shoved inside the other in a messy ball shape.

Shifting a few piles of clothes out of the way, Emory sat next to Byron and reached across him. He passed her a small bunch of clothes, and she got to work folding while he finished the socks.

"Tucker's coming tomorrow," she said with a yawn. "You can't join the meeting, but I told him to come here for dinner."

"I'm serving beef." Byron grunted a satisfied laugh.

"I will buy something vegan on my way back from the office tomorrow. You can cook beef for the rest of us."

Just like back when they were flooded into the farmhouse, Byron still did all the cooking. It suited Emory just fine, considering she despised being in the kitchen most of the time. Besides, she was generally too exhausted from work anyway. Marketing was her passion, but working full time was tiring. Byron had taken his role of house husband very seriously, even in the years before he was actually her husband. He didn't just cook, he did most of the laundry, and he became the default parent for Clayton, organising everything they needed for his transition through preschool and into the primary school he was still attending. Byron even coached the basketball team, despite never having played a game in his life. He was perfect.

The only thing that made it better was the small ceremony they held back at the farm a little over a year ago. Mya had become a celebrant just to be the one to officially marry them, after years of questioning why they were waiting so long. Emory knew why Byron was waiting, though, and it didn't bother her. Clayton and Miff had been their ring bearers. Emory twisted her wedding band on her finger, remembering the way Miff had slept at their feet through the ceremony. It was nice, having that lovely memory of her that she could carry with her always.

Tucker had, of course, been their first witness, and, after a few years of slowly coming to terms with the new family arrangement, Jaxon had been their second. Things were still sketchy, at best, but he was there. They were all trying to make things right.

Emory's stomach grumbled. "How long until dinner is ready?"

"I can start serving it up now, if you want?"

Emory climbed onto Byron's lap and settled between his legs. "In a minute," she mumbled against his lips. "You know, all those years ago, I never thought this would be where we'd end up."

Wrapping his arms around her, Byron held her close as he kissed her deeply before whispering in her ear, "I'm pretty fucking happy that we did, though."

Acknowledgments

Finishing this one feels bigger than the ones that came before. Maybe because it's about 70,000 words more than I ever set out for it to be. Short story who? Certainly not Byron and Emory. They had far too much story to tell.

I wouldn't change it, but I think because of the changing plans, I never realised I was writing the book that would come after my debut series until I'd already finished writing it. So, looking back at it now has me in all kinds of feels. Publishing any book is equal parts thrilling and terrifying. There's so much hope that readers will relate to the characters and fall in love with the story, but there's just as much trepidation because what if they don't? What if it's *too* different to the books that came before? I hope it's the former. I hope you found something in Byron and Emory's story that you loved.

As with any book any author ever writes, I have a huge list of people to thank. I never set out to have my acknowledgements read like an Oscar's speech, but I guess that's kind of what they are. So here goes.

Thank you, of course, to my husband, Shannon. Without you I would not know what true love looks like, and I wouldn't be able to write happily ever afters. Thank you for being my rock, my sea, my spotlight, my biggest supporter.

Emma Mugglestone, Holly Brunnbauer, and Renae Black, thank you for convincing me not to give up on this story, even when things weren't going the way I hoped.

Elise Helliwell and Casey Nott, this book would never have made it this far if it weren't for your expert advice. Thanks for reading an early draft, not hating it, and helping me make it shine.

Thank you to my editor Laura, for squeezing this book into an already tight schedule. Thank you for helping it shine.

I am fortunate enough to have a whole crew of bookish friends and supporters who go above and beyond to help make my books shine. Chloe from The Berry Agency, Paige @paigersturnspaiges, Ellie from Love Notes PR, and my incredible Street Team, all deserve immense levels of thanks and love.

And you, dearest reader, because I couldn't do this whole author thing without your support. Thanks for continuing to pick up my books.

About the Author

When she was 10, Santa brought Devon a "how to write a book" journal. Publishing her debut novel more than 20 years later, she's glad it finally got put to good use.

Devon May resides in Melbourne, Australia with her husband and the two tiny humans who call her mum. When she isn't breaking up fights, she enjoys books that either break her heart, or turn her on. She carries her emotional support Kindle everywhere, should probably drink more water, and will never be caught without a hair tie on her wrist.

STAY UP TO DATE

For bonus content and monthly book recs, sign up for Devon May's newsletter subscribepage.io/devonmay or join her Facebook readers group for weekly discussions and first looks www.facebook.com/groups/devonmaysreaders

instagram.com/booksbydevonmay

tiktok.com/@booksbydevonmay

threads.net/@booksbydevonmay